PUFFIN BOOKS

ABERRATIONS

THE BEAST AWAKENS

Also available by Joseph Delaney

THE SPOOK'S SERIES
The Spook's Apprentice
The Spook's Curse
The Spook's Secret
The Spook's Battle
The Spook's Mistake
The Spook's Sacrifice
The Spook's Nightmare
The Spook's Destiny
I Am Grimalkin
The Spook's Blood
Slither's Tale
Alice
The Spook's Revenge

The Spook's Stories: Witches
The Spook's Bestiary

The Seventh Apprentice
A New Darkness
The Dark Army
Dark Assassin

ARENA 13 SERIES
Arena 13
The Prey
The Warrior

ABERRATIONS SERIES
The Beast Awakens

ABERRATIONS

THE BEAST AWAKENS

JOSEPH DELANEY

PUFFIN

PUFFIN BOOKS

UK | USA | Canada | Ireland | Australia
India | New Zealand | South Africa

Puffin Books is part of the Penguin Random House group of companies
whose addresses can be found at global.penguinrandomhouse.com.

www.penguin.co.uk
www.puffin.co.uk
www.ladybird.co.uk

First published 2018

002

Text copyright © Joseph Delaney, 2018
Map illustration by Matt Jones

The moral right of the author has been asserted

Set in 10/15.5 pt Palatino
Typeset by Jouve (UK), Milton Keynes
Printed in Great Britain by Clays Ltd, Elcograf S.p.A.

A CIP catalogue record for this book is available from the British Library

ISBN: 978-0-241-32099-0

All correspondence to:
Puffin Books
Penguin Random House Children's
80 Strand, London WC2R 0RL

For Marie

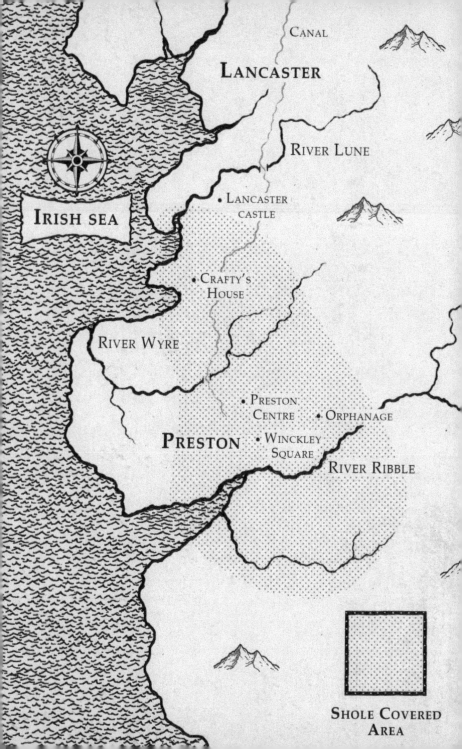

CANAL

LANCASTER

RIVER LUNE

IRISH SEA

• LANCASTER
CASTLE

• CRAFTY'S
HOUSE

RIVER WYRE

• PRESTON
CENTRE   • ORPHANAGE

PRESTON   • WINCKLEY
SQUARE

RIVER RIBBLE

SHOLE COVERED
AREA

THE CELLAR

Crafty was listening to the whispering from his brothers' graves.

He sat at the three-legged table, watching the shadows slither slowly towards him and staring at the far wall of the darkening cellar. Leaning against that far wall was a tall, decrepit, narrow cupboard, which without the wall's support would long ago have collapsed. Once it had been well stocked with food. Now the cupboard was bare.

Crafty had checked it every hour or so, but whenever he'd carefully pulled back the wooden doors, groaning in agony upon their rusty hinges, it was empty. He'd left the cupboard doors open now to save himself the trouble of checking, but he was sure it would never fill itself again. The magic controlling it – a porter spell that instantly sent objects over long distances – had finally faded and died. Benign

Fey magic never lasted long here within the Shole; here, it was malevolent magic that ruled.

Crafty shuddered just to think of what lay outside the cellar walls, and then hunger made his stomach rumble. At least there was a fire to keep him warm and fend off a little of the cold and damp. All that remained now were glowing embers, the last of the wood from the beds of his dead brothers.

Taking his eyes off the cupboard for a moment, he glanced round at the large wooden bookcase on the other wall. One of the shelves was sagging under the weight of the books that were so precious to him. He'd read them over and over again to keep at bay the tedium of life in the cellar. Although many were gone now, fed to the fire to keep it burning, there were some he couldn't bear to sacrifice. These were the gardening books that had belonged to his mother.

A lump came to his throat as he thought of her. She'd been dead for almost a year now, but the pain of her loss was still there. He missed her badly, and the happy home she'd made for him and his brothers. But now he had to leave everything behind. He had to leave this refuge. He had to leave it or starve.

Crafty didn't want to go. He wanted to stay here, with the memories of his mother and his two dead brothers.

Brock and Ben had been twins, two years older than him. They had been good to him; looked after him – so it didn't scare him when they whispered to him. Sometimes he would kneel on the earthen floor and place his left ear close to their gravestones, listening carefully, trying to hear what they said. Sometimes he heard them calling his name.

'*Crafty! Crafty! Crafty!*' they whispered.

Other times they'd weep and, feeling full of pity, he was tempted to raise the stones and release them. But Father had told him never to go too near the graves – Crafty wasn't sure why; he didn't know about the whispering. He'd told Crafty that he was thirteen now, and must be brave, calm and dutiful – just like his brothers. They had lived their lives, and now they were resting in the cold earth. Crafty should leave them be.

And maybe, he thought, it might not be too bad down there. At least they weren't hungry. They didn't need to leave the safety of the cellar and face the dangers outside it alone.

Crafty's thoughts turned back to his father.

I have to go away again, he had said, wrapping his black woollen scarf tightly about his thick neck, buttoning up his greatcoat and tugging on his big boots. Courier Benson had been summoned to the castle once more and had no choice but to obey; couriers, Crafty knew, were valued members of the Castle Corpus. *Be brave, Crafty . . . let's hope you're still here when I return.*

His father had said it with a smile, as if he was joking. Whenever there was danger, he usually joked about it.

Crafty was still here, and still waiting, but he feared that this time his father wouldn't return in time to save him. His father should have returned long before now. Something must have gone wrong.

There was a tiny breeze in the cellar, and Crafty could smell warm candlewax. He'd always liked that smell, but now it worried him. Something worse than hunger would force him out of the cellar; something more insistent than his empty grumbling belly.

The cellar was only safe when it was lit by the magical candles his father had left. There were three of them positioned to form a triangle, each impaled on a spike on its own heavy metal stand. The huge candles had burned brightly with barely a flicker, but his father had been away too long and their benign magic was almost depleted. One by one they had been going out. Now there was only one still alight, and it had burned very low. If Crafty didn't leave soon, he'd hardly be able to find his way to the door. And once the final candle guttered out, the cellar would no longer be safe.

In the fading light Crafty took a look around the cellar for the last time. It had been home to him, a mostly comfortable refuge, for almost a year. It was time to go.

He headed towards the silver-alloy stairs that led up from the cellar to the door; beyond that was another staircase that led to the kitchen. Those silver stairs were another protective ward his father had provided for the cellar.

Just as he reached the bottom step, there was a sudden noise behind Crafty that halted him in his tracks.

It was not the whispering of his dead brothers. It was not the clamour of their cries.

It was the sound of something thrusting upwards through the earthen floor.

I was so close . . . Crafty thought as his heart thumped against his ribs.

The final candle guttered out, plunging him into total darkness.

THE BOG QUEEN

Crafty held his breath and kept perfectly still. Perhaps the thing that was emerging from the earth wouldn't notice him.

Thud! Thud! Thud! went his heart. How fast could it beat without bursting out of his chest?

He knew exactly what was happening. During the past week the cellar had come under attack several times – the worst occurring just after the second candle had gone out. It had begun with thumping and banging in the rooms above. It had sounded like something big striding back and forth, bumping massive shoulders into doors and walls and trying to destroy the house.

That had distracted Crafty from the main attack. While he was gazing fearfully at the ceiling, something had risen into the cellar through the floor. Long, thin, bony fingers had twisted upwards through the soft earth in search of prey.

Those fingers had been green, covered with brown warts and tipped with razor-sharp nails that were encrusted with dried blood.

Crafty had leaped back in alarm. As if sensing the movement, those threatening fingers had lurched further upwards, revealing the hand almost as far as the wrist. But in doing so the fingers had passed out of the shadow cast by the table, to be bathed in the yellow light of the final candle.

The warts had burst like boils lanced with a hot needle, the skin had sizzled and burned; and from deep under the earth had come a scream – followed by a groan of anguish. The hand had been withdrawn and the danger had passed, much to Crafty's relief.

But now there was no magical candlelight to repulse the threat.

Swallowed by complete darkness, he now heard squishing, slithering, sucking sounds as something began to free itself from the soft, clinging earth. He could smell the loam. He turned, horrified, to see a brown glow emerging as a head came pushing up through the soil like a mushroom.

And then Crafty breathed out slowly, with some relief. There was no danger. He knew this creature, and she'd never hurt him before.

Her name was Bertha, and she was the only living friend Crafty had (if you didn't count his father). Throughout the time he'd been confined in the cellar she'd come visiting. For some reason the three candles hadn't been able to keep her away.

Now she sat cross-legged facing him, just behind the muddy hole she'd emerged from. The soft glow she gave off illuminated her whole body, revealing a slim, brown-skinned girl. Her eyes were large and green, and she appeared to be wearing no clothes, but that was because the garments that had once covered her had become fused with her skin, making it look like stretched brown leather, criss-crossed by lines, folds and creases. Her hair cascaded to her shoulders in gleaming black leathery coils, and atop her head was a slim golden crown with a single large green gem affixed to the front.

She was the Bog Queen.

She'd once been the warrior queen of the Segantii, a tribe who'd lived in Crafty's area in ancient times. Led by Bertha, they'd won many battles, but then they had finally come up against the Romans, with their daunting shield-walls and long spears.

The Roman invaders had proved such a formidable enemy that Bertha's priests thought they couldn't be defeated without divine help. So they had offered up Bertha's life to their gods. They'd sacrificed her, cutting her throat and then slicing off the forefinger of her right hand – though why they'd done that, Crafty couldn't imagine. Once dead and buried, she'd slowly sunk further into the bog and had lain there, silent and still within the slime, for a very long time. Then the Shole had engulfed her burial place, and had returned her to life. Those who slew her were long dead, while she now lived again. Crafty often wondered if Bertha took any satisfaction from that.

Now she opened her mouth. The Bog Queen always spoke softly, and in a strange accent, and her meaning was sometimes hard to divine. So Crafty leaned forward and listened very carefully.

'I tickled your brothers' feet as I passed beneath them,' she said, widening her eyes. 'You should have heard them chuckle!'

'All I can hear is their whispering,' Crafty admitted sadly. 'I wish *I* could hear them laugh.'

'Don't be sad, Crafty. They're just resting. You know nothing that's dead here stays dead forever. It's the dying that's hard. That can hurt. But all that's behind them, and now they're just waiting till it's time to wake again.'

Crafty had once asked her when that would be, but Bertha had become stubbornly silent. Either she didn't know or she wasn't telling.

'It's been a long time since you last visited me,' he told her now. 'Have you brought bad news again?'

Earlier in the year, in the happier times when his brothers were still alive, Bertha used to visit them all in the cellar at least once a day; she would sit and talk for hours. Then, for the last seven months, ever since his father had taken Brock and Ben to the castle, returning only with their bodies to bury, Crafty had been alone. At first his loneliness had been terrible, and but for Bertha's frequent visits he would have

9

lost his mind. But now she rarely came to see him, and when she did she usually brought bad tidings.

Indeed, just now her face looked grim. 'Yes, the news is bad, Crafty, but it's always best to know when danger is approaching so that you can face it with your eyes wide open. I've come to warn you. Your father's on his way back.'

How could that be bad news? Crafty wondered in surprise.

'Good. I'm looking forward to his return,' he told her with a smile. 'I've been alone for far too long. He's never stayed away as long as this before. I hope he's bringing me another book to read.'

The Bog Queen did not reply immediately, and her face remained very serious. 'He's carrying a black hood, and a knife with a long sharp blade,' she told him.

Crafty's heart sank. Now he understood why this was bad news. Once before, his father had returned to the cellar with those items. On that occasion he'd taken Crafty's brothers back with him to the castle – supposedly to be tested by someone called the Chief Mancer for a job there. It was the Chief Mancer who coordinated the teams of people, the Castle Corpus, who tried to learn more about the Shole and perhaps halt its relentless advance northwards; an advance that was now threatening the castle itself.

Each brother had been hooded and, as they left, Father had gripped the knife so tightly that his knuckles had turned white.

Neither brother had returned alive, and Crafty's father had refused to discuss the matter. Crafty wondered if the 'test' they'd had to take was very dangerous. Was it his turn now? he wondered. Would he die too? At that thought his heart hammered in his chest again and his palms began to sweat.

There was a rumbling noise from somewhere on the upper floors which, although preferable to anywhere outside the house, weren't as safe as the cellar. Could it be another aberration? Crafty heard a door slam, and then big booted feet began walking down towards the cellar. It was his father.

'It's time for me to go, Crafty,' Bertha said. 'Goodbye.'

'Bye, Bertha,' he whispered, his throat dry.

She gave him a little wave with her right hand, the one without a forefinger, and with a sad smile slid into the hole, feet first. The last thing he saw was the top of her brown head with its pointy crown, and then the earth closed over her and she was lost to sight.

3

DISTANT BREATHING

Crafty's father closed the door behind him. He was wearing his black lambswool greatcoat and carrying a candle which sent his gigantic shadow flickering up the wall behind him. He began to descend the steps, his big boots ringing on the silver-alloy stairs.

Crafty glanced up at him fearfully and saw that Bertha had been correct. His father was indeed carrying a black hood and a knife with a long sharp blade. He reached the bottom of the stairs, walked across the room and placed both items on the triangular table before him.

He turned to face Crafty with a frown. 'Cheer up, Crafty,' he said, his voice a deep growl. 'Things could be worse.'

As usual, Crafty thought, his father seemed cool and detached. He made no mention of Crafty's situation, alone here in the dark, or of the danger he'd faced. Father had changed since the death of Crafty's mother, and although Crafty was pleased to see him, he couldn't help feeling hurt.

'Where have you been, Father? I'm hungry,' he complained, 'and I'd almost given up on you returning in time to save me. The third candle went out not long ago.'

'Well, the one I'm holding will only last a few more minutes, so we've no time to waste. I'm taking you to the castle. You'll be well-fed there, so that deals with the first of your concerns. Put on your jacket. It's very cold out there.'

Crafty promptly did as he was told. It was always cold in the Shole, even in daylight.

'Now turn and face me.'

He did as he was commanded – and saw that his father was holding out the black hood.

'This is for your own good, Crafty. We're not sure about the extent of your powers yet – whether they'll protect you. But there are things out there in the Shole that would freeze the marrow in your bones and give you a lifetime of nightmares. You might even panic and run, and who knows if I'd be able to reach you in time to help. So it's better if you don't see them just now.'

Crafty stared at the hood dubiously. He'd never experienced the Shole directly – all he knew about it was the little that his father or Bertha would tell him, and none of that was good. He didn't like the idea of not being able to see what was going on.

Noticing his reluctance, his father softened a little. 'Don't worry, I'll keep my hand on your shoulder and make sure you don't stumble. I won't deny it – this is going to be difficult, because I've got to protect you as well as myself. But it can be done as long as you keep calm and follow my instructions immediately. Understand?'

Crafty nodded warily.

'Good lad. Now, are you ready?'

He nodded again.

His father eased the hood over Crafty's head. Now he could see nothing.

'What do they want of me at the castle?' he asked, his voice muffled by the hood. He could hear his father moving around the room as he answered, no doubt gathering up the last of their meagre belongings. He clearly hoped that they wouldn't be coming back here again.

'The Chief Mancer has sent for you. He needs to test you for something, Crafty. It's nothing to worry about. If you pass, you won't need to stay here in the cellar any longer. You'll be able to work with him and help him to perform his duties.'

'What's the test?' Crafty asked. 'Is it the same one that was given to my brothers?'

'It is indeed, Crafty, but it really is nothing to be concerned about. You'll pass – I'm sure of it.'

'Couldn't I be a courier like you, Father? Couldn't you train me?' Crafty begged. He'd be far happier working with his father than with the Chief Mancer in a castle full of other strangers.

'No, Crafty. You're far too young to train as a courier. Anyway, you don't have a choice. You can't stay here – I see that the porter spell on the cupboard has failed, so I won't be able to get food to you any more. Now come on, no more talking. Let's be on our way.'

Crafty felt his father's hand on his shoulder, guiding him towards the steps. Soon their boots were clanging on silver as they began their slow ascent.

Bye, cellar, Crafty thought with some sadness. *Goodbye, my brothers . . .*

They came to a halt on the top step. Crafty heard his father turn the handle and open the door. Once through, they were climbing again, Crafty carefully feeling his way in the pitch-black of the hood. This time there were only seven steps; they were made of wood, and their boots no longer made a clanging sound. Then there was another door – and now they were on level ground.

Crafty's father guided him forward, but Crafty could have managed this part without help. He'd grown up in this house. He knew they were passing through the kitchen where, as a child, he'd watched his mother making jam butties and baking scones. He gave a half-smile at the memory. Then they went out through the back door.

The cold took his breath away. It was summer out in what was now known as the Daylight World, but here in the Shole it was said that the temperature never rose much above freezing. It certainly felt like it to Crafty, who immediately began to shiver.

They began walking and, as they did, their feet made squelching noises in the soft ground.

'We're following the curve of the bog until we can go directly north towards Lancaster,' his father said, keeping his voice low.

The bog was where Bertha had been buried – it was her home. Crafty suddenly wondered if he'd ever see her again.

After about ten minutes Crafty's father spoke again, his voice hardly more than a whisper.

'We're on a track leading north now. There's a wood to our left, but it seems safe enough. I can see a cottage in the distance to our right, so we'd better be extra careful. Buildings can be dangerous, Crafty. All sorts of terrible aberrations make them their homes. But most only come out at night. At the moment it's not long after noon, which is the safest time. We should be fine for a while, and we've only a few miles to go.'

They walked on in silence for another half-hour. Everything was deathly quiet. There was no birdsong. All Crafty could hear was the sound of his own breath, and their boots, now crunching across firmer ground. It became even colder, making him wonder if there was frost or snow underfoot.

Suddenly his father gripped his shoulder and brought him to an abrupt halt. He leaned down so that Crafty could feel his warm breath against his right ear.

'Don't speak or move. There's something big through the trees to our left. If we're lucky, it won't notice us.'

Crafty could hear it. Something was moving ponderously through the undergrowth, brushing through the grass and crushing twigs underfoot. He could also hear heavy distant breathing.

His father's hand kept a tight grip on his shoulder. Was Crafty imagining it, or was he trembling?

Eventually the breathing and the rustling and cracking grew quieter. Within minutes it had faded away altogether, and they began to move forward again without saying anything, though Crafty couldn't help letting out a small sigh of relief.

Another half-hour passed. Then: 'Nearly there, Crafty! Just a few more steps!'

And suddenly he could feel warmth on his face. Crafty gasped. It had to be the sun! He hadn't seen it in over a year. Even through the thick black hood, he could see light.

They'd emerged from the Shole and survived! Crafty almost laughed with relief.

'Stand still,' his father instructed.

He obeyed, and the hood was gently eased off his head. Then he stood there, blinking up at white clouds drifting across a blue sky and feeling the sun on his face.

His father returned his long knife to the sheath on his broad leather belt, stuffed the hood into his pocket and let out a huge sigh of relief too.

Crafty looked around, and saw that, just north of them, there was a glittering canal, and behind that a hill with Lancaster Castle atop it, multi-coloured flags flying from the battlements. There were people in the narrow, cobbled streets leading up to it, but nowhere near the crowds he'd fought his way through on his last visit, well over a year ago. Even so, after the time he'd spent in that dark cellar the sight was almost overwhelming.

Then he turned to look south, gazing back at the threatening darkness of the Shole. It was like a huge black curtain, stretching from the ground right up into the heavens, enveloping and hiding everything within it. It looked like the edge of a storm – a wall of dark cloud that might sweep over them at any moment and obliterate what was left of the Daylight World.

Crafty knew that the few people who managed to survive within the Shole itself were usually changed by its dark magic. Some were extremely dangerous, according to his father. Most didn't attempt to leave, but the few who did were slain on sight by the castle's border patrols.

Others became marooned on what were known as the Daylight Islands – patches of land surrounded by the Shole. These people depended upon couriers such as Crafty's father to carry messages back and forth and keep them in touch with the outer world, and sometimes even bring them medicine or magical artefacts. Some islands didn't have enough land to grow food, and so it had to be delivered to them by means of a porter spell, just like Crafty's cupboard in the cellar. But it was a complicated process and often failed – as it had with Crafty.

And so all those who were trapped – good or bad – had to stay within the Shole and survive as best they could.

Crafty heard a noise behind him, and saw four guards from the border patrol rushing down the hill towards him and his father, swords drawn, chain mail gleaming in the sunlight. But as they drew nearer and recognized Crafty's father as Courier Benson, they slowed to a walk, sheathing their swords.

As a castle courier, he was permitted to both enter and leave the Shole. Anyone or anything he brought out was considered to be under his protection and, subject to a subsequent examination by the castle authorities and ratification by the Duke, they were usually permitted to live. The judgement of couriers was generally trusted – after all, they knew the Shole better than most.

Crafty's father hailed the guards, who nodded at him without smiling and, at a leisurely pace, continued their patrol of the boundary between the Shole and the Daylight World.

As they continued on their way, Crafty looked at the houses and saw broken windows and doors hanging from their hinges. They'd been abandoned, and he thought they'd probably been looted of any possessions their owners had left behind. People with any sense were moving on before the Shole got any closer.

Because it's always moving, always advancing, thought Crafty.

Mainly it moved north, but he'd heard that there was also expansion to east and west, making the Shole wider. But it no longer expanded southwards. Nobody knew why.

And sometimes no amount of foresight could save you. Although the Shole usually crept forwards by no more than a few inches each week, sometimes it could surge by as much as several miles. Those sudden movements were unpredictable.

Crafty's mother had been at the local market when the Shole suddenly engulfed the whole area – and killed her. *Or changed her*, Crafty thought, though he didn't like to dwell on that. Although Crafty's father had searched for weeks, he had never found her body. They'd had to assume the worst.

Afterwards his father had tried to make the cellar safe for Crafty and his brothers, using all the skills and knowledge he'd acquired as a courier. But that had only bought them time. He'd known that eventually the creatures of the Shole – the aberrations – would overwhelm them.

So Crafty's father had offered his sons' services to the Chief Mancer, who was a powerful man. Working for him would allow them to escape from the Shole. But escape to what – death? In order to work for the Chief Mancer you had to pass that dangerous test – whatever it was. Crafty's brothers had not survived it. Crafty's stomach turned over in nervous anticipation.

They crossed the nearest bridge over the canal and walked up Market Street towards the castle. Stalls lined the cobbled streets, displaying merchandise that few people were around to buy. All sorts of food were on sale: hot pies, steaming joints of meat waiting to be carved, parched peas and chips. But the strongest smell was that of sea creatures. Lobsters slowly writhed in big bowls of water, and there were shrimps and mussels from Morecambe Bay. Crafty's stomach rumbled, and he wondered what he'd be given to eat at the castle.

As he looked around, it seemed that people were simply carrying on with their lives and ignoring the threat. But a closer study of their faces suggested otherwise. They were anxious and fearful, their minds never at rest.

If you looked north, ignoring those haunted faces, everything did indeed look normal – but to the south there were only the abandoned buildings beyond the canal and the dark wall of the Shole.

They walked up to the main gate of the castle and, at a nod from his father, the guards allowed them to pass under the portcullis and through the gate into the flagged courtyard beyond.

'This is my son,' Crafty's father called to another guard, who had come over to intercept them. 'The Chief Mancer is expecting him. He's to be interviewed tomorrow.'

The guard glanced at Crafty – was that pity he could see in his face?

'Go with him, Crafty,' his father said, turning to face him. 'Get an early night so that you're at your best tomorrow. And good luck. I'll be back soon to see how you're getting on.'

Crafty hesitated, hoping that his father might give him a hug. But then he remembered that, since the death of Crafty's mother, his father had become more distant, a little colder. All he got was a nod as his father turned and walked away. It brought a lump to his throat, but he knew he had to be strong.

Until his father said that he was to be interviewed the next day, Crafty had expected to be taken straight to the Chief Mancer. Instead he was led up a series of spiral stairs to a small room in one of the towers, with a bed, a chair and a small table, and a narrow window that offered a good view south over the city. On the table, he saw immediately, there was a plate of cheese, bread and ham. His mouth began to water.

When the guard left, he locked the door behind him – though Crafty was too hungry to let that bother him much. He raced over to the table and quickly cleared his plate. The minute he'd finished he suddenly felt exhausted. He hadn't slept much the previous night, and it had been a very tiring day, so he undressed and crawled into bed, expecting to fall asleep immediately. But he was still wound up by the events of the day. He tossed and turned, and then started thinking about his mother. An early memory came to him from when he was no more than five or six, the Shole still far to the south of their home.

It had begun in darkness with the sound of weeping.

The noise had woken him up, and brought him stumbling downstairs. He had stepped into the kitchen to see his mother kneeling on the flagstones, gazing into the glowing embers of the fire. Tears were streaming down her cheeks and dripping from her chin.

'Mama! Mama!' he cried, his own tears falling as he ran towards her.

She gathered him to her and he pressed his face into her long hair as she consoled him.

'What's wrong, Mama? What's wrong?'

She lifted him up, carried him over to a chair and sat him on her knee, her arms still wrapped around him. 'Nothing's wrong, Crafty. It's just that I miss your father, and he's been away so long this time. I wish he'd hurry back.'

They stayed like that, not saying anything. He was happy to be in her arms and glad that she was no longer crying. At last he looked up at her and spoke. 'When I grow up, I want to be like my father. I want to be big like him and wear a uniform and be a courier and visit the castle.'

'Maybe you'll get your wish,' his mother had said, smiling down at him. 'You're Fey – you're different from other people. It's a job you might well be able to do.'

'How am I different, Mama?'

'You just are, that's all. We won't know how different until you're grown. You and your brothers and your father are Fey; when you're older he'll tell you all about it, no doubt.'

'The boy next door said that I'd grow up to be a warlock and they'd lock me in a dungeon and throw away the key and give me maggots to eat and stick hot needles into me. His big brother laughed.'

His mother had frowned and held him a little tighter. 'Take no notice, my love. People always make fun of those who are different. Children are the worst of all. Don't bother your little head about it.'

Crafty pushed the memory away. Only now that he was older did he realize how scared his mother must have been after each departure, fearing that her husband would fail to return – that he'd be killed down south in the Shole and she'd never see him again.

It must have been hard for her as the only member of the family who wasn't Fey. It wasn't just children who were cruel – adults were wary of Fey folk. They kept their distance and talked behind your back. Neighbours shunned them – if his mother went out to hang up her washing, those in the next-door garden would immediately go inside. Their children were happy to talk though – happy to torment Crafty and his brothers.

Crafty realized that his mother must have been very lonely at times. It was unusual for a normal human to marry a Fey. People looked down on it. She must have been very brave to do so.

Now she was dead, slain by the Shole, and he would never see her again.

4

THE COMMON PEOPLE

The next morning Crafty awoke to see the dawn light pink against the pointy window of his little room. He didn't rush to get out of bed – he was still thinking about his childhood. Tears came into his eyes as, once again, he pictured his mother kneeling on the cold flags and weeping.

But it was no good crying, he told himself. He tried to recall happier memories. His had once been a happy family. He remembered sitting at the kitchen table, his feet not yet long enough to reach the floor, listening to his father's story of why he was now called *Crafty* instead of his proper name, Colin.

'You never learned to crawl, son,' he had said, beaming down at him. 'You didn't need to. You were hardly more than a baby when you found your own method of moving. You'd spy something with your beady little eyes, get your body into the right position, and roll over and over until it was within reach. You rolled rather than crawled! You've always had your own crafty way of doing things.'

Crafty wondered if that would help him now.

A guard brought him some breakfast – bacon and eggs that had grown cold – and left without a word, again locking the door.

Crafty was still starving, so he wolfed down the food, then tried to be patient as he waited to be summoned. No doubt the Chief Mancer was a busy man; administering the test would be only a small part of his duties for the day.

Then, late in the afternoon, there was a knock on the door. Crafty was escorted from his room by a different guard: a big man with an even bigger frown and a wooden club at his belt. They walked down many steps, and then along windowless corridors, and then down more steps, and soon Crafty could tell that they were below ground level. The guard didn't speak, even though Crafty tried to initiate a conversation – he just pointed, prodding him hard in the back with his fat forefinger if he hesitated. Crafty had to walk in front and it wasn't always clear which direction the guard wanted him to take, so he got prodded a lot.

At last they arrived at a stout oaken door with a silver knocker in the shape of a narrow skull. It wasn't a human skull: it had horns, too many teeth and a long jaw – Crafty had never seen anything like it in his life. He wondered what it was.

Above the knocker there was a big brass plaque:

CHIEF MANCER

Crafty took a deep breath. Here it was – the place where his test would take place.

The guard rapped three times and took a step back. The door opened, but Crafty could see only darkness beyond. Fear began to prickle the back of his neck. He didn't like the idea of entering that room at all. But the big guard prodded him hard in the back again and, when Crafty hesitated, simply pushed him through.

Crafty heard the door close behind him and kept perfectly still, hoping that his eyes would adjust to the darkness. He could make out a vague shape directly in front of him – was it moving? Was it coming towards him? His heart began to thump.

Crafty gave a cry of surprise at the sudden glare of a light from where he'd seen the movement – and then he saw the outline of a tall thin man with a taper in his hand and a fat black candle now flickering on the edge of the desk. The man blew out the smoking taper.

He must have been sitting in the dark. Why on earth had he been doing that? Crafty wondered. It was a strange way to start the test.

In the dim candlelight Crafty could see that the room was extremely cluttered. The desk was piled so high with books and manuscripts that there was hardly room for the candle.

The wall was lined with shelves of leather-bound books – and everything was coated with a thick layer of dust.

The man behind the desk got up and took a couple of steps towards Crafty. His eyes bulged as he took in Crafty carefully. He looked like he needed a shave, and there were food stains down the front of his black gown.

If this is the Chief Mancer, he's surprisingly scruffy, Crafty thought.

The man's hair was black too, but greying at the temples; although he was by no means an old man, he was definitely well past his prime.

At last the man spoke.

'Well, young man, has the cat got your tongue?' he demanded. 'You'd better ask your first question before I start to get impatient.'

'Question?' Crafty asked. He was surprised – he'd assumed that *he'd* be the one to be questioned.

'Yes, *question*! You must have some. How can you hope to find out what's expected of you if you don't ask any questions?'

Crafty wasn't sure what was going on, but he did have some questions.

'Are you the Chief Mancer?'

'That's what it says on the door. Who else did you expect to find in my office?'

'And what does a mancer do, sir?' Crafty asked.

The Chief Mancer raised his eyebrows as if Crafty was some sort of idiot, so he kept talking.

'Oh, I know you deal with the Shole – but what are the practicalities of that, exactly?'

There was a long silence while the man stared at him. When he spoke again, his voice was much softer.

'*Practicalities!* That's a big word for a little man. You'd be surprised what the *practicalities* are. But I'm afraid they're Guild secrets, not to be divulged to the uninitiated.'

'But I *will* be initiated if I pass your test, won't I, sir? When I become your apprentice, won't you have to teach me everything?'

The Chief Mancer's face went red. At first Crafty thought he was angry, but then he began to laugh out loud as he paced up and down. Eventually he pulled himself together and came to a halt in front of Crafty. He shook his head.

'Foolish boy! Passing the test won't qualify you to become my apprentice. There's no way that you could *ever* become that. It takes the right breeding, the right lineage and a very special type of mind to become a gate mancer. Your father's a good enough man and an excellent courier, but he comes from common yeoman stock – as, I believe, did your mother. The blood that runs through your veins is very ordinary, make no mistake about that – at least with regard to the social hierarchy of this city. You are a commoner – you could never become a mancer.'

'Then what does my passing the test lead to, if not to becoming your apprentice?' Crafty was struggling to be polite. He hated the way the Chief Mancer had called him and his family common. It reminded him of the teasing he'd suffered for being Fey – people always thought they were better than him.

'You'll find out tomorrow exactly what it entails but, to put it bluntly, you'll be what's usually called a *gate grub*. I've left it too late to do the test today, so I'll administer it at midday tomorrow,' said the Chief Mancer. 'It's the best time for it. By far the safest hour.'

Crafty didn't like the sound of his new title. Who would want to pass a dangerous test just to become a grub?

'It can't be *that* safe, sir,' he told him. 'It killed my two brothers, and I suppose I'll be next.'

But the mancer shook his head. 'Oh, no. It wasn't the test that killed them. They both passed with flying colours. The test just tells me whether you're up to the job. It's the work you're being tested for which is dangerous – very dangerous; much riskier than the test. And it's that experience which might kill you – or drive you mad . . .'

With that Crafty was dismissed and escorted back to his room by the same silent guard. Once again, he was locked in and left to his own devices, the only interruption being a meagre supper of cold ham.

Crafty wanted to get the test over and done with, and the longer he waited to take it the more nervous he became. Consequently, it took him a long time to get to sleep, but this time he didn't dream.

The following day, just before noon, the same guard delivered Crafty back to that same room, prodded him inside and closed the door behind him. It was just as dark as before and, once again, the Chief Mancer lit a single candle.

'Why do you sit in the dark, sir?' Crafty asked.

'It's one of the *practicalities* of my calling, young man. Now, come and sit over here, close to this curtain.'

Crafty saw a sturdy chair facing a black curtain which dropped from the high ceiling right down to the floor, covering the wall.

Immediately two things worried him. Firstly, the chair was bolted to the floor, and two pairs of brown leather straps which appeared to be restraints were attached to it. The higher two straps would bind the chest; the lower two, the legs.

Secondly, he didn't like the look of that black curtain. At first glance it seemed ordinary enough – a screen that could be closed for privacy or to keep the light out. But this room was surely a long way underground. If there was a window behind that heavy black curtain, there could only be rock or soil beyond it –

'Sit down!' the Chief Mancer commanded, clearly tired of waiting.

So Crafty obeyed, expecting the mancer to bind him with the straps. But instead he pulled the curtain aside, and Crafty gazed in astonishment at what was revealed.

Within an alcove in the wall was the strangest contraption he'd ever seen. Four ornate iron legs supported what at first glance appeared to be a large circular mirror, about five feet in diameter. Its thick frame appeared to be silver, but within it there was no glass. Crafty could see no reflection – just a swirling darkness.

'This,' said the Chief Mancer, 'is a silver gate. Each gate mancer is in charge of one. It is their main tool for exploring the Shole.'

Suddenly Crafty noticed something else. Something very disturbing.

On either side of the gate – just in front, between his chair and the silver circle – stood two shiny metal poles. They drew his eyes up to the sharp horizontal blade that seemed ready to descend.

It was a guillotine.

'Oh, don't worry about that,' said the mancer. 'I work it using this . . .' He pointed down to a wooden pedal on Crafty's left (and out of his reach). 'At the moment it has the safety catch on and it's locked in position. We won't need it for this test.'

'What's it for, sir?' Crafty asked, his mouth suddenly very dry.

'It's used to chop off appendages,' the Chief Mancer replied calmly, as if it was the most obvious thing in the world.

'What's an appendage?' Crafty asked.

'You have the word *practicalities* in your vocabulary, and yet you don't know what an appendage is? That surprises me, young man, so let me educate you. It's an accessory – something attached to the body. It could be a human limb, or simply part of one, such as a hand or even a finger. It could also be a tentacle or a claw. Sometimes we find it necessary to chop 'em off!'

Crafty was appalled, but the Chief Mancer went on.

'I press that pedal with my foot, and the blade falls and does the deed.' He smiled strangely at Crafty. 'Believe me, it's very sharp.'

Crafty gulped. The guillotine was very close, and he felt his body begin to tremble.

THE TEST

Crafty stared up at the mancer. 'Are the straps for me, sir?'

'They could certainly be used to keep you in the chair – and they may well be, if you pass – but not on this occasion. Don't worry, young man. Everything will be explained to you later. But I am not going to waste my time teaching you until I'm sure that you *will* become a gate grub – so let's get started.'

He moved round to the side of Crafty's chair. 'Now, concentrate! Stare into the centre of the circle and tell me what you see.'

Trying to ignore the guillotine, Crafty did as he was instructed. Though what *was* he supposed to see?

'All I can see is darkness,' he replied. 'It seems to be moving.'

'Concentrate and look more closely!' the Chief Mancer commanded.

Crafty stared hard into the circle – and now, to his surprise, he saw that something had changed.

'The darkness is swirling,' he reported; 'it looks like dark clouds moving anti-clockwise.'

'Good! That's right. It's moving in what we call a widdershins direction. Now, look more carefully. Try to see through the cloud. Can you see any claws or teeth? Or maybe big eyes staring back at you?'

Crafty was immediately on his guard again. What on earth did that mean? Could something dangerous be watching him from within that cloud?

Maybe, if he couldn't see anything but the cloud, he would fail the test? he thought. But there was no point in lying. His father always said that it was better to tell the truth, no matter how painful it was. If you told one lie, it usually meant telling more of them to support it.

'All I can see is the dark cloud, sir.'

To Crafty's surprise, the mancer seemed pleased with his answer.

'That's good. Excellent! It means that you are difficult to detect. That's vital in our line of work. Some potential grubs can find things but are visible to anything that's hungry. Were you easy to find, they would have found you by now.'

'*Who* would have found me, sir?'

'The aberrations of the Shole – who else?' The Chief Mancer seemed annoyed by Crafty's ignorance.

Crafty knew that the term 'aberrations' referred to those who had been changed by the Shole – but he didn't know much more about them than that.

The mancer went on. 'Being detected is one of the biggest dangers of using the gate. However, the creatures will have dined last night and are always at their most sluggish at midday, which is why it's safer to conduct the test at this time. So now we'll move forward to the next stage. You're hard to detect, but can you *find* things? Let's see . . .'

'Find *what*?' Crafty asked.

'Well, some things are easier to find than others. In general, finding things is a skill that gate grubs can develop with practice. But all the practice in the world won't help unless you have a basic talent. Do you have that spark of ability? Your brothers had it, so you *should* be the same. If you do, you'll have inherited it from your Fey father.'

Again, Crafty didn't know very much about being Fey – his father had kept saying he'd tell him more when he was older – except that most Fey inherited some kind of magical potential. And it was just that – *potential*. There was no guarantee that a Fey would develop a useful gift, but as a rule the Fey were immune to the effects of the Shole: they couldn't be killed or changed by it. Although they were at risk from the creatures that dwelt there, for some reason they were less visible than other humans. This was why couriers were always recruited from among the Fey.

The only useful Fey gift Crafty was aware of was his ability to hear the whisperings of his dead brothers. He realized that the Chief Mancer had to perform the test in order to check that he had the same talents as his brothers and father. It suddenly occurred to him that he might fail. He could still be returned to the cellar – and if he was, without his father's wards and magic he would face certain death.

'You had a family pet, I believe?' the Chief Mancer asked, interrupting his thoughts.

Crafty was taken aback. What did that have to do with anything? He simply nodded – and felt a pang of loss as he did so. He had loved that dog.

'Yes, we had a dog. She went missing,' he told the mancer. 'The Shole took her. She was called Sandy.'

It was on the terrible day he'd also lost his mother to the Shole.

'So try to find it,' said the Chief Mancer. 'It would be easier if you had a piece of its fur, but as it was your dog, you should be able to use the emotional bond you once had with it. I gave your brothers the same task and they both succeeded. Let's see what you can do!'

Crafty stared doubtfully into the swirling cloud within the silver frame. He was starting to get annoyed. The Chief Mancer wasn't giving him much help.

'How?' he asked.

'This is the second part of the test!' he was told sternly. 'What you see through the gate is the Shole. You are looking at a random location somewhere within it. It could be on the very edge – say, south of the canal – or it could be deep inside it, somewhere near that cursed place called Preston where all our troubles first began. You can change the location with your mind. You can move it to find your lost dog. Just think about your dog. You can either do it or you can't. But find it, and you've passed.'

'How long have I got to find it, sir?'

'I'm a busy man. The most I can allow you is five minutes. It begins . . . now.'

Crafty stared into the cloud again, trying to block everything else from his mind and concentrate on Sandy. It wasn't easy. He was nervous, and his mind kept drifting back to his fate if he failed. Then he remembered his last game with her. They'd been playing in the garden and he'd just thrown a stick for her to fetch. He'd thrown it too far and it had gone over the hedge into the field beyond. Sandy had burst through the hedge and dashed after it, barking delightedly.

Then Crafty's father had started shouting at him through the open door. 'Get in here! Get in here now!'

He had stared at him, dumbfounded – until his father had pointed at the dark curtain racing towards them.

Crafty had just managed to get into the house before the Shole reached them.

Sandy hadn't.

As those painful memories filled his head, Crafty continued to gaze into the swirling cloud, the image of his dog clear in his head.

Then he heard a distant barking. It was coming from inside the circular gate! Suddenly the clouds cleared, and he found himself looking through the gate at what appeared to be a deserted farmyard, with a barn and a surrounding fence. Everything was dim and grey, but he could see big, bare animal bones lying on the ground. Then a dog was bounding towards him, barking madly.

It was Sandy!

Crafty leaned forward eagerly as she came into view – then jerked back and glanced at the Chief Mancer. The alarm on the man's face matched Crafty's.

If the dog bounding towards him was Sandy, she was barely recognizable as the border collie bought as a pup from a local farmer. She'd been mainly black, with a broad white stripe running down the centre of her face. This dog had the same markings, but that was where the resemblance ended. This creature looked ferocious, and at least three times Sandy's size. Its jaws were wide open, revealing three rows of sharp killer teeth, angled back like those of a shark. Crafty had never seen such terrible teeth in any kind of dog.

If this was Sandy, she had been dramatically changed by the Shole, transformed into a monster.

Crafty could see saliva dripping from the dog's jaws. It looked hungry, its eyes fixed on him. It was almost upon him now, and he began to edge backwards in his chair. Could it leap through the gate? Could it bound into this room?

Crafty heard a click and looked at the Chief Mancer again. He'd pressed something with his left foot. He must have taken the safety catch off that contraption! Now his right foot was positioned over the pedal that released the guillotine.

'Sit well back!' he was told. 'Don't worry – I've never missed!'

Crafty suddenly realized what was going to happen. When his dog leaped through the gate, the mancer would bring that sharp cruel blade slicing down into her. Sandy would be cut in half.

She had changed, but Crafty felt sure that, underneath, she was still Sandy. He couldn't let this happen to her.

'No!' he cried, leaning forward towards the gate. He had to stop Sandy leaping through to her death.

Without thinking, Crafty reached forward into the chill air of the Shole, towards the dog's huge jaws and sharp teeth. Then terror struck him like a spear of ice penetrating his heart. Sandy's eyes were full of hunger and rage and her jaws were widening, ready to bite off his hands at the wrists.

But then, suddenly, her eyes softened in recognition and she began to lick Crafty's hands. He stroked her flank and patted her head and started to push her back.

He glanced round at the Chief Mancer, who was looking furious, his foot still positioned over the pedal.

Crafty could see his knee trembling.

6

THE WAITING ROOM

The blade of the guillotine gleamed in the candlelight. Crafty looked up at it fearfully – it appeared to be trembling in time with the Chief Mancer's knee.

Crafty leaned further forward, his head now partially through the gate too: he could feel damp, chilly air on his face. If the blade fell now, it would cut off his head.

He patted Sandy, saying hello, then tried to push her back again.

She resisted. She wanted to come through the gate, and she was too big and strong to push away.

Then Crafty suddenly had one of his clever ideas.

'Fetch, Sandy! Fetch!' he cried, making a throwing motion with his arm.

He'd played that trick on Sandy before, and she'd always gone after the imaginary stick, returning moments later to play the game again.

It worked! As she turned and bounded away, Crafty withdrew his head from the gate, leaned back in his chair and thought of the cloud. Nothing but that dark cloud he'd seen swirling in the circle. The farmyard was quickly obscured, so he relaxed and let out a deep breath. Crafty realized that he'd instinctively worked out how to leave a location within the Shole. He wondered if the Chief Mancer would be impressed.

He wasn't.

'That was an extremely reckless and dangerous thing to do!' he shouted. 'It is vital that a gate grub obeys the commands of his mancer instantly.'

'That was my dog, sir. I knew she wasn't going to harm me. I'm sorry, but I couldn't allow her to be cut by that blade!' Crafty said, pointing upwards.

'I've a good mind to fail you,' retorted the mancer angrily. 'You *must* obey immediately. You must *never* question a decision made by a gate mancer. It's for your own safety, as well as that of the castle.'

Crafty understood his reasoning, but he still felt cross. 'You said that my brothers found Sandy too. Didn't you know that the dog had been changed and could be dangerous?'

The Chief Mancer shook his head. 'We can't predict how long it will take for the Shole to change a person or creature trapped within it. In this case it took much longer than usual. Your dog didn't look like that when your brothers found it. It has changed since. You were lucky to survive the encounter. The guillotine may seem cruel, but you must understand that it is vital. When we look into the Shole, dangerous aberrations could easily enter the Daylight World through the gate.'

Crafty was still angry, but he didn't want to be returned to the Shole, which would mean certain death. He might not like the mancer's methods, but it seemed that being a gate grub was the best he could hope for, and it was still preferable to going back to the cellar.

With this in mind, he put on his most innocent and compliant expression. 'I'm sorry, sir. Please don't fail me. I won't disobey you again.'

The Chief Mancer stared at him for a long time, then nodded. 'I am inclined to give you another chance, Benson. After all, your brothers had it far easier: they were facing a normal dog. Besides, we've had a few . . . unfortunate accidents recently. We need a replacement grub urgently. So – are you clear on what this is all about?'

'You mean being a gate grub, sir?'

'More than just that, young man. I mean what everybody in this castle is trying to do?'

Crafty thought for a moment, then answered, 'You're trying to fight the Shole. That's what my father told me. He said it was a war between the Daylight World and the Shole, and that things would get a lot worse before they got better.'

The Chief Mancer gave a strange smile. 'I suppose that's one way to describe it. We, the Castle Corpus, are a dedicated team of people. We divide up into groups with different specialities, but we work together in order to discover as much as possible about the Shole, in order to learn how to deal with it. Our work is urgent. Do you understand?'

Crafty nodded.

'Good. Then welcome to the castle. You are now officially a gate grub. Training will be provided on the job . . .'

Crafty was marched back to his room by the same grim-faced guard, who once again locked him in – though he returned about an hour later with a bundle of clothes.

'Put these on, boy, and report downstairs. Ground-floor corridor, the Waiting Room – and don't be late!'

The guard went out, slamming the door behind him – but this time he didn't lock it.

Crafty looked at the clothes. There was a pair of leather boots with shiny steel toecaps. The trousers were black, and there was a short-sleeved shirt in a shade of red which he thought was called maroon. Stitched on the left shoulder was a badge: it was a white triangle around the black letters *GM*. It seemed he'd been given the uniform of a gate grub.

There was also a long black military greatcoat, similar to the one his father wore on his journeys across the Shole. Crafty tried it on. It was very heavy, and came down almost to his ankles; he felt completely lost in it. *Maybe I'll have grown a bit by the time winter comes*, he thought. But for now, as it was the middle of summer, he hung the coat on a hook on the back of the door.

He quickly shrugged on the rest of the uniform, not wanting to risk being late. He noticed that the other clothes were also slightly too big for him. He wondered who they had belonged to previously, and what had happened to the owners. *Had they belonged to one of my brothers?* he thought with a shiver.

Crafty pushed the thought to the back of his mind and set off, slowly making his way down the steps towards the ground floor. He came to a long corridor lined with closed doors, the name of each room inscribed above them: THE DEAD ROOM, THE FORENSICS ROOM, THE RELIC ROOM, THE OPTIMISTS' ROOM, THE PESSIMISTS' ROOM and THE GREY LIBRARY were just a few. Crafty wondered what went on inside. He was puzzled by some of the names. Why would a library be grey? Why would anyone choose to be called a pessimist, always looking on the dark side of things and fearing the worst?

Luckily THE WAITING ROOM was easy to find. He knocked softly on the door.

Nothing happened. He listened. Silence. He knocked again.

There's probably nobody inside, thought Crafty, so he turned the handle and opened the door.

He was wrong, for at the head of a very long table, their backs to him, sat a girl and a boy. On the table stood a grubby white box, but otherwise it was bare.

Crafty entered, closed the door behind him and walked cautiously towards the table.

Now the pair twisted round to look at him. They appeared to be a couple of years older than Crafty and were wearing the same uniform. He noticed that their heavy greatcoats were draped over the backs of their chairs, and hoped he wouldn't need his. Crafty was also surprised to see that the girl was wearing trousers too. In his experience, women always wore dresses or skirts. Perhaps trousers were more practical for this job.

The girl herself was very slim, with long brown hair that fell to her shoulders. She was very pretty, but Crafty recognized the look on her face – he'd seen it on the faces of those who judged him on his appearance before they'd even heard him speak.

He decided to try to win her over. 'Can I sit down?' he asked politely.

The boy next to her smiled. Crafty noticed that two fingertips were missing from his left hand and his nose was broken and squashed into his face.

'You *may* sit down!' the boy replied with a grin. 'Whether you *can* or not depends upon your physical dexterity!'

Crafty looked at them both in puzzlement. If this was some sort of joke, he didn't understand it.

The girl started grinning too. 'Sit down,' she invited. 'We're only having a bit of fun. He's just pointing out that you should say "may" when you're asking for permission, that's all. You'd better get used to that sort of thing because the Chief Mancer is a real stickler for grammar. Well, he's a stickler for everything, really. His real name's Wainwright, but everyone calls him Ginger Bob.'

'Why do you call him that?' Crafty asked, remembering the Chief Mancer's black hair.

'You'll find out soon enough,' she replied with an even wider grin. 'So, did he correct your grammar when he tested you?'

Crafty shook his head. 'No, but he was a bit sarcastic when I used the word *practicalities*. He said it was a big word for a little man.'

'Sounds like typical Ginger Bob,' said the boy with the missing fingertips. 'He's an important man in this castle, boss of all the gate mancers, and he likes to think he knows everything. By the way, my name is Pete Proudfoot, but my friends call me Lucky. And this –' he smiled at the girl – 'is Donna Henderson. What's your name?'

'Colin Benson, but my family call me Crafty.'

'You're Brian Benson's son?' Lucky asked, clearly impressed. 'Big Brian, the courier?'

'Yes, that's him.' Then something occurred to Crafty. 'You two must have met my brothers, Brock and Ben. They were gate grubs too – they died.'

Lucky shook his head. 'Before our time. I'm sorry about your brothers, Crafty, but nobody lasts long being a gate grub. We've only been here for a few months ourselves. I've done three and Donna has done nearly four. And we're told that nobody's ever survived more than a year. It's a scary and dangerous job and it never gets any easier.'

'That's because there's no proper training,' Donna added angrily. 'You learn on the job, so the first mistake you make can cost you your life.'

Lucky nodded. 'Lucky for me I only lost two fingertips...' He waggled his stumps. 'A lot depends on which gate mancer you work for. The youngest one's a nasty piece of work – he's caused the deaths of four grubs already. His name is Vipton, but we call him Viper because he's a real snake in the grass who takes chances with other people's lives. Be warned: he likes to play tricks – especially on new grubs.'

Crafty didn't like the sound of that at all. The Chief Mancer – Ginger Bob, as they called him – was a bit pompous but seemed to know what he was doing, and he definitely took his job seriously. Surely he wouldn't place a grub in danger unnecessarily. But if you had to work with reckless mancers like Viper, when the work was already so dangerous . . .

Crafty decided to focus on something else. He pointed to the letters on the front of his uniform. 'Why does it say *GM*?' he asked. 'Shouldn't it be *GG* for gate grub?'

'That,' said Donna scornfully, 'shows our lowly position here in the castle. Our role doesn't even have an official title. "Gate grub" is just a joke, something made up by the mancers. We're just wriggling little grubs, used like bait on the end of a hook to go fishing in the Shole. *GM* stands for gate mancers. We aren't part of their guild but we belong to them. That's what those letters tell you!'

Crafty's father was a member of the Castle Courier Guild. He knew they had rules to guide their behaviour and secrets that had to be protected from outsiders. Courier craft – the special use of Fey magic that had kept Crafty safe in the cellar for so long – was just such a secret, and his father hadn't been allowed to teach it to his sons because they weren't members of the guild. There were long waiting lists to join guilds, and even if your father was a member, that didn't guarantee the same for you.

'So when do we start work?' Crafty asked.

'Well, we usually just wait here until somebody needs us,' said Donna, turning away from Lucky to face him. 'If we're lucky, it'll be a quiet day and nobody will come. It's boring waiting, but it's better than sitting in that chair facing the gate. Sometimes we play draughts,' she said, nodding towards the white box. 'Just before noon they bring us sandwiches and apple juice, but I'm afraid you've missed that. We're usually on duty until dusk, and then it's a light supper in your room and bed. But we get Sundays off. The guild rules say that mancers have to attend church twice – once in the morning and once early evening.'

Crafty was about to ask why when the far door slammed open. A scowling young man in a gleaming white shirt strode into the room and glared at them.

'You!' he called out, pointing a finger at Crafty. 'New boy! Come with me. I have a job for you . . .'

THE SPADE

Crafty followed the young man out of the door and down three flights of steps. They were heading deep underground, and although Crafty would have liked to quiz the mancer about where they were going, he was now striding along way ahead. When they eventually came to a door, Crafty groaned silently as he spotted the name on the brass plaque:

S. W. VIPTON

This was Viper.

Inside, the room was already lit by a flickering candle and was just as gloomy as the Chief Mancer's den. It was also smaller, but where his had been cluttered with books and manuscripts, this room was extremely tidy. A few leather-bound books were stacked on shelves but, apart from the candle, the desk was bare and free of dust. Crafty also saw a stack of neatly folded white shirts on another shelf beside a cupboard. But this room did have one other thing in common with the Chief Mancer's: a chair was bolted to the floor in front of a black curtain. And Crafty knew what it concealed.

'Stand there!' Viper commanded, pointing to the floor beside his desk.

He hasn't even asked me my name, Crafty thought, but he did as he was told.

Viper circled him three times, slowly. He was taller than Crafty, but he didn't seem *that* old. Viper couldn't have been more than twenty years of age. Although his shoulders were muscular, he was slim, with a thin face and a slightly hooked nose. His mane of hair, swept back and gleaming with oil, was the colour of midnight. His face was pink and, unlike Ginger Bob's, closely shaven. But it was the immaculate white shirt buttoned up to the neck that drew Crafty's eye. This was a young man who was – to use a word that would have impressed the Chief Mancer – fastidious; he was precise, fussy and painstaking in his dress and appearance.

The man in question halted, staring down imperiously at Crafty. When Crafty looked up and stared back, attempting a smile, Viper hissed angrily through his teeth. 'Look down at your boots!' he snapped. 'I'll have no insolence from a young whippersnapper like you.'

Crafty took that to mean that he didn't like him staring back at him, so he dropped his eyes.

'Why aren't you in full uniform?' demanded Viper.

At first Crafty couldn't think what he meant. Then he remembered the long black coat he'd left in his room.

'I – I thought that the coat was only for winter, sir,' Crafty stammered, sensing that this wouldn't go down well.

'Well then, you've made your first big mistake, grub,' sneered Viper. 'In some parts of the Shole it's always winter; so cold that you can freeze to death in less than half an hour.'

With a shock Crafty realized the implications of what Viper was saying. Did he mean that he would sometimes have to go through the silver gate, out into the Shole? He'd assumed that a gate grub just sat in the chair and found things.

He was about to ask, but before he had time to open his mouth, Viper walked over to the black curtain and drew it back to reveal the gate, set within an alcove.

'Sit!' he commanded.

Crafty decided not to aggravate him any further; he clambered into the chair and looked at the silver frame with the dark clouds swirling within. It looked identical to the one in the Chief Mancer's room. The chair had similar straps too.

But Viper didn't bind him to the chair. He gave a sly smile that Crafty found disturbing and, when he spoke, his voice was softer but somehow more menacing.

'No doubt Mr Wainwright, the Chief Mancer, has explained to you that the primary function of a gate grub is to locate things within the Shole. This can mean objects, creatures or places. But once that task has been achieved, the gate mancer can usually, but not always, return to the same spot by using this ratchet-dial on the gate,' he said, pointing at a circular dial. 'We call these spots "fixed locations", and we use them to do further research on the Shole.'

'What's a ratchet-dial, sir?' Crafty asked, putting his grievances aside. He was still eager to learn all he could about his new job; any information might be useful in the future.

'It's a dial with metal teeth so that it cannot slip backwards and change location accidentally. That's what I intend to do now – take us to a fixed location. Once there, I want you to retrieve something for me that was left behind by another grub.'

As he turned the dial, it made an ominous clicking sound.

'There!' Viper pointed into the centre of the gate.

The cloud had cleared, and Crafty found himself looking at a desolate landscape with a single tree at its centre. The ground was covered with snow, and the branches of the tree were heavily laden too. Leaning against the tree was a spade.

'Get me that spade!' Viper commanded. 'Don't worry – the area is quite safe at present.'

The spade appeared to be about a hundred yards away.

'You want me to climb through the gate?' Crafty asked, hoping he'd somehow misunderstood.

'Of course I do, grub. I don't think your arms are quite long enough to reach it from here!' Viper gave a nasty laugh.

'Could you please move the gate a bit nearer to the spade, sir?' Crafty asked. Despite what Viper had said, there was something about the bleak landscape that made him fearful. He couldn't see any danger, but he didn't want to be there any longer than was strictly necessary.

'That's not possible. It's a fixed location.'

'Maybe *I* can move it nearer . . .'

Crafty wondered whether, if he concentrated hard on that spade, the gate would move towards it. He'd got pretty close to Sandy when she was located. But before he could try, Viper gripped his left shoulder and pulled him backwards so fiercely that he cried out with pain.

'How dare you! A grub obeys instantly and *never* questions the order of a gate mancer! Do as I say immediately or I'll take you to the Chief Mancer this instant, and you'll be returned from whence you came. Did you know that we discuss grub candidates at meetings? Oh yes, I know all about that miserable year you spent in the Shole. How would you like to be back in that cellar?'

Crafty knew he was right. It was better to be a gate grub than back there, waiting to die. The moment Viper released his shoulder, he gave a grimace, got to his feet and, gripping the frame with one hand, clambered through the silver gate.

The cold instantly snatched his breath away. What a fool he'd been not to bring his greatcoat! Crafty glanced up at the sky. There was no sign of the sun, just a drab uniform greyness.

He didn't want to give Viper the satisfaction of seeing him look back, so he simply started walking towards the tree. His boots crunched as they made contact with the snow.

The air was freezing, and each breath he exhaled erupted into a cloud of mist.

When he was halfway there, Crafty risked a glance back at the gate. To his surprise, he saw that it no longer looked like a silver frame mounted on ornate iron legs. From this side, only a shimmering blue circle was visible. He noted with alarm that it didn't seem to have any real substance – it looked like something that could fade away at any moment. He began to walk faster, shivering violently.

He glanced behind him again, and for a moment the circle seemed to change into the huge gloating face of Viper. Crafty blinked in astonishment – was he seeing things? – and when he looked again, it was just a blue circle once more.

Crunch! Crunch! Crunch! went his boots on the frozen ground. It was the only thing he could hear. The Shole was utterly, eerily silent.

He'd almost reached the tree when he heard a terrifying sound: a shrill cry, rapidly descending through several octaves before erupting into a booming roar. What type of creature was that? Although distant, the beast was clearly something huge. Did it know that he was here? Had it got his scent? Was it bounding towards him right now?

Crafty began to run towards the tree; he seized the spade and turned to sprint back towards the gate. He'd only taken three steps when he halted in horror.

The gate had vanished!

Trying to control the panic that tightened his throat and stifled his breathing, he headed for the point where he thought he'd last seen it. But there was no sign of it at all. Had he made a mistake? Set off in the wrong direction?

He lost track of time as he paced backwards and forwards, searching for the blue circle, always keeping the tree in sight. Had it been minutes or only seconds since he'd heard that awful cry? He was getting colder and colder: his fingertips were already numb and he could feel the cold like pinching fingers busy working on his nose, lips and cheeks.

Then it began to snow. It was heavy snow too; huge flakes whirling down so that he could hardly see the tree in the distance.

There must have been a problem with the gate, he thought. Perhaps the dial had slipped ... But then he remembered that this wasn't possible – that ratchet locked it into position.

Viper would sort it out, wouldn't he? He'd come back for him. Surely he would. With that in mind, Crafty decided to head back towards the tree again. If he wandered too far afield, Viper would never be able to find him, but he'd see him next to that tree.

Crafty leaned against the trunk anxiously, still gripping the spade. He looked down and saw that his fingertips were turning blue. If the gate didn't open soon, he would die here, he thought. If the cold didn't get him, whatever it was that had made that sound would.

His body and his mind were now both numb. Neither was working properly. He was shaking violently, and finding it difficult to think. He had no idea how long he'd been out there.

Then, suddenly, there was a shimmer right in front of him. To Crafty's astonishment, the gate reappeared close to the tree. He remembered vaguely that Viper had said he couldn't move the gate, but he had certainly done so now.

Thank goodness, he thought, relieved at the thought that his ordeal was nearly over.

Still carrying the spade, he was about to clamber through the gate when he heard Viper shout, 'Put the spade back against the tree. We won't be needing it.'

Crafty thought he'd heard him wrong. But, when he hesitated, Viper shouted even louder. 'Do as I command!'

Numb with cold and disbelief, Crafty walked stiffly over to the tree and left the spade there. Then he turned, came back to the gate and, with great difficulty, pulled himself through.

Viper was standing beside the chair, smirking down at him. 'Feeling a little chilly?' he asked.

Crafty nodded slowly, still dazed. He stamped his feet weakly to get the circulation going again; snow dusted the floor around them.

'Well, let that be a lesson to you, Benson. Next time I expect you to report in full uniform. Now get back up to the Waiting Room.'

So he knew my name after all, thought Crafty.

THE SNATCH

Back upstairs, Crafty joined Lucky and Donna in the warm Waiting Room. He was still shivering violently.

Both stared at him, waiting for him to speak, but Crafty was too cold and exhausted to even open his mouth.

'What happened?' Lucky asked. 'What did you have to do?'

Crafty grimaced, and told them about the spade.

'Ugh! It's his idea of a joke,' Donna said angrily. 'I was afraid of that. I'm really sorry you had to go through that – especially without a coat!' And she gave him a warm smile that animated her whole face.

Crafty's heart jolted with emotion as he remembered his mother giving him that same sympathetic smile. In fact Donna did look like his mother might have looked as a young girl – from her lips to her soft brown eyes.

'I had a really bad time of it,' Lucky told him. 'I got frostbite and ended up losing two of my fingers,' he said, holding out his left hand. 'Some joke, eh?'

'I'm sorry about your fingers,' Crafty told him. 'I thought that was because of an accident with the guillotine.'

'An easy mistake to make,' Lucky said, his grin turning into a grimace. 'Viper is reckless with that guillotine. The last two grubs who died working with him met their end under his blade. One boy's arms were chopped off at the elbows and he died from blood loss.'

Crafty didn't reply. What a horrible story! He was glad to be out of the cellar, but had he stepped out of the frying pan into the fire? Viper seemed capable of turning his life as a gate grub into a nightmare.

'How did the other two grubs die?' he asked.

'One supposedly went missing – he simply didn't return to the gate. It's not impossible, but we never venture more than fifty yards away – we're usually in view of the mancer the whole time. I expect Viper abandoned him. The other was caught by aberrations and ripped to pieces.'

'I suppose they could all be accidents,' Crafty mused.

'Oh, he killed them all right!' insisted Lucky, raising his voice. 'But according to the castle, there was no evidence. The guillotine deaths were written off as accidents too. Viper claimed that an aberration came through the gate in pursuit of the grub, so he had to stop it getting into the castle. They were very close together and, when the blade came down, it killed the gate grub along with the aberration. It's happened twice though. At best Viper's reckless; at worst he's a killer. My instinct tells me it's the latter.'

'I wish I'd been brave enough to tell Viper to go through the gate and get the spade himself,' Crafty fumed, angry at himself.

'That would have done no good. He'd have just reported you to Ginger Bob and done his best to get you the sack. As for Viper going out into the Shole, he couldn't even if he wanted to,' Donna told him.

'That's right. Viper and the other mancers can't go through the gate. Not even Ginger Bob can risk it,' Lucky confirmed.

'Why's that?' Crafty asked.

'It's part of our talent – that's why we're chosen as grubs,' Donna answered. 'It's because we're Fey and have the abilities that come with it. We can be trained to do magic and are good at finding things with a silver gate. More importantly, the Shole itself doesn't kill or change us. It's something we've inherited from our parents – that's why your dad is able to be a courier, Crafty. Anybody else who stepped through would be dead – or worse – within seconds; there would soon be nothing left but their bones. Either that or they'd slowly start to change into something terrible. You know what? I think we have a great deal more ability than the mancers, despite what they say. Some people believe they can only control the gates because of what's mixed into the silver of the frames.'

'I heard it was the ground-up bones of dead gate grubs,' said Lucky, grim-faced.

But Crafty shook his head. 'That can't be true. My father brought back my brothers' bodies and buried them in our cellar.'

He didn't mention that he could hear them whispering. He'd told nobody about that – even keeping it a secret from his own father. He didn't feel ready to discuss it with anyone. In any case, he didn't know Lucky and Donna well enough to trust them just yet.

'They wouldn't need to use them all! Besides, your father's a courier. I bet they wouldn't dare do that to his dead children.'

Crafty winced at the thought of his brothers being ground up to make gates for people like Viper to use. He still had no idea how they had died. His father had never discussed it and Crafty had been too upset to ask.

Donna sensed his pain, and tried to cheer him up. 'Look on the bright side, Crafty – tomorrow's Saturday. Survive that, and then Sunday is our day off, and we'll get paid! We'll show you around the city and then the castle.'

'Well, the parts of the castle they allow us to visit,' added Lucky. 'Whole sections of it are out of bounds and heavily guarded.'

'Thanks,' said Crafty with a smile. Things were definitely strange here, but he liked this pair, and felt that they might become good friends.

*

None of them were called again, and the afternoon passed quickly. But when Crafty got back to his room, he began to brood about his father. He was very surprised not to have heard from him by now. After all, he'd promised to check up on him soon; Crafty guessed he was busy with his courier duties, and would visit as soon as he returned. Other dark thoughts churned through his head: of his once happy family, he reflected, his two brothers and his mother were dead, his father constantly away on dangerous missions.

The following day, when Crafty went down to the Waiting Room, he made sure he brought his heavy coat and draped it over the back of his chair. He wouldn't be caught out again.

The three grubs were left alone all morning, and even managed to play a few games of draughts. But just after lunch, which they ate in the same room, the far door opened.

Crafty's heart sank – until he saw that it was 'Ginger Bob'.

The Chief Mancer approached them with a serious expression on his face. 'Benson, come with me. I've a task for you.'

Crafty got to his feet and reached for his coat.

'You won't need that. It's a chair job,' he was told, so he left it behind.

He followed the mancer down the steps and through the open door of his untidy study. As usual, it was gloomy, lit by a single candle.

The black curtain had already been drawn back, away from the gate, and Ginger Bob simply nodded at the chair.

As soon as Crafty sat down, the mancer started to bind him with the leather straps: first his legs and then his chest.

'Not too tight, are they?' he asked.

'The one across my chest is a little uncomfortable, sir,' said Crafty, though he was more uncomfortable about the fact that he was being strapped in for the first time. What was all this about?

'Is it restricting your breathing?'

Crafty shook his head.

'In that case, we will leave it as it is. Those straps have an important function. A little discomfort is preferable to being dragged out of the chair and through the gate into the Shole by something that wants to eat you – as I'm sure you agree.'

Crafty did, but it didn't make him feel any better.

'Our next task is dangerous, but provided you do exactly as I tell you, all should be well. We are about to carry out what we refer to as a *snatch*. You're going to grab something in the Shole, and then drag it back through the gate so that our experts can examine it and increase our knowledge about the Shole and its aberrations. Here, put these on . . .'

Ginger Bob handed Crafty a pair of black leather gauntlets. They were tight but supple, and he had no difficulty in easing them on. Now he understood why their uniforms had short sleeves. The gloves reached as far as his elbows, and the palms had rubber grips.

'Now, do you know what a fixed location is, young man?'

In the nick of time Crafty managed to stop himself from using Viper's nickname.

'Mr Vipton explained it to me.'

'Good. I'm pleased to see that your training is already progressing well. Now, I will take the gate to a fixed location within the Shole, near the centre of Preston. As you know, this is where the Shole first began, and so it is very dangerous. However, because you won't have to worry about finding the place, you can simply focus your attention on making a successful snatch.'

Crafty didn't think there was anything 'simple' about it, but refrained from saying so. 'What am I going to snatch, sir?'

'We'll be going to the site of what was once an orphanage. You're going to snatch a child and drag it back through the gate into this room so that it can be studied.'

Crafty's heart sank. He didn't like the sound of this at all. 'A child, sir?' he asked.

The mancer saw the dismay on his face. 'Look – don't think of it as a *child*. It's been changed by the Shole and is no longer human. That's why we want it. Our experts want to study the changes and learn more about this particular aberration.'

There was a yellow rope hanging from the ceiling directly above the Chief Mancer's desk. He reached up, tugged at it, and somewhere in the distance a bell rang.

Crafty heard boots hurrying down the stairs, and then there was a triple rap on the door.

'Enter!'

Two large guards came in, carrying between them something that looked like a huge birdcage. They supported it on their shoulders, using a long metal bar that went through a ring attached to the top of the cage. The guards carefully lowered it to the floor and, after removing the lock, one of them opened the barred door.

Crafty eyed it up. It would be uncomfortable, but he reckoned he could have just about fitted inside if his knees had been touching his chin. He wondered about the creature they were going to be snatching. How much would it have changed?

'Prepare yourself, young man.' Ginger Bob snapped his fingers to get Crafty's attention and pointed towards the gate. Crafty sat back and stared through the swirling cloud, uncomfortably aware that the guards had taken up position on either side of his chair. They were clearly getting ready to grab whatever it was that he was snatching. However, he was happy to note that the guillotine foot-switch was still locked. That sharp blade made him very nervous.

He heard the ratchet-dial behind him click three times, and suddenly the swirling clouds parted so that, within the frame, he could see a narrow cobbled street. At the end was a large stone building. The sign above its metal gate read:

MOUNT STREET ORPHANAGE

It doesn't get much grimmer than this, thought Crafty warily.

Beyond the gate he saw the open wooden door to the orphanage. It was hanging off its hinges, and broken glass littered the entrance. Peering through, he could only really see darkness, but he thought there might be something moving in the shadows.

'They're watching us.' Ginger Bob confirmed his thought. 'Hopefully one of them will come out to investigate. Then you can snatch it.'

'Can they see me?' Crafty asked, dropping his voice to a whisper.

'They see what they most want to see,' replied the Chief Mancer. 'I am deploying what we call a *lure*. From their side of the gate, the magic makes the silver gate take on the form of their heart's desire. They're probably very hungry, so most likely it'll be their favourite food – probably raw meat, dripping with blood. That's what most aberrations are after.'

Almost as soon as he'd finished talking, something small scurried out through the dark doorway, emerging into the dim light. At first Crafty couldn't see what it was. It had two arms, two legs and a head that looked human, but there was something strange about its jerky movements. It scuttled forward like an insect, then halted; moved, then halted again, coming directly towards them all the time.

Was it really seeing raw meat dripping with blood? Crafty shuddered at the thought.

The mancer was suddenly very businesslike. 'Be ready to make the snatch! When it gets close enough, grab it by the forearms! Don't let go, whatever you do.'

When it was very near the gate, the creature lifted its head, apparently staring right into Crafty's eyes. Ginger Bob had told him what they were going to snatch, but nothing had prepared him for this. He jolted back in shock – for though this had clearly once been a child, it was horribly changed.

Its eyes were red, the pupils thin vertical slits. It opened its mouth, and Crafty saw triple rows of sharp teeth inside – smaller than Sandy's, but no less deadly. Had this creature really once been a human child – an orphan, taken by the Shole? Was he really supposed to grab it? It was no larger than a five-year-old, but as soon as he got close, those teeth would surely tear hungrily at his flesh?

'Now! Do it now!' the Chief Mancer ordered.

OLD NELL

Terrified of the consequences if he disobeyed, Crafty thrust both arms through the gate and attempted the snatch. Although his left hand missed its target, his right closed around a thin forearm and he gripped it as hard as he could.

The creature whipped its head round faster than he could blink. It hissed horribly, and then bit hard into Crafty's hand, the jaws bearing down on it with incredible strength. Crafty yelped with pain, but still managed to jerk the thing towards him, through the gate and into the Chief Mancer's office.

The two guards obviously knew their stuff. They were fast and efficient, and it took them only a couple of seconds to drag the screaming beast off Crafty and hurl it, screeching, spitting and snarling, into the cage.

Once the door was locked they bowed politely to Ginger Bob and, without saying a word, carried the yowling creature out of the office by means of the long pole balanced on their broad shoulders. Now Crafty could see why they needed it – the cage was kept well away from them as the thing inside reached out through the bars.

Crafty examined his right gauntlet. His hand was throbbing, and there were tooth marks in the leather. When he removed it, he saw that the skin was red, but the bite hadn't drawn blood.

'That will turn into a nasty bruise, but it could have been worse.' There was genuine kindness in Ginger Bob's voice, but then, to Crafty's surprise, he changed the subject completely. 'Do you like biscuits, young man?'

Crafty nodded, dazed.

After carefully drawing the black curtain across, the Chief Mancer unstrapped Crafty, then beckoned him towards his desk. He gestured to the smaller of two chairs facing his. Crafty noticed that, as well as being cluttered with books and papers, the desk was covered in crumbs – as was the floor surrounding it. Ginger Bob was a mouse's best friend.

The mancer rooted through a pile of manuscripts until he found a blue tin. He eased off the lid and then handed Crafty a large ginger biscuit.

'This is a custom I always observe,' he said, taking a biscuit for himself. 'After the successful completion of a mission my assistant and I always celebrate by nibbling ginger biscuits.'

Another mystery solved, thought Crafty. Now he knew how the Chief Mancer had got his nickname.

'You did well, young man,' the mancer continued. 'Even though you grabbed the aberration with only one hand, you still had the presence of mind, the speed and the strength to complete the snatch. You have made a promising beginning. Now, do you have any questions?'

'About the snatch, sir?'

'About anything to do with the Shole.'

Crafty thought for a moment before speaking. He certainly had questions, but where to start?

'Do we know how it began, sir? The Shole, I mean. I know there are lots of theories, but are we any nearer to the correct one?'

The Chief Mancer stared at the ceiling and then closed his eyes as if deep in thought. 'We know that the Shole was first observed in a small street called Water Lane close to Fylde Road, a busy thoroughfare in Preston. It's not that far from the orphanage you just saw. Over the next ten years it gradually expanded to cover most of the town centre. At first it was a rough circle, but the second stage of its expansion has been more erratic, and mainly northwards. The Shole is like a great beast which is gradually awakening, growing and becoming increasingly dangerous.

'Now, almost seventy years later, it has extended much further, and even threatens the heart of Lancaster and this castle. But why and how it began we still don't know. That is why the gates are so important. The work we do feeds the research that may one day explain everything and offer a solution. We can only hope that we will be able to reverse the expansion of the Shole, or even end it altogether.'

Crafty suddenly thought of another question – something that had been puzzling him since he first found out about the gates.

'Couriers are used to carry messages to and from the Daylight Islands. Wouldn't it be easier to use the gates to go to those communities directly?'

The Chief Mancer shook his head. 'The capabilities of the silver gates are limited. They can only be used to visit places directly *within* the Shole. The Daylight Islands are small patches which the Shole has missed and moved round. Besides, couriers have plenty of other important functions. On their travels through the Shole, they record any changes, along with locations that might be of interest. Essentially, they patrol the Shole.'

They'd almost finished their ginger biscuits, so Crafty quickly got in another question before Ginger Bob could send him back to the Waiting Room. 'Why do we call it the Shole, sir? I remember hearing it called the Shadow Land and the Shade, and once the Curtain, but since then it's always been the Shole. It's the only name my father uses.'

'Well, those other names are good descriptions of what we see and experience. It is very much like a dark curtain advancing across our county, or indeed a shadow world. But *Shole* is the name that has stuck. Originally it was formed from the words *Sink Hole*: when whole farms suddenly disappeared, leaving only a darkness behind, folk thought they had fallen into a sink hole. But the word is also an adaptation of *Sheol* – and that, Benson, is another name for Hell . . .'

Crafty went back to the Waiting Room, carefully mulling over what Ginger Bob had told him. The Shole terrified him, but he couldn't help finding it interesting. What it was and what it did had aroused his curiosity, and he knew there was much to be learned from studying it. For the first time since he'd arrived at the castle, he wondered whether he might enjoy being a gate grub after all.

The following day was Sunday – their day of rest – and, as promised, Crafty was shown around the city and the castle. As Lucky and Donna led him through the streets, they pointed out the main routes across the city and the best shops for warm, freshly baked bread and sausage rolls. They weren't wearing their uniforms, and Donna was now dressed in a skirt and blouse with a cardigan buttoned to the neck against the chilly air. It didn't feel much like summer.

Donna took the lead, striding along energetically. There was something gawky about her slim body, as if she hadn't yet learned how to control her limbs.

They halted outside an apothecary's window. 'This is the best cure-all shop in the city,' Lucky announced. 'They've got potions for colds and the flux, and, if you're really ill and need bleeding, those little beauties will do the trick!' He was pointing at a box with a glass lid. It was full of fat brown leeches.

'Think what the Shole would do to those creatures,' Donna said, pulling a face. 'Imagine one of them, the size of a big dog, slithering on to your body. It'd drain your blood in no time!'

Crafty shuddered – he knew that doctors used leeches to suck the bad blood out of a diseased body, but he'd never been convinced that bleeding worked, and neither had his mother.

'Why is the city so quiet?' he asked, turning away from the window to glance down the almost deserted street.

It was long after the Sunday morning church services; by now the lanes should have been busy with people enjoying their leisure time. After all, it was their one free day. On Sunday afternoons Crafty's parents had sometimes brought him and his brothers into Lancaster. In summer the streets had been thronged with people – you'd had to almost fight your way through the crowds.

'A lot of people are leaving, more and more each week,' Donna answered. 'They're going north to live in Kendal or even Carlisle. Everyone knows that the Shole is getting closer. There's a real fear that it will soon surge again, engulfing the castle and the rest of the city. People are getting out while they still can.'

As he walked back up the hill towards the castle, with Lucky and Donna chatting beside him, Crafty tried to dispel the image of the giant leech that Donna had conjured up. He was beginning to realize that the Shole changed things in terrible ways. It could take something small and innocuous – like a child – and turn it into a ravening monster. Leeches already loved sucking blood; what if they were a whole lot bigger, and ferocious to boot? He shuddered again at the thought of it.

It was definitely chilly for summer, and a strong north-east wind was blowing them about, but they started their tour of the castle up on the battlements anyway. Crafty was keen to see the view. Outsiders weren't permitted up there but, as part of the Castle Corpus, they were allowed access.

To the north he could see the river Lune winding around the northern limits of the city before making its way west towards Morecambe Bay. To the south was the canal. In one direction it carried barges towards Kendal and the north; in the other it went as far as Preston. But no barge ever travelled south from here. The canal was cut off by the Shole.

Crafty's eye was caught by the county flag fluttering in the wind – a red rose on a white background. The whole country was divided into territories called *counties*, and theirs, Lancashire, was one of the largest. As its ruler, the Duke of Lancaster (called that because Lancaster was the main city) was a very important man, with the power of life and death over its inhabitants; only the King had more power.

The wind was gusting so hard it was difficult to stay upright, but that didn't stop Crafty noticing something he hadn't spotted from his bedroom window. The dark wall of the Shole didn't reach up into the sky as far as he'd thought. To the south-east, the green summits of the Bowland Fells protruded from it like islands in a dark sea. Unlike the Daylight Islands, those fell tops were uninhabited. Once there had been sheep, but by now they would probably have wandered down into the Shole – to die or be changed.

'Windy enough for you?' Donna asked with a grin.

Crafty grinned back and nodded, laughing. She beckoned to Lucky and they all made their way down into the castle. Soon they were peering into the huge bustling kitchens, where aproned cooks were serving lunch. People were eating at long wooden tables. The aroma of food was tantalizing and the murmur of conversation even louder than the background clatter of dishes.

'Why don't *we* eat here?' asked Crafty. Apart from lunch, which they ate in the Waiting Room, all his meals had been brought up to him in his room. No one had said as much, but it was clear that you weren't meant to visit other people's rooms.

'Only general workers eat here. Some of the guilds, such as gate mancers, have their own private dining rooms. Being mere gate grubs, we don't rate that. It's because the Chief Mancer doesn't like us to *fraternize*, as he calls it. We're kept away from other castle workers in case we give away secrets or learn theirs – that's what I've been told, anyway. We're not supposed to tell anyone what we do in the Shole. There's a lot of secrecy here.'

Crafty remembered what Ginger Bob had told him when they first met: *We, the Castle Corpus, are a dedicated team of people. We divide up into groups with different specialities, but we work together in order to discover as much as possible about the Shole, in order to learn how to deal with it.*

Maybe that wasn't actually true at all . . .

Before long Crafty found himself walking past the Waiting Room. He pointed to the other doors. 'What goes on in these rooms?' he asked.

'I think that one –' Lucky pointed to the one on the right – 'the Relic Room, is where they keep any objects brought back from the Shole. It's a big laboratory and museum, where they study, catalogue and store anything we find. But as for some of the other rooms – well, what happens there is anyone's guess. Like I say, people work within their own guilds, keep to their own specialities and don't talk about what they or others do. It's a sort of unwritten law for those who work here.'

'The Optimists' Room and the Pessimists' Room . . . sounds like a joke, I always think!' Donna laughed.

Crafty grinned. 'And the Dead Room sounds like somewhere I'd rather not be.'

'Well, that's just about everything,' Lucky told him, coming to a halt at the top of a spiral staircase.

'Can't we go down?' Crafty asked.

'We can visit a few other places, like the mancers' rooms, but only when we're summoned. To be honest, most of this place is out of bounds,' Lucky explained. 'Somewhere down below there's a room they call the Menagerie. That's where they keep the live aberrations we snatch. Some people say there's also a labyrinth of tunnels that goes deep under the castle, and that some passages emerge at different places in the city – but I think it's just speculation.'

Donna shuddered. 'We think they conduct research down in the Menagerie. At night you can sometimes hear screams . . . it's horrible. There's one other place we could show Crafty,' she suggested to Lucky, 'but we'll need to go out into the yard to reach it.' She turned to Crafty. 'It's called the Witches' Well. That's where they keep witches, either when they're awaiting trial or before they hang them. There have been a lot of trials recently – the Church is getting very strict. If you slip the guard a coin, he'll let you go down and see a witch up close. You can even talk to them.'

'Aren't they dangerous?' Crafty asked.

He wasn't too keen on seeing a witch up close, and certainly didn't want to talk to one. There had always been witches in Lancashire, and for the most part they'd been considered pretty harmless; most were healers, or would summon a bit of benign magic to help you – so long as you paid. But since the coming of the Shole it was thought that they had become more powerful, their magic slowly gathering strength. People were becoming more and more afraid of malevolent magic, which could be used to harm people.

Of course, lots of things were blamed on the Shole. But there was no denying that witches could be dangerous – and the Church had taken full advantage of the situation, claiming to be fighting harmful magic. Which was probably why, Crafty thought, so many witches were being arrested and tried.

'Yes, there are some witches you need to be wary of, but there's only one down there at the moment, and she's really old and a bit soft in the head,' Lucky explained. 'She couldn't hurt a fly even if she wanted to. They call her Old Nell. She's from a local village, the Crook o' Lune, and folks there protested when she was arrested. She used to cure warts, ease the pain of toothache and see into the future a bit. But the villagers' complaints did no good. The Church Court decided that she was a witch and now she's going to hang.'

A pang of sympathy went through Crafty, and he saw that Donna was pulling a face too. Poor Old Nell – it didn't sound like she'd been doing anyone any harm.

They came out into the yard and headed towards a big rusty gate set into the far wall. Beyond it Crafty could see a steep staircase leading down, and a red-faced guard with a club at his belt standing just to the left.

'Well, young sirs and madam, no doubt you're wanting to talk to Old Nell,' the guard said with a grin as he saw them approaching. Then he rubbed his thumb and forefinger together, indicating that he would need payment for the privilege.

Grumbling, Lucky handed him a coin and the man eased it into his trouser pocket before unhooking a big key from his belt. After dealing with the rusty padlock, he pulled back the gate, which creaked loudly on its hinges, the base grating across the flagstones.

'If you're not back in ten minutes, I'll come down with a small sack and bring up any bits of flesh and bone that are left once the witch has finished with you,' he said, his face very serious.

Crafty knew that he was joking, but it still didn't do his nerves any good.

The steps were dark, but there was a glimmer of light from below. Crafty followed Lucky and Donna down until they emerged into a big cell illuminated by a single flickering wall torch. It smelled terrible. There was no furniture, just a bundle of dirty rags in the middle. For a moment Crafty's heart pounded as he wondered where the witch was – could she have escaped? – but then he saw a leg protruding from the mound, and realized that it was fastened by a chain to a ring set in the floor. Slowly the bundle of rags sat up to reveal a wrinkled old face, eyes like tiny brown buttons and a shock of white hair streaked with dirt.

'Well, well!' the witch croaked. 'If it isn't three gate grubs come to talk to Old Nell. Come to hear your fortunes, have ye?'

None of them replied. Crafty couldn't imagine how she'd known that they were gate grubs. None of them were wearing their uniforms. Was it a lucky guess, or was she using some kind of magic?

'But what sort of grubs are ye?' she continued, unperturbed by their silence. 'Do you serve a silver gate or a black gate?'

'We serve silver gates, Nell,' Lucky replied in a shaky voice. 'I've never even heard of a black gate.'

'Then let me be the one to reveal a secret of this ancient castle. Let Old Nell put ye right. A silver gate is a portal to the Shole, whereas a black gate is a portal to Hell.' She cackled wildly, causing them all to jump back a little.

'It can take you to Hell?' Lucky asked dubiously.

'Yes, to Hell, little grub. Ye might've heard of it!' the witch said sarcastically. 'It's where the damned go after death – both humans and other creatures. It's where I'll go once I've swung on the end of the hangman's rope and stretched my neck a bit more than I'd like. A lot goes on under this castle, far from the light o' day. Aye – there are gates that take you to Hell just as easily as to the Shole.'

Crafty saw Donna shake her head slightly. She didn't believe the witch either, though she certainly looked scared.

But Crafty wasn't so sure. He'd been able to hear the whispering of his two dead brothers. He knew there was more to the afterlife than just being buried. Why shouldn't there be gates to where the dead were – to where they went after they'd finished whispering?

'So do you want to hear your fortunes or not?' Old Nell persisted. 'Don't be shy. I'll start with you, skinny girl!' she cried, pointing at Donna, who gasped. 'You've not long left on this earth. Enjoy your last bit o' daylight. You'll be the first o' these grubs to die. And it'll be very soon. Not a nice death either, I'm afraid. Hanging would be less painful – although I must say *I'm* not looking forward to it much.'

'Take no notice, Donna,' Lucky said, his voice filled with anger. 'Why say such cruel words, Nell? We came to talk to you. We thought you'd like a bit of company!'

'*A bit o' company!* Don't make me laugh, boy. You came to gawp at an old witch and have a bit o' fun. I know your game. And just so you know, *you'll* be the second to die. Hope you're enjoying my company, young scallywag!'

Crafty was alarmed by Old Nell's tone, which was mirthless and bitter. She didn't seem to be joking.

Then her brown button eyes fixed on him and her mouth cracked into a horrid smile. 'Come a little closer, Crafty,' she said, beckoning him with a finger, its nail cracked and bloody.

How did she know his name? Crafty shivered, but took a couple of steps towards the old witch, obeying without thought.

'No, Crafty!' yelled Lucky. 'Don't go any nearer!'

But he was unable to stop himself. Was this magic, or simple curiosity?

He took another couple of paces, and suddenly Nell lunged forward and grabbed his ankle. Donna and Lucky shrieked, but didn't dare come any closer.

The witch squeezed his ankle tightly. Her hand was very cold, and his eyes were drawn to hers as she held him with her fierce gaze. He couldn't move – not even to raise his little finger. He could barely breathe.

'Well! I don't know what to make o' ye, Crafty. You're not like your friends. There's more to *you* than meets the eye. The *Lord of the Gates* – that's what you be, make no mistake. But that's only if you live long enough.'

She stared at Crafty for a minute longer – he felt her eyes looking right into him. Then, suddenly, she released his ankle and he staggered backwards.

'Be off! All three of ye, begone!' Old Nell hissed fiercely.

Terrified, and not needing a second invitation, they made a dash for the door. Then:

'Stop!' Nell shrieked, and they came to a sudden halt, limbs in a tangle, almost jammed together in the doorway in their frantic haste to escape.

'Don't think too much on my words,' she went on, her voice much softer, almost wheedling. 'I was only having a bit o' fun. Maybe ye'll live long lives, but it's a dangerous job, being a gate grub. So I'll send ye away with a kindly curse that will either help ye or make things worse. To all three of ye, I say this: *May you get what you deserve!'*

And with that, they turned tail and scrambled up the stairs, Old Nell's laughter ringing in their ears.

Once back in the yard, they were quiet for a while, but as they wandered through the castle gardens, Lucky and Donna soon cheered up and started cracking jokes, mainly at Crafty's expense – calling him the Lord of the Gates.

'Is there actually a Lord of the Gates in the castle?' Crafty asked.

'No – not unless you count Ginger Bob!' laughed Lucky. 'You're the only one we've got!'

Crafty didn't mind the jibes. He knew they weren't meant unkindly, and he was beginning to think of Lucky and Donna as friends – and he hadn't had friends in a very long time.

Nobody really trusted Fey folk or wanted to get too close to them. Crafty and his two brothers had been the only Fey in their boys-only school, and Brock and Ben had been in a different class. As a result, he had often felt lonely, especially in the playground – though never as lonely as during his last few months in the cellar. It felt good to have someone to share a joke with.

Although his friends didn't refer to it for the rest of the day, Crafty knew that they were still thinking about Old Nell's curse. He certainly was.

Was it good to get what you deserved?

Perhaps it depended on how you lived your life.

10

A DANGEROUS JOB

That night Crafty found it hard to get to sleep again. There had been no sign of his father, and he resolved to ask a gate mancer about him the next day.

His thoughts turned to his new friends. He'd been lonely for such a long time, he reflected – although that wasn't quite true, he realized; he'd been forgetting someone.

Bertha had been a good friend to him. They'd often sat cross-legged on the cellar floor, facing each other as they talked. Bertha's slim golden crown sat perched on the dark coils of her hair, reflecting the light of the three candles. Beside them was the mud hole from which she had emerged. Although the candles kept aberrations out of the cellar, for some reason they couldn't prevent Bertha coming to see him. This wasn't something he had revealed to his father. He was afraid that he'd try to keep her out. He wouldn't trust an aberration, no matter how friendly she seemed.

Bertha had told Crafty all about the distant past. At first, she'd been happy as the warrior queen of the Segantii. They had defeated all the local tribes, but then a powerful new enemy had invaded their lands.

'What were they like, the Romans?' Crafty had asked.

'They were big tall men with short swords, long spears and curved oblong shields – but they always worked together. They built long straight roads so that they could move their warriors from place to place very quickly. And when they fought, they stood shoulder to shoulder and locked their shields together to form a wall. We couldn't break through it – lots of us died trying. But then I got an idea . . .'

'Something to break through their wall of shields?' asked Crafty, leaning forward to catch Bertha's reply. She spoke very softly, her accent making it difficult to understand what she was saying.

'Yes – I got the idea after watching a hedgehog curl up into a spiky ball when a dog tried to eat it. The poor dog got a sore nose and ran off howling. The hedgehog used those spines as a form of defence, but I saw how that shape could be used to attack. I designed a weapon and got our blacksmiths to make it for me. It was a heavy iron orb covered in sharp spikes and attached to a long chain. I practised using it. When I whirled it above my head, it made a strange whooshing sound; I could build up a tremendous speed and force. I knew I could use it to batter gaps in the

Romans' shield-wall, and my own warriors would then pour through and defeat them.'

'Did it work?' Crafty asked.

Bertha shook her head sadly. 'I never got the chance to try it out in battle. Our tribal priests were very powerful and, even though I was their queen, I was seized and slain. They thought that, by sacrificing me, giving up something that was important to our tribe, they'd win the favour of our gods. So they killed me and buried me in the bog.'

'Well, it didn't work. The gods didn't listen,' Crafty told her. 'The Romans conquered the whole land and stayed here for hundreds of years. Those priests would have done better to let you fight on.'

Bertha's big green eyes went wide, and she smiled at him. 'But it all worked out for the best. If they hadn't put me in the bog, I wouldn't have been brought back to life, would I? And we wouldn't be talking now.'

Yes, thought Crafty. They'd had so many long, interesting talks like that. Bertha's friendship had made it possible for him to endure those long months in the cellar. He owed her a lot.

He wondered what she was doing now.

Monday meant that they were back in the Waiting Room.

'What would you do if you really *were* the Lord of the Gates and could tell all the gate mancers what to do?' Lucky asked casually as Crafty sat down. He and Donna grinned at each other, and Crafty rolled his eyes. It looked as if the joke was going to continue.

'Well, for one thing I'd give proper training to gate grubs,' he replied, joining in. 'And anyone who played silly, dangerous games like Viper would be sacked on the spot!'

But before he could carry on, the far door opened and three mancers walked into the room. One of them was unknown to Crafty, and it made him wonder how many gate mancers there were.

The Chief Mancer was in the lead, an unknown large, plump man came in at his heels, and Viper brought up the rear of the grim-faced procession.

'We have an emergency,' Ginger Bob announced solemnly, glancing at each of them in turn, 'so this will be a combined operation. You, Henderson, will go with Mr Vipton; Proudfoot, you're with Mr Humperton, and you, Benson, will come with me.'

With that the three mancers turned on their heels and, carrying their heavy greatcoats, the three gate grubs followed. Crafty felt sorry for Donna. He was certainly glad *he* hadn't been assigned to Viper.

In Ginger Bob's office he was invited to sit down by the desk. The mancer sat facing Crafty.

'Now, young man. I want you to understand that what I am about to tell you must never be divulged to anyone other than those involved – by which I mean anyone other than the three gate mancers and the three gate grubs involved in this operation. Breaking that rule will have dire consequences.

Give me your word that, whatever results from what we are about to undertake, your lips will be permanently sealed.'

'Yes, sir, I give you my word,' Crafty told him. What else could he say? He wondered what the punishment would be for breaking the rule. The Chief Mancer seemed to be taking this mission pretty seriously.

'Well. You will have heard about the Duke of Lancaster's eldest son – the one who was trapped on a small Daylight Island when the Shole surged about a year ago . . .'

'No, sir, I didn't know that.'

'Ah, of course, I suppose it is understandable that you wouldn't have heard . . . you would have been trapped in the Shole when it happened. Well, he was visiting a small village called Penwortham, west of Preston. When the Shole suddenly expanded, the village became a new Daylight Island. Since he is the son of our county ruler, his rescue was considered a priority. Not long ago, the very best people were sent to bring him safely through the Shole and back to this city.'

'So the Duke's son isn't Fey, sir?' Crafty asked. Some people didn't like the Fey, others even had a hatred for them, but they had useful powers. The Duke liked power, so maybe, like Crafty's mother, he had married a Fey – but then hidden the fact in order to be more popular? Crafty's father had once hinted that such things were not unheard of.

'Of course not, young man!' Ginger Bob looked shocked. 'That's why the task was so difficult. He could not be brought through the Shole without risking death or change. But after months of effort and experimentation, our brightest boffins have devised a shielding material that offers protection against the Shole. It was fixed around a sedan chair . . .'

Ginger Bob paused as he saw the bewildered expression on his gate grub's face. Crafty didn't know what a sedan chair was – he'd never even heard of such a thing. Nor had he known that they'd found a way to protect humans from the Shole – did this mean they could begin rescuing more people? He made a mental note to ask the mancer about it later.

'A human passenger may be carried in a sedan chair,' Ginger Bob continued. 'This one has a door and a roof but no windows. It completely encloses its occupant – like a giant box. It has no wheels, but is supported by two long wooden poles that rest upon the shoulders of the bearers. In this case, the people entrusted with bringing the Duke's son home were couriers, who could make it safely through the Shole. Three of our best men were given the job – two to carry, one to guard.'

'And did the shielding material work?' Crafty asked.

The Chief Mancer looked a little shifty, as if he was hiding something. 'It was tested extensively,' he said. 'The Duke himself was happy for the rescue attempt to go ahead. I am confident that whatever has gone wrong has nothing to do with the shielding material.'

He was *definitely* looking a bit shifty, thought Crafty. He wondered if the shielding material had been *his* idea, and he was worried about getting into trouble.

'Anyway – starting from a point west of the river Ribble,' the mancer continued, 'they had to go deep into the Shole in order to cross a bridge leading to the safest routes north towards Lancaster. Despite that detour, the couriers should have been back with the Duke's son by now. But they aren't. They are already almost twenty-four hours overdue. It seems that something may have happened, so we need to find them.'

A frightening thought lurched into Crafty's head.

'Was one of the couriers my father, sir?' he asked, his voice shaking.

The look on the mancer's face confirmed the worst, and he sighed. 'I'm sorry to have to tell you that your father was indeed one of the couriers assigned to the task. But in finding the chair and the Duke's son, I hope that we will also find your father and the other couriers.'

The blood began to pound inside Crafty's head and he fought to hold back tears. What if something had happened to his father? What if he never saw him again? He had already lost his mother to the Shole, and then his two brothers – he couldn't bear the thought of losing his father too.

But Ginger Bob clearly didn't have any time to waste on sympathy. He pulled a silver watch out of his pocket and consulted it. 'It's nearly ten minutes to noon. Almost time to get you into the chair, young man. Before we proceed, have you any questions?'

'Are we going to attempt a snatch, sir?' Crafty asked. 'Are we going to try and bring them all back through a gate?' He wanted to help the Duke's son, but his main concern was for his own father's safety.

'The first priority is to locate the chair and its occupant. Then, depending on the situation, we may indeed attempt a snatch. But this is more likely to be what we call a *combined field operation*. It will involve all three of you grubs going through gates into the Shole and working together. What happens after that depends on the situation you find. So initially I won't be strapping you in. Leave your coat there for now,' the mancer said, pointing at a chair.

He led Crafty across to the curtain and pulled it back; Crafty took his seat, gazing into the opaque swirling clouds inside the silver gate. After once more consulting his watch, the Chief Mancer reached into his breeches pocket, pulled out a small scrap of black cloth and handed it to Crafty.

'This is a piece of the shielding material that clads the sedan chair,' he said.

Studying it closely, Crafty could see that it wasn't simply black. There was a background of dozens of tiny glittering specks that made him think of stars in a clear night sky.

'Now concentrate, Benson. You should be able to find the same material. Find that, and you've found the Duke's son – and maybe your father too.'

Crafty concentrated as hard as he could, trying to sense the material within the Shole. The clouds in the gate cleared, and suddenly he was looking through the grey gloom towards some leafless trees. To the right was a low wall, and beyond it he could see a row of buildings maybe three storeys high. Nothing was moving. The ground by the trees was sparsely covered with grass and dead leaves ... and then he noticed a large object lying on its side.

He could see two poles on the grass beside it, and the black, glittering material covering it – it was a box that had a door but no windows. It was the sedan chair.

But there was no sign of his father or the other couriers.

Crafty suddenly felt very sorry for the Duke's son. To have to travel like that, in total darkness, listening for any noises. It must have been terrifying. But then, he thought, it was no different to his own experience in the Shole, when his father had pulled a hood over his head.

The Chief Mancer interrupted his thoughts. 'Well done, young man. You've found the sedan chair, but things do not look promising. Note that the door is open, with no sign of the Duke's son or the three couriers. And I know this location. At midday this area should have been without risk. Although the Shole is riddled with dangers, there are safe routes that couriers take through this part of Preston, which explains why they cut across these gardens.'

'Where are we, sir?' asked Crafty.

'Somewhere called Winckley Square. Thanks to its proximity to the river Ribble, it used to be favoured by Preston's wealthiest citizens – this was a large central garden owned by the gentry who inhabited those townhouses. Now it all belongs to the Shole, and its aberrations dwell within them. But fear not – they will not emerge until darkness falls. You have plenty of time to investigate.'

Great, Crafty thought to himself. *Just what I need – a chance to spend time in the Shole . . .*

The mancer walked across to his desk and returned carrying Crafty's greatcoat. Crafty came to his feet, pulled it on and buttoned it up to the neck; he knew just how cold the Shole could be.

'Check to see that – as I predict – the sedan chair is empty. If the Duke's son is still inside, he could be either dead or terribly changed, so take care. If he's not there, then the three of you must make a thorough search of the walled garden, but do *not* venture outside it. Then, young man, you must report back. Report back *only* to me. Do you understand?'

'Yes, sir,' Crafty replied as he clambered through the gate.

'Speed is of the essence!' Ginger Bob called after him. 'If the Duke's son is alive, there is a slim chance he may still be himself. We must rescue him before he starts to change!'

It was not as cold as when Viper had played that trick on him, but Crafty was still glad of his coat. A chill breeze was blowing directly into his face, numbing his nose. In the distance, through the trees, he could see two circles of blue light. Lucky and Donna must have spotted the chair too.

He reached it before they did, and cautiously looked through the door.

Whoever had constructed the sedan chair had tried to make it as comfortable as possible. It had a soft leather seat and was lined with blue velvet. But it was empty.

Crafty's mind raced. What had happened here? Why had the door been opened? Where had the couriers gone? Where was his father? And where was the Duke's son?

Lucky and Donna joined him, and peered inside.

Crafty told them what Ginger Bob had said to him. 'One of the three couriers was my father. He's missing with the others – he's lost somewhere in the Shole.'

'Oh, Crafty, I'm really sorry,' said Donna, patting his shoulder sympathetically. 'I know it must be hard for you to come searching for the Duke's son when it's your father you'd really like to find.'

Crafty found he had a lump in his throat; he couldn't reply.

Lucky gave him a pat on the back. 'It may not be as bad as it seems,' he said. 'Couriers have gone missing in the Shole before and found their way back.'

For a moment there was silence – none of them knew what to say next. Crafty surreptitiously wiped away his tears, while Donna and Lucky pretended not to notice.

'Well, we'd better begin our search,' Donna said at last, assuming command. Four months' service made her veteran. She had more experience than Lucky, and definitely more than Crafty.

'If we split up, we could do it faster,' Crafty suggested, looking at her.

'No, Crafty, that's the worst thing to do,' she replied. 'Sticking together and helping each other is the best way to survive here. Let's see if there are any tracks.'

The ground around the sedan chair was soft and muddy, and they quickly found four sets of footprints. It was easy to distinguish those of the Duke's son from the couriers'. The men's big boots left deep prints and showed that they had headed up the slope. The Duke's son appeared to be wearing narrow, delicate shoes with slightly tapering toes, and his footprints led in the opposite direction.

The group had split up. But why?

'We'll follow the tracks made by the Duke's son,' Donna declared.

Crafty would much rather have followed those of his father and his companions, but how could he argue? Their duty was to find the Duke's son. At least they knew in which direction the couriers had headed.

When he glanced behind him, Crafty could see no sign of the blue circles that marked the positions of the three gates. He crossed his fingers that they could find their way back.

Although this place had once been called Winckley Square, the garden itself was oblong in shape, and they hurried along it on a downwards sloping path. There were rustlings all around them, and Crafty's eyes darted left and right. He felt as if they were being watched, and he could see that Donna and Lucky were nervous too. Their expressions were worried as they glanced around.

The creatures he'd been warned about were supposed to be asleep in the houses that bordered the garden. But what if there were other things of which the Chief Mancer was unaware – something new that had attacked the rescue party and their cargo?

At the bottom of the slope the ground became very soft again, and the sound of their squelching boots was all Crafty could hear. Then, suddenly, he thought he heard a cry. Donna held up her hand as a sign that they should halt.

They listened intently. The cry came again, so they cautiously set off towards it. A prickle of dread ran up Crafty's spine – and within moments they had found the Duke's son.

The Chief Mancer had never mentioned his age, but Crafty had expected him to be young, perhaps even younger than them.

He was wrong. This was a youth of perhaps eighteen or nineteen, and he was weeping softly. He was stuck up to his waist in what appeared to be a small bog.

Crafty had never seen him before, but his clothes betrayed his standing. People who walked the streets of Lancaster didn't wear clothes like that. Around his neck was a big white ruff above a purple silk tunic with silver buttons. This was definitely the person they were looking for.

Still sobbing, the lad stared up at them. He had a smooth round face and the faintest of blond beards at his chin. His eyes were red from crying.

'Help me! Please help me!' he begged pitifully.

'Don't you worry, sir,' Donna told him, trying to sound cheerful. 'We'll have you out of there in no time at all.'

But it wasn't easy. Their first attempts to reach him were cautious – they didn't want to get sucked down into the bog themselves. However, although the ground was soggy, it proved to be relatively firm, and after a bit of testing they found they were in no real danger. It seemed that the Duke's son had been unlucky enough to find a small spot that was soft enough to suck him in.

Soon all three of them were close enough to tug him free. But no matter how hard they tried, they could barely budge him. And as they struggled and strained, he kept wailing and sobbing. Then there was a squelching sound as, at last, with a Herculean effort, they managed to raise him a couple of inches.

It was then that they became aware of the full horror of the situation.

They realized that the Shole had indeed changed him: he no longer had any legs.

His whole lower body had been transformed into a mass of twisty, fibrous, woody roots.

11

SHARP PRUNERS

Finding the gate without trouble, Crafty ran to report back to the Chief Mancer.

Ginger Bob stared at him through the circle. His face was impassive, and Crafty hadn't a clue what he was thinking. He assumed they'd be told to leave the Duke's son where he was. Surely nothing could be done to help him now . . .

But he was wrong.

'Well, Benson,' said the mancer, 'the Duke's orders were very clear. Even if his son had been changed by the Shole, he wished him to be brought back to the castle – no matter what the difficulty or cost. He is the Duke of Lancaster and his word is law. We must obey him. Wait here,' he added. 'I'll arrange for the necessary implements to be brought to you.'

Crafty waited anxiously in the cold, wondering what the Chief Mancer had meant by 'necessary implements'. When he returned, Crafty understood with a chill of horror exactly what they were going to have to do.

Through the gate he was handed three spades – and what at first glance looked like a large pair of scissors. Then Crafty realized that they were for pruning trees. His mother had had a similar pair.

'Bring him back to this gate,' the Chief Mancer ordered sternly. 'Only *this* gate. And do whatever it takes.'

Crafty shuddered, and headed back towards Donna and Lucky. He knew that they were being ordered to cut through what had once been the young man's legs, pull him free and bring back what remained of his body. It would be a grim task.

'We have to dig him out as best we can and take him to Ginger Bob's gate,' he told the others, in a voice too low for the whimpering young man to hear.

Donna nodded. Wasting no time, she took one of the spades, strode over to where the Duke's son was buried and started to dig energetically. Her limbs looked uncoordinated, but she was using the spade effectively, chucking earth back over her left shoulder.

'Donna certainly doesn't mess about!' Lucky observed. 'Just gets on with what needs doing.'

Crafty had a bad feeling about that. Perhaps Lucky did too, because at first they both simply watched from a distance without making any attempt to help.

All at once the youth's whimpers erupted into a shrill scream of agony.

Donna stepped back, clearly appalled. It seemed that cutting through the roots would cause the lad terrible pain, just as if they were his legs. Crafty's heart sank – he'd wondered if that might be the case.

'Donna!' Crafty called, beckoning her towards him. Donna came over, looking doubtfully at the spade she was carrying.

He led her further away so that they were completely out of earshot of the trapped young man. Lucky followed, casting an anxious look over his shoulder.

Crafty laid out his plan. 'My mother liked gardening, and sometimes I used to watch her work. I even helped her out from time to time – I've read all her books on the subject,' he told them. 'If the Duke's son was a small tree, his roots would be spread out quite a way, further than you might think. We need to start digging a lot further out. If we make a large enough hole around him, we might be able to tug him free without using these,' he added, showing them the sharp pruners.

Lucky and Donna both squirmed – they were clearly as unhappy as Crafty at the idea of snipping through the young man's roots.

'We're bound to hurt him a bit – we can't avoid cutting through some of the finer roots,' he continued. 'But there may also be what's called a taproot. It's the main central root, which is often very thick and goes deep into the ground. We mustn't damage that or I think it would kill him.'

Donna nodded. 'Fine. You seem to know what you're talking about, Crafty, so we'll do as you say. I only have one worry. This'll take quite a while, and the longer we stay beyond noon, the more dangerous it will get. We don't want to be here when it gets dark.'

Crafty knew that it got dark in the Shole a lot earlier than it did in the Daylight World. Once the sun grew low in the sky, it could no longer penetrate the gloom, and that could happen as soon as late afternoon, even in summer.

So they set to work as quickly as they could, all three of them digging with the spades, creating a wide pit around the youth. Occasionally he gave a yelp, but after a while they saw that he had lapsed into unconsciousness. Maybe he'd fainted from the pain and fear, thought Crafty. He was certainly in a sorry state.

Then Crafty had another dark thought. Maybe the Duke's son was continuing to change . . . Perhaps in time he'd be completely made of wood, the blood in his veins and arteries replaced by sap, his brain changed to fungus? Maybe if that happened, he'd feel less pain. But could they be sure of that? Some people thought plants did feel pain. Perhaps a weed screamed silently when you pulled it up, tearing it free of the earth? Crafty shook his head at the idea and got back to work.

It took hours. As the three grubs got closer to the young man's body, they saw that the roots became thicker. They dug around these very carefully and then eased them free of the slimy soil. At last they reached a big root that went down directly below him. Crafty's prediction had been correct: this was the taproot, and they had to dig very deep before it grew thinner. They tugged at this together – until at last they pulled the youth free with a loud slurping, sucking sound.

Only then did the Duke's son open his eyes. He stared around in terror before his gaze settled on Crafty.

'I feel dizzy,' he complained. 'The whole world is spinning . . .'

'Don't you worry, sir,' said Donna, smiling kindly in an attempt to reassure him. 'We'll soon get you safely back to the city. The worst is over.'

But it wasn't. At least not for them. Their troubles had only just begun.

They lifted the young man up as gently as they could and carried him towards the Chief Mancer's gate. He began to moan, and Crafty knew that dragging his roots across the ground was causing him pain. But what else could they do? They were trying their best – they just wanted to get out of there as soon as possible.

Crafty was pleased that he'd been able to suggest a way to free the youth. Donna's method would have caused him terrible pain, and the Chief Mancer's sharp pruners might have killed him on the spot. Now at least there was a chance that he would survive. Maybe one day the people in the castle laboratories would be able to reverse the effects of the Shole, he thought. For now, maybe they could plant the young man in soil again? But would he want to live like that? Was it really preferable to death?

Soon the three gates were in sight, and they carried their strange burden towards the Chief Mancer's. Through the circle Crafty saw a couple of guards standing behind him, peering curiously at them through the gate's shimmering blue frame. All three figures in the room recoiled when they saw the Duke's son.

Crafty, Donna and Lucky carefully eased him through, head first, and the guards gingerly took up the burden.

'Well,' said Ginger Bob when the youth had been taken away. 'Henderson and Proudfoot, go back to your own gates. I only want one pair of muddy feet tramping through my office, thank you very much.'

Crafty shivered. It was starting to get dark, and the danger from the creatures in those houses would be increasing by the minute. Surely it would be better if all three of them came through *this* gate. After all, the mancers' offices were only a few doors apart. And who cared about a bit of mud? Yet here was Ginger Bob, pointing at the gate and asking Donna and Lucky to take a very risky walk of at least fifty yards!

Then the mancer turned to Crafty. 'You, Benson, had better go and get the spades and the pruners and bring them back here. We can't afford to lose castle property.'

Crafty looked at him in dismay, but saw that he meant it. He turned to look at the gathering gloom.

Donna must have guessed what he was thinking. She shook her head and said, 'We'll come with you, Crafty, and help you collect the tools. It's getting more dangerous by the minute.'

Lucky murmured his agreement. 'We can't let you go back alone.'

Crafty felt a rush of relief, and thanked them for their offer. He knew they'd probably get into trouble with Ginger Bob – they were disobeying orders, after all – but he would be really glad of the company.

All three of them hurried back. The visibility was deteriorating rapidly; in the garden now only the nearest trees could be seen. The wall and the houses beyond were already lost in darkness.

They soon approached the place where they'd left the tools, though they could barely see anything now. Then Crafty heard the first howl, quickly followed by another and another. Those chilling cries turned the blood in his veins to ice. The three of them stopped and looked at each other in horror.

'Forget the spades!' Donna shouted, pointing ahead. 'Run for your lives – back to the gates!'

A pack of four-legged creatures came bounding towards them over the wall, saliva dripping from open jaws. Howling with hunger, they sounded like wolves but looked like giant hairy cats. Huge fangs curved down over their lower jaws, and their long limbs ended in long sharp claws. The three gate grubs turned and ran.

For a few seconds they kept together, panting hard. But soon Crafty found himself in the lead, with Lucky at his shoulder. He glanced back and saw that Donna, sprinting as best she could in her uncoordinated fashion, was falling far behind. And the beasts were gaining on her – fast.

Crafty realized with a jolt that they should have all headed for the nearest gate – Ginger Bob's – in spite of their orders. No doubt Donna and Lucky were panicking just as much as him, because they had split up, each making for their own gate.

It was then that the howls came again, much louder this time. Crafty could hear the fanged predators bounding along behind him, getting closer and closer. His breathing was ragged now, his legs trembling with effort and fear. It was going to be a very close-run thing – for the first time he wondered if he might not make it to the gate in time!

Crafty risked a glance back, and saw that one of the creatures was practically upon him. His heart pounding, he raced up to the gate and dived through. The Chief Mancer was standing to one side, his foot positioned over the guillotine pedal. But Crafty immediately turned and focused his mind on the gate, thinking of clouds. The swirling opaque barrier filled the frame, and the danger was over.

He lay on the floor, panting and trembling. That had been close – too close.

'I see that you didn't manage to recover the tools,' Ginger Bob said, raising his eyebrows.

'It was either that or be eaten alive!' Crafty told him, astounded that he should even mention the tools now. Didn't he realize that they'd nearly *died*?

But the mancer just nodded and gave a little smile. 'Yes, of course. We can recover them another day. Well, go and get some rest, Benson – go straight to your room. There'll be plenty of time tomorrow to talk things over with your colleagues. I'll order a hearty supper to be brought up to you. Well done on the mission today – you did well.'

So Crafty trudged wearily back up to the tower. He was almost too tired to eat the bread and ham that were delivered to him.

But he wouldn't have been able to eat at all if he'd known what had happened.

Not all of them had made it back through their gates.

12

HANGING THE WITCH

When Crafty awoke, the aching muscles of his arms and back reminded him of what had happened the previous day. But there was a sense of accomplishment too – and a touch of exhilaration. He had helped rescue the Duke's son, and he was looking forward to talking it over with Lucky and Donna.

As usual, Crafty ate breakfast in his room and then reported directly to the Waiting Room. He was normally the last to arrive, but to his surprise only Lucky was sitting at the table. Crafty was just about to ask him about Donna when the far door opened and the Chief Mancer came in. His face looked particularly sombre. Crafty and Lucky exchanged a look. This couldn't be good news.

The mancer gave a little cough before speaking. Crafty thought he was about to make a snide remark about Donna's absence, but instead, to his astonishment, he began to applaud their achievement.

'I must congratulate you both on your exemplary conduct yesterday. Despite the danger, you worked long hours in treacherous conditions, and freed the Duke's son from that terrible predicament with minimal damage to his somewhat . . . transformed person.'

Ginger Bob paused and gave another cough. 'However, I do have some rather dreadful news. Unfortunately . . . I'm sorry to say . . . Henderson died at the scene.'

For a long time nobody spoke.

Crafty couldn't believe it. Donna was *dead*? A sudden pain in his chest made it difficult to breathe. Crafty hadn't known her long – less than a week – but so much had happened in that time, and they'd spent long days together. Donna had quickly become his friend.

He was angry with the Chief Mancer. If he hadn't sent him back to collect the tools, it wouldn't have happened. Then, if Donna hadn't insisted on helping him to collect them, she'd probably still be alive and chatting to them now. And now he'd never see her again – just like his brothers, his mother . . . and maybe his father.

'How did she die, sir? Was Donna caught before she reached the gate?' Lucky's voice sounded choked and quavery.

'She reached the gate, Proudfoot, but the aberrations that pursued her were close on her heels – extremely close. It was necessary for her mancer to use the guillotine. Unfortunately, it was brought down just too soon, and it severed Henderson's legs as she came through the gate. The poor girl died of shock and blood loss.'

Out of the corner of his eye Crafty saw Lucky's face twist in rage and pain. They could only imagine the agony Donna must have suffered. Lucky looked ready to explode. Then Crafty heard him suck in a big breath, clearly trying to calm his fury as he bowed his head and stared at the floor.

Crafty was seething too. Viper had killed other gate grubs before – two of them with the guillotine. Now he'd done it again. How could he possibly be allowed to continue as a mancer?

'As is customary following the death of a team member, you will not be required to work today. Donna's death is very sad and a great loss. You will of course report for work at the usual time tomorrow morning.'

With that the Chief Mancer left the room.

'I need to get out of here,' Lucky said, his voice full of bitterness, his eyes brimming with tears. 'I'm going out into the city. Want to come?'

Crafty nodded silently. He wished there was something he could say to comfort Lucky – after all, he'd known Donna much better than Crafty had – but nothing seemed right.

Five minutes later they were tramping through the cobbled streets of Lancaster, neither of them saying a word. They followed a rough circle, with Lucky setting a furious pace – up Meeting House Lane, then round the back of the castle and down Church Street. They were about to cross over to Market Street when they saw a procession winding away to the east.

'What's going on? Where's everybody going?' Lucky asked of a ragged old man at the back who was struggling to keep up.

'They're going to hang the witch,' he wheezed. 'Up on Gallows Hill. There'll be a big party afterwards. But bring your own drink!' Crafty saw that he was clutching a large bottle of ale in his hand.

'Let's follow them, Crafty,' Lucky said. 'I'd like to watch that old witch die.'

Crafty wasn't keen on the idea, but felt unable to protest. There was something newly grim and determined about Lucky. He'd always seemed a cheerful lad – though maybe a little fatalistic. He was clearly taking Donna's death very hard.

They began following the raucous crowd, many of whom seemed to have been drinking already: they were singing bawdy songs, and stumbling around. Lucky walked with his head down, hands firmly in his pockets.

Crafty noticed that in among the crowd there were groups of two and three wearing grey cloaks and hoods. He pointed them out to Lucky.

'Are they some sect of the priesthood?' he asked.

'They're a sect all right, but nothing to do with the Church,' Lucky replied. 'They call themselves the Grey Hoods – they've a religion of their own. They worship the Shole.'

'That's so stupid!' Crafty said, astonished. 'Why would anyone want to do that?'

'It works for some people,' Lucky told him. 'Mostly crazy people . . .'

Crafty was intrigued and wanted to find out more, but he could tell that Lucky was in no mood for talking.

At the top of the grassy slope – Gallows Hill – they saw a big wooden platform upon which a gibbet had been erected. It was a vertical post with a horizontal arm, a noose suspended from it. Beneath the rope stood a barrel, waiting for Old Nell.

The cart carrying the witch had just reached the platform. She was hauled off and pushed towards the steps. She shuffled slowly up, and when she reached the top the crowd began to jeer and shout in excitement. Crafty could see that Nell had been gagged, no doubt to stop her casting spells, and her hands were tied behind her back.

Lucky was trying to get a better view, but that was the last thing Crafty wanted. He was beginning to feel sick at the prospect of witnessing this poor old woman's death. Fortunately the crowd was too dense for them to see anything much. As Crafty gazed around, he saw people sitting down having picnics, taking advantage of the dry grass. Unusually for a Lancashire summer, it hadn't rained for at least a week – though Crafty could feel a strong wind blowing in from the west, straight from the sea, and clouds were building. It was going to rain, and soon.

On the platform men wearing black robes started making speeches while Old Nell stood calmly by, waiting to die. The speakers seemed to be priests, but the wind carried their words away and Crafty couldn't catch what was said. Those nearer the platform kept cheering, so he guessed they were being given a list of Old Nell's supposed misdeeds, the Church making it clear what her sins were and why she was being executed.

The whole thing disgusted him. As far as he knew, she hadn't done anyone any harm, yet here she was, her death to be used as entertainment. Everyone seemed to be treating it like a fun day out. At one point the crowd at the front surged to their feet and began clapping, but those nearer the back roared at them to sit down because they were blocking their view.

After ten minutes of speeches they got on with the hanging. A hood was placed over Old Nell's head, bringing back to Crafty the horrifying memory of being hooded when his father had led him through the Shole. It was all too easy to imagine what Nell was going through now. How terrible it would be – to know that in minutes you'd be strangled and, soon after that, dead.

Next they stood her on the barrel, and positioned the noose around her neck. The crowd was in a frenzy now, screaming and shouting at the executioners to get on with it. Finally they tightened the noose – and kicked the barrel out from under Old Nell's feet. Everybody but Lucky and Crafty clapped and cheered.

Crafty watched as Nell's legs kicked and her body twisted on the end of the rope. At one point a big gust of wind blew her ragged skirt up above her head, showing her undergarments. That got another big cheer.

Suddenly Lucky jolted forward, away from Crafty. 'Die, witch! Die!' he screamed.

Crafty gazed at him in astonishment, surprised by his hatred. What had got into him?

But Lucky's shout went down well with the crowd around them, and it was quickly taken up as a chant:

'*Die, witch, die! Die, witch, die! Die, witch, die!*'

Old Nell was still dancing at the end of the rope, but her movements were feebler now, hardly more than a twitching of the knees.

'Why do you hate her so much?' Crafty asked Lucky, unable to contain his feelings any longer. 'She's just a poor old woman – and even if she did have some magical ability, she didn't use it to harm people. She just cured warts and toothaches. Do you really think she deserves that?' he asked, pointing towards the gibbet.

The body of the witch was still now. She was dead, and out of her misery.

'Yes, I do,' Lucky said bitterly. 'She foretold Donna's death, and then she cursed all three of us. She said we should get what we deserved. Well, Donna was kind and helpful, and brave. Did she really deserve to die like that? To have her legs chopped off by a sadistic, reckless idiot? What do *we* deserve – the same?'

Crafty didn't reply. Lucky was furious, and he'd begun to wish he'd kept his mouth shut.

'And you know what?' Lucky continued, his fists balled up tight by his sides. 'Poor Donna won't even get a funeral because she's an orphan and has no family to care what happens to her body. They'll just grind up her bones and use them in the frame of a new gate.'

While he was speaking, it had finally begun to rain – great drops were being blown almost vertically into their faces. The people around them lurched to their feet, quickly gathering up their possessions and beginning to leave.

Crafty and Lucky stayed where they were, and within five minutes the hillside was almost deserted. The men on the platform were lifting Old Nell's body down from the gibbet. They still had a job to do, in spite of the torrential rain.

Crafty and Lucky were already soaked to the skin but still neither of them moved.

Lucky spoke again, more softly this time. 'Don't feel too sorry for her, Crafty. Tomorrow her family will come for the body and, if the rumours I hear are true, they'll carry it into the Shole under cover of darkness. They say most witches come back from the dead if they're buried there.'

'How can witches' families carry their dead into the Shole if they aren't Fey?' Crafty asked. 'Are witches Fey?'

Lucky shrugged, and a drop of rain fell from the end of his nose. 'Some think that witches have their own resistance to the Shole. But it's probably just talk.'

Crafty hesitated, unsure whether to take Lucky into his confidence. But he was a friend, wasn't he? So he blurted out the truth.

'The Shole *does* bring people back from the dead – that's a fact, not just superstition,' he said. 'And they don't have to be witches, either.'

Lucky turned to him. 'You know that for sure?' he asked, sounding disbelieving.

'Yes. When I was trapped in the Shole, I was visited by a girl who'd died hundreds of years ago – maybe thousands, for all I know. I called her the Bog Queen because she wore a crown; she'd been sacrificed by her own people, then buried in the bog. Her real name was Bertha.'

Lucky looked shocked. 'What was she like? Weren't you scared of her?'

'No. She was kind to me. I spent almost a year shut up in a cellar, and during the last months, after my brothers died, I was mostly alone. My father's job meant he was often away. She made my life bearable. I owe her a lot.'

Lucky put his arm round Crafty's shoulders in sympathy. 'You've had a hard time, Crafty, and I'm sorry for it. But things here are bad too. As gate grubs, our lives are worthless – we're at risk every day. And do you know what we have to do to make things better?'

Crafty shook his head.

So Lucky told him.

'We have to kill Viper.'

13

SMALL AND SCRAWNY

'You can't mean that!' Crafty protested. He hated Viper – of course he did – but he didn't want him *dead*.

'I do mean it,' Lucky spat. 'It's either him or us. At some point one of us will be assigned to him again, and we'll get hurt. Give him enough time, and eventually he'll kill us both. He'll either abandon us to die in the Shole – he's done that with other grubs – or slice us up with the guillotine. We've got to kill him first.'

Crafty didn't reply. What Lucky was saying shocked him. He knew he wasn't capable of murdering anyone – not even Viper.

'Come on,' Lucky demanded. 'You're supposed to be the crafty one – now live up to your name. How can we do it without getting caught? You need to come up with some clever scheme.'

'I'd like to try something else first,' replied Crafty carefully, hoping he could dissuade his friend from such a reckless course of action. 'I'll go and talk to Ginger Bob and tell him what we think – that Viper is dangerous and reckless and –'

'No!' interrupted Lucky. 'He won't listen. Look what he did – telling you to collect the tools, even though it was so dangerous out there. And mancers always stick together.'

'Let me try anyway. Please.'

Lucky looked cross, but sighed. 'Suit yourself. But when you've failed, we'll do it *my* way. Deal?'

Reluctantly Crafty nodded. 'Why do you think Viper behaves the way he does?' he asked. 'Does he simply get pleasure out of killing gate grubs?'

Lucky shrugged. 'Who knows what's going on inside his head. There are some people walking among us who look fine on the outside; but if you could read their thoughts you'd realize you were dealing with monsters. And there are other possibilities . . .'

Crafty looked at him, but he seemed reluctant to continue. After a long pause he began again: 'This is just speculation, but I've thought about Viper a lot during my three months at the castle. You know that crazy cult that worships the Shole – the Grey Hoods who were in the crowd earlier? They want the Shole to take over the whole world. They think that it will bring their dead families and friends back, and they will all live forever. The priests don't like it, and the Church has persuaded the Duke to come down hard on them. Some have been imprisoned, and now they are allowed out in public only in groups no larger than three. But they seem to be getting stronger. Although they kept within the law, there were still a lot of them about today. I've always wondered if Viper was one of them . . .'

'I suppose, being a gate mancer, he'd have opportunities to undermine the fight against the Shole,' said Crafty. He'd never heard of this weird cult until today, but then, he had missed a lot during his year in the cellar.

Lucky nodded. 'I think so. He could give them bad information, pretending it was research. Also gate grubs are getting harder to recruit, and the death toll isn't helping.'

They left Gallows Hill and made their way back to the castle in silence. They had a lot to think about, and they were both still mourning Donna.

Crafty spent the rest of the day in his room, pondering on all that had happened to him since he came to the castle. He wished he could talk to his father; his advice was always sound and wise. But now he was missing, and no one knew where he might be. Crafty wondered if the Duke's son had recovered yet. If he had, maybe he'd be able to tell them what had happened and why the three couriers had left him and gone up the hill.

Crafty sighed. *Come back soon, Father . . .* he thought. He didn't let himself wonder if his father might never be coming back. But the fear was there in the back of his mind.

The next morning Crafty walked into the Waiting Room to find Lucky at the table, his head on his arms.

'Tired?' he said, joking weakly.

But when Lucky lifted his head and looked at him, Crafty saw that his cheeks were streaked with tears, his eyes red and swollen. Before he could apologize, the far door opened and the Chief Mancer came in.

'I sincerely hope that we will not need your services today,' he began, 'but life must go on, and we must continue with our work. We are attempting to recruit a replacement gate grub, but it is proving somewhat . . . difficult.' He looked worried.

Crafty raised his hand, signalling that he wanted to say something.

Ginger Bob looked at him, and gave the faintest of smiles. 'Yes, Benson, what is it?'

'Could I have a word with you, sir?'

'Of course. Metaphorically speaking, I am all ears,' he said, waiting expectantly.

Crafty paused. 'I'd like to speak to you in private, sir.'

The Chief Mancer stared at him, and so did Lucky. They were both wondering why Crafty couldn't just say what he needed to. But the truth was, Crafty was worried about Lucky. He wanted to talk to Ginger Bob about Viper, and having Lucky around might put him off. There was also the danger that Lucky might interrupt and spoil things, especially in his present state of mind.

'Very well,' replied the mancer. 'I'm about to put a candidate through his paces, so come and see me this afternoon. Make it three on the dot.' And he turned and left the room.

'I don't know why you couldn't speak to him in front of me. What are you afraid of?' Lucky said immediately.

But before Crafty could think up an answer, the far door opened again and he gave a silent groan. It was Viper.

'Come with me, Proudfoot. I have a job for you!' he commanded.

Lucky glanced at Crafty, his eyes wide with fear.

'Now!'

Lucky dragged himself to his feet, and reluctantly followed Viper out of the room.

Crafty was simultaneously worried and relieved. He couldn't help but feel glad that Viper hadn't taken *him*, but he was very concerned about Lucky. Would Viper try to strike again immediately? he wondered.

He grew ever more anxious as time passed and Lucky didn't return. At first he tried to occupy himself by running through what he was going to say to the Chief Mancer. He knew he probably had only one chance to tell him how dangerous Viper was, so he had to get it right. He knew that Ginger Bob was a stickler for the rules, but surely he could be made to see how reckless Viper had become?

Three more hours passed, and then, finally, it was time to go down and talk to the Chief Mancer – and there was still no sign of Lucky.

Crafty knocked on the door and was invited to enter. The room was gloomy as usual, with a solitary candle flickering on the untidy desk. Ginger Bob pointed to a chair, and Crafty sat down opposite him. He couldn't help glancing over towards the black curtain.

'Did the candidate pass the test, sir?' he asked, wondering if a new gate grub would be joining them.

'Unfortunately he failed. Well, Benson, get to the point. What can I do for you? I'm afraid if you're here to ask about your father, I've not heard anything. All three couriers are still missing.'

Crafty's heart plummeted. He'd been hoping, if the conversation went well, to ask about his father – but now it seemed there was no need. He had a job to do, and he'd better get on with it. He cleared his throat.

'I was wondering if I could ask you a couple of things about Donna's death . . .'

Ginger Bob frowned, but gestured for him to go on.

Crafty took a nervous breath, and made his first point.

'Firstly, sir, I believe that each gate grub should have some sort of weapon to fend off aberrations from the Shole.'

'A weapon?' the Chief Mancer exclaimed, raising his eyebrows in astonishment.

'Yes, sir – perhaps some sort of spear to keep attackers at bay. Or at least a knife –'

'A knife? Preposterous! You are gate grubs, not warriors.'

'But, sir, couriers are armed. My father carries a knife with a long blade.'

'That is because couriers have to cross miles and miles of the Shole in order to reach distant Daylight Islands – alone, I might add – whereas gate grubs spend hardly any time on field operations, and rarely venture more than fifty yards from the nearest gate. You may also have noted that couriers are big men, strong and brawny. It is not for nothing that they call your father Big Brian. Gate grubs are small and scrawny. You don't have the physique to use weapons.'

'Perhaps, sir, that's because none of us live long enough to grow up and develop that physique.' Crafty could feel himself getting cross. Ginger Bob wasn't listening to him at all!

Anger clouded the mancer's face, and Crafty knew he'd made a mistake.

'I don't like your tone, Benson. Have you anything further to add? If not, return to the Waiting Room. I'm a very busy man.'

Crafty should simply have left the room then, but he was angry too. The Chief Mancer had dismissed his suggestion about weapons out of hand. Something had to be said.

So he said it.

'I do have something further to add. Sir, I am unhappy about the way Mr Vipton conducts himself. Donna was the third gate grub he's accidentally killed with the guillotine, and I believe that he has left others to die in the Shole. He's been involved in too many fatal accidents – he should no longer be trusted. I would respectfully suggest that Mr Vipton needs a period of retraining before he is permitted to be in charge of another gate grub.'

By now the Chief Mancer was on his feet. He looked ready to explode.

'You have gone too far, Benson – *much* too far,' he said, his voice low and dangerous. 'You have spoken completely out of turn. How dare you criticize a gate mancer! This is a breach of professional etiquette!'

He reached for the bellrope and tugged it, gesturing that Crafty should stand. Almost immediately there was a knock and, on being told to enter, two guards came into the room.

'Take this boy down to the lowest, darkest and dampest of the cells. He is to spend the night there. Bring him back to me at dawn tomorrow,' Ginger Bob ordered them.

Crafty's heart dropped like a stone. He tried to protest, but the guards seized him by the arms and marched him swiftly through the doorway.

Down and down through the castle they went. He couldn't believe that the dungeons were so much further below them. The corridors seemed endless, and all Crafty could hear was the drip of water and the stamp of the guards' boots. There was a dark passage ahead of them – they had reached the last torch. The guard on his left pulled it out of the wall sconce and used it to light their way.

Eventually, after what felt like miles of passageway, they thrust Crafty into a cell. It was bare but for a heap of straw in one corner, and it smelled as if somebody had died and they'd forgotten to remove the body. There was another smell too – even worse than the soldiers' latrines downwind of the castle barracks.

'Where am I? You can't just leave me here!' he cried.

But his pleas fell on deaf ears. Worse still, when the guards left him, they took the torch – Crafty couldn't even see his hand in front of his face. It was terrifying, and claustrophobic. He lay down on the floor, and was disturbed to find that it didn't make any difference whether he had his eyes open or closed.

But then, after a while, he did begin to see things. His imagination began to conjure up apparitions – or at least he *hoped* it was his imagination. At one point he thought he could see Old Nell. Her neck had been twisted and stretched by the hangman's noose and she gave him an evil grin. He even thought he heard her malevolent cackle. He shook his head to make the vision disappear.

He'd had no supper but he didn't feel the slightest bit hungry. Fear, combined with the stink in the cell, would have spoiled anybody's appetite. *All this*, he thought, *just for trying to do the right thing*.

He knew he'd never trust Ginger Bob again, not like before. He'd thought him reasonable, maybe even kind – certainly compared to Viper, but his reaction proved that he had as little regard for the gate grubs as everyone else.

Crafty tried to sleep, but it was bitterly cold and he kept shivering. At last he drifted off and was immediately plunged into a nightmare. He was back in the cellar, trapped in the Shole again.

His brothers were whispering . . .

'Crafty! Crafty! Crafty!'

He knelt down and put his ear close to the floor, trying to

catch what they were saying. Suddenly four thin bony arms sprouted from the soil and reached out for him. They gripped his shoulders, their fingernails sharp, like talons; he could feel them cutting into his flesh.

He tried to fight them off, but they dragged him down into the mud. Why were they doing this? Why would Brock and Ben want to hurt their own brother? he wondered. Down and down they dragged him. Crafty's mouth was filled with earth, and he choked.

Suddenly he realized what they wanted. They'd been buried for months – they must be hungry. They were going to *eat* him!

Crafty woke up abruptly, trembling, relieved to find that it had only been a nightmare. But he was too scared to go back to sleep. He didn't want a repeat of that terrible dream.

After a while he calmed down, but each time he was on the verge of sleep he'd hear a scream in the distance and jolt awake again. He wasn't sure if it was his imagination or not. Did they torture people down here? Or were those the cries of aberrations being studied and cut up for research?

Then he heard something new – something outside his cell door; something slithering across the flags. All at once the sound stopped, and Crafty wondered if it had just been his imagination again. He listened hard, and eventually heard another distant cry echo down the corridors towards him.

That seemed to be the signal for the slithering to start up once more. It sounded louder. Was it getting nearer? Was it approaching the door of his cell? Now the slithering stopped and there was a new sound: a scratching, like sharp claws against the stout wooden door. Was something trying to get in? Surely the door was too thick? he told himself. What could it be?

Crafty's mind darted about as he wondered how something that slithered could also have talons. It had sounded like a snake, but it also had arms. That was no longer impossible; not with the coming of the Shole. This creature could well be an aberration – something that had escaped from the laboratories or the Menagerie.

The scratching went on and on, getting more and more frantic. Could the beast gouge its way through the wood? Crafty's heart was beating fast and the cold sweat of fear was running down his forehead to sting his eyes. It suddenly occurred to him that there might be a gap under the door. If the aberration was like a snake, it could slither underneath . . .

Suddenly the scratching noise stopped. Then he heard the slithering again – though it was getting fainter, moving away from the door.

At last there was silence, and very slowly Crafty's racing heart returned to its normal speed. But he didn't sleep again that night.

14

THE PRACTICALITIES

In the morning the guards took a dishevelled and thoroughly miserable Crafty back to the Chief Mancer's room.

Ginger Bob stared coldly at Crafty from the chair behind his desk; this time he didn't invite him to sit down.

'What do you have to say for yourself, Benson?' His tone was like ice.

Crafty knew that he wanted him to apologize, and although he didn't think he had much to be sorry for – indeed, he thought the mancer should be apologizing to *him* – the thought of another night in the cell made him only too eager to oblige.

'I'm really sorry, sir, if I spoke out of turn. It won't happen again.'

'Indeed it won't, Benson. Another incident like this and you will immediately be returned to the Shole. Of course, I felt professionally obliged to tell Mr Vipton about your accusations. He was far from pleased. You owe him an apology too. Go back to your room and clean yourself up. Then report to the Waiting Room.'

Crafty could tell that the Chief Mancer was still furious with him; he wouldn't forget this breach of etiquette in a hurry.

Back in his room, Crafty washed himself thoroughly, trying to scrub the horrible stink of the cell off his skin. He noticed that a clean uniform had been laid out on the bed for him. This was surely Ginger Bob's work – he seemed to think of everything. He'd known that Crafty would be dirty and smelly from his night in the cell and would need fresh clothes; that was kind of him. But then he'd felt it necessary to inform Viper about his complaint; he'd been 'professionally obliged' to do so.

Now there would be consequences.

Viper was certain to want revenge.

When Crafty had eventually cleaned himself up, he went down to the Waiting Room – and got a shock.

There were two people already sitting there, both dressed in the uniform of gate grubs.

He was relieved to see that one was Lucky. The other was a girl.

Lucky was sitting further up the table, four chairs away from her. The girl was reading a book, its jacket covered in brown paper so that the title wasn't visible. Her hair was cut short like a man's – Crafty had never seen a girl with a haircut like that. She looked about Lucky's age, or maybe a little older. She had a pert nose and an intelligent expression that was also cold and aloof.

Crafty sat down just one chair away from the girl. Lucky caught his eye and shook his head at him. Crafty wondered what he meant by that. It seemed like some kind of warning – but the girl was surely friendly enough? They were all gate grubs together now, after all.

'Hello,' Crafty said, introducing himself. 'My name's Crafty. What's yours?'

Very slowly the girl raised her head from the book, frowned, and fixed him with a gaze of intense displeasure.

'I don't speak to boys. I don't like boys. Go and sit with your ugly friend and leave me alone!'

Crafty didn't need telling twice. He was astonished! So much for being friendly. By the time he'd stood up, the girl's nose was already back in her book.

Crafty went and sat beside Lucky. He knew he hadn't deserved such treatment, but he felt even more annoyed on Lucky's behalf. It wasn't his fault that his nose was broken and squashed. It was cruel to call him ugly.

'I did try to warn you!' Lucky murmured. 'At least she said something to you – she's just been ignoring me. So, how did it go when you spoke to Ginger Bob? How did he react?'

Although Lucky had kept his voice low, Crafty suspected that the girl could still hear them. Maybe she was only pretending to read that book? Was she listening to every word they spoke – spying ... but for who? Viper? Crafty decided that, if this was the case, she probably already knew what he was about to tell Lucky anyway.

'When I complained about Viper, he was annoyed, to say the least,' Crafty replied. 'He said it was "a breach of professional etiquette" for me to question Viper's methods. I spent the night in a pitch-black, smelly dungeon. What's even worse, he told Viper about my complaint.'

Lucky screwed up his face as if he'd been punched. 'Now it's even more urgent to carry out *my* plan! If we don't, you won't last the week.'

Crafty's blood ran cold. He was very afraid of what Viper might do to him. He looked at the girl again, and then, on impulse, spoke to her. 'I'd like to give you a warning. There's a gate mancer called Vipton who's more than likely to take you out on your first job. He'll leave you in an extremely cold place, and you'll think you've been abandoned to freeze to death. But don't be afraid. Just keep calm. He'll be back. He has a twisted sense of humour – it's a trick he plays on all new gate grubs.'

The girl didn't even bother to look up. 'I'm quite capable of looking after myself,' she replied coldly, 'and I certainly don't need any advice from you,' she added, her eyes never leaving the page.

Then, as if on cue, Viper came through the door at the end of the room.

'You!' he called out, pointing a finger at his prey. 'New girl! Come with me. I have a job for you!'

Crafty inwardly gave a sigh of relief. He'd expected Viper to be thirsty for revenge and choose him first. He watched the girl wriggle into her greatcoat and push the book into the right-hand pocket. She hadn't made the same mistake as him, then. At least she'd be a little warmer, depending on how long Viper kept her waiting before he returned to collect her.

The mancer turned and walked down the length of the table, the girl following him. But just before he reached the door, he paused, turned again and pointed at Crafty.

'I have a job for you too, Benson, but it'll be later in the afternoon. I look forward to the pleasure of your company then,' he added with a little smirk.

Crafty's heart sank. So he hadn't got away with it after all.

After the door had closed, Lucky leaped to his feet and began to pace up and down. 'You know what "later in the afternoon" means, don't you? It gets dark much earlier in the Shole. By then it'll be very dangerous. He's obviously hoping to find some excuse to leave you there – or maybe watch you get eaten by aberrations!'

Crafty knew his friend was right, but could see no way out of it. 'Well, there's nothing I can do about it, is there?'

'If it came to it, would you fight him?' Lucky demanded.

'Of course I would, if it was possible! But he probably won't give me the chance. He'll either choose to slice me with the guillotine blade when I enter or leave the gate, or, as you say, he'll put me in a situation I can't hope to get out of.'

Lucky gritted his teeth in frustration, then asked, 'Did you do as I asked – did you think it through? Did you use that crafty brain of yours to work out the best way to kill Viper?'

In fact Crafty *had* thought about it during his long night in the cell, but he still paused before telling Lucky. After all, it was a serious step; they were talking about murder. But suddenly he remembered poor Donna, and how she had died. He didn't want that to happen again – not to him or to Lucky. Also, if he was dead, who would look for his father?

So, with a sigh, he told Lucky his plan.

'We need to take him by surprise and drag or push him through the gate and into the Shole. Then, from this side, I can make the gate go opaque. He'd be left behind, and the Shole would soon have its effect.'

'Not bad, Crafty!'

'But I haven't had time to work out the practicalities,' countered Crafty. 'He's bigger than me. A lot would depend on where he stands in relation to the gate. And I'd need an element of surprise. Then there'd be the problem of explaining to the Chief Mancer what had happened and convincing him that it was an accident.'

'A combined operation, when we're all in the field, might be our best chance,' Lucky said. 'If the gates were far enough apart, the other mancers wouldn't be able to see what was happening – we could all help to push or pull him through. If Donna was still here, it would certainly be possible, but that new girl might be a problem . . .'

Crafty thought about it. 'A combined operation. That's a good idea. That might work,' he said.

He'd actually already thought of this, but he let Lucky take the credit. Of course, he hadn't foreseen the arrival of the girl. Lucky was right. She might be a problem.

'Why did you warn the girl about Viper?' Lucky asked, and Crafty was pleased to change the subject. 'She didn't deserve our help.'

'If we try to be kind to her, then perhaps we can win her round,' Crafty suggested. 'And if she works with Viper and sees how he behaves, she might be on our side.'

Lucky gave him an evil grin. 'Don't be too sure about that. They're both nasty pieces of work! Maybe they'll get on well together!'

The girl came back a couple of hours later. She removed her coat, pulled her book out of her pocket and started to read again. Not one word did she say to either Crafty or Lucky, and she didn't seem perturbed in the slightest. She wasn't even shivering.

The boys had just finished a game of draughts but, instead of putting the pieces back into the box, Crafty turned to the girl and asked, 'Would you like a game?'

'I prefer reading,' she said, not bothering to meet his eyes. 'Besides, draughts is far too easy. I prefer chess.'

After that they ignored her. The afternoon dragged on, and Viper left it very late to collect Crafty.

Lucky mouthed a 'good luck' as he left the room, and Crafty could tell that he was really worried about him. The girl didn't look up from her book.

Once they were in his office Viper pointed to the chair in front of the black curtain, so Crafty sat down. He could see a few faint stains on the tiles there. Was that Donna's blood? he wondered.

Don't think about that, he told himself. *You'll drive yourself mad.*

Viper didn't strap him in, but Crafty noticed that, before drawing back the curtain, he unlocked the guillotine with his foot. Crafty's mouth went dry.

'We're going to a fixed location,' Viper said curtly, the dial clicking as he turned it.

Seconds later the swirling clouds within the frame of the gate vanished to reveal a place that Crafty recognized immediately. It was Winckley Square in Preston, where they'd gone to rescue the Duke's son – and where Donna had died.

'You know where you left the tools, Benson,' Viper said with a sneer. 'Go and find them and bring them back.'

Clearly, the spades and the pruners could have been collected at a safer time, but Viper had deliberately brought Crafty here now, when it was almost dark. Those fanged beasts would be waiting in the houses beyond the garden wall, and he had to cover at least fifty yards to recover the tools.

Wasting no time, Crafty buttoned his greatcoat to the neck, then clambered through the silver frame and out into the freezing air of the Shole. He quickly followed the sloping path down through the trees, noting that the gloom was already darkening into full night. He soon reached the swampy hole from which they'd freed the Duke's son, tucked the pruners into his coat pocket and picked up the three spades. They were heavy and cumbersome, and it would be hard to move fast when carrying them by himself. The sooner he got back to the gate the better.

As he turned towards the gate, Crafty heard the first screeching howl. He began to run, but the three spades were hampering his progress, and as he sprinted up the slope he tripped over a tree root and fell headlong. Scrambling to his feet, he grabbed the spades and raced onwards, straining to see the blue shimmer of the gate. What if Viper had abandoned him already?

But there was the gate. He forced himself on, hoping that it wouldn't wink out. As he drew near, he glanced over his shoulder and saw a dozen of the cat-like beasts bounding along, closing in on him rapidly.

Ahead, through the gate, he saw Viper smirking at him. 'Hand the spades to me one at a time, Benson!' He took great delight in taking each one as slowly as possible.

Behind Crafty, the howling of those hungry beasts was getting ever louder. Was that what Viper wanted – to allow one of them to leap through the gate with Crafty so that he could chop them both with the guillotine? That way it would look like an accident.

When Viper had finally taken all the tools, he beckoned to Crafty. Sweating and shaking with fear, Crafty saw that Viper's foot was positioned over the guillotine pedal, ready to bring it down into his flesh and bones. He could almost feel the blade.

But now the beasts were almost upon him. His heart pounded as he scrambled through the gate, expecting to hear the guillotine coming down at any moment –

Then he was there. He slumped on to the chair and turned in relief – and saw fierce open jaws almost filling the frame before him, slaver dripping, the eyes above glittering with blood-lust.

Desperately he willed the clouds to return . . . and then the danger was over. But, looking down, Crafty saw that one of his feet was still under the blade of the guillotine! He quickly pulled it back, but not before Viper had caught his eye and smirked.

'Stand up!' the mancer commanded, his face becoming stern.

Crafty obeyed, his legs still wobbly.

'Go over there, away from the chair! There – in the centre of the room.'

As Crafty stumbled over, his heart slowly returned to its normal rhythm. Viper couldn't hurt him now – could he?

The mancer began to circle him slowly, like a predator considering the best moment to leap upon its prey. In his right hand he was holding what looked like a length of black string – Crafty suddenly realized that it was a shoelace.

All at once Viper struck him with it twice across his right shoulder. *Flick! Flick!*

It didn't hurt because of the thickness of his greatcoat, but Crafty still found it annoying. He wondered if Viper was trying to provoke him into losing his temper?

Flick! Flick! He did it again, a nasty smirk on his face.

'You're afraid of that blade, aren't you, Benson?' he said, pointing up at the guillotine.

'Of course I'm afraid of it! Who wouldn't be?' Crafty snapped back, not bothering with the 'sir'.

Viper leaned down until their noses were almost touching. 'I don't like working with sneaky little cowards,' he said, spitting the words into Crafty's face.

'I'm not a coward, but I *am* afraid of working with you. You killed Donna Henderson,' Crafty retorted. 'You've killed other grubs too.'

'All grubs die eventually – it's just a matter of time,' Viper said. 'In the Shole there are more ways to die than you can imagine. Being Fey won't save you. I remember one gate grub who died a particularly horrible death. You see, he had worms . . .'

Crafty looked at him in astonishment. *Worms?* What did that mean?

'Worms, Benson!' Viper said, rubbing his stomach theatrically and giving him an evil grin. 'There were parasites in his belly – probably from eating undercooked pork or fish from the market. The Shole didn't harm him directly because he was Fey like you. But it changed the worms. The following night he was in terrible agony. You see, those worms had grown teeth. They ate their way out of him. Nothing could be done. In the morning he was found lying in bed, full of holes. The sheets were covered in the nasty writhing things, and each one left a trail of blood.'

Crafty felt sick – he thought he might throw up right there and then. He remembered what Donna had said about the leeches – it seemed it hadn't been far from the truth.

Sensing his horror, Viper nodded vigorously. 'Yes – one way or another, you were going to die eventually, maybe weeks or even months from now. But then you ran and told tales to the Chief Mancer, and I'm afraid that's unforgivable.

'Your time will come much sooner now, Benson!'

15

THE COLD DEAD FINGER

The following morning, after yet another sleepless night, Crafty gave Lucky a detailed account of what had happened. They sat a long way from the girl so that she couldn't possibly hear what they were saying. Once again, her nose was stuck in that mysterious book.

'He actually said that to you, Crafty?' Lucky asked, aghast.

Crafty nodded.

'It's an open admission that he intends to kill you. We can't delay any longer! The first time we're sent on a combined field operation, we should take our chance and sort him once and for all.' Lucky spoke quietly, but his voice seethed with anger.

Despite what had just happened, Crafty still didn't like the idea. He knew that 'sort' meant kill. It would be murder. But if they didn't do something, then one of them – probably him – would die soon. There had to be another way of dealing with Viper, but even Crafty's clever brain couldn't think of one.

'How long before we're likely to have another combined operation?' he asked.

'That's the problem,' Lucky explained. 'You can't predict it. The rescue of the Duke's son was the first we'd had in weeks. But then sometimes you have a cluster. Once we had three in five days – that was awful. I suppose we'll just have to cross our fingers that the next one comes sooner rather than later.'

'Do you think that story he told me – about the worms eating their way out of that poor gate grub . . . Do you think it was true?' Crafty asked.

'Could be,' Lucky said. 'I've never heard of anything like that, but the Shole has been around for seventy years, growing and getting more dangerous as time passes. Almost anything could have happened – things so scary they've had to be hushed up. There are many things that aren't public knowledge, but somewhere in the Grey Library there'll be a record of everything that's happened, you can be sure of that.'

'I wish we had access to that library,' Crafty said. 'We're the ones risking our lives – we deserve to know what's waiting for us out there in the Shole.'

He glanced back at the girl, wondering what on earth that book was. She certainly seemed to be enjoying it – it totally absorbed her. Crafty missed his books. Apart from talking to Bertha – and his father on his occasional brief visits – that had been the only good thing about his stay in the cellar. There were no books in his current room – perhaps the castle assumed that gate grubs wouldn't be able to read . . .

Later that morning the far door opened.

Crafty's heart was in his mouth, but to his relief it was the Chief Mancer who entered the Waiting Room.

He looked at the girl and smiled. 'Miss Crompton-Smythe, please come with me. I have a job for you – one that you might find rather interesting.'

Crafty and Lucky braced themselves, expecting the girl to make some kind of rude retort – but instead, and to their complete astonishment, she actually smiled back at him. Then she tugged on her greatcoat, stuffed her book into its right-hand pocket and followed him out of the room.

'Well – at least we know her second name now,' Lucky observed.

'You mean her *two* second names!' Crafty said with a grin. 'That's a very posh double-barrelled name.' Lucky looked blank so Crafty filled him in. 'It suggests that her father and mother came from such well-connected, wealthy families that they wanted to keep both names.'

'Not many of the Fey are wealthy. We get the jobs others don't want. Hmm. Ginger Bob was very polite to her too – makes sense if she's posh. Even someone from the Fey gets respect then. Since when did he care whether *we* might find a job interesting?' asked Lucky. 'I've never heard him address a grub like that before.'

'Viper wasn't very polite to her yesterday,' Crafty pointed out.

'But Viper's rude to everyone, isn't he?'

'True,' Crafty agreed.

They lapsed into silence. Crafty was worrying about his next job with Viper; Lucky was deep in thought too, staring down absently, but suddenly he started in surprise. 'Hey – look at that!' he cried, pointing to something on the floor next to the girl's chair. It was a piece of paper with writing on it. The girl must have dropped it – perhaps it had fallen out of her book, Crafty thought.

He went to pick it up, then brought it back and spread it out on the table.

'Her handwriting's terrible!' Lucky exclaimed.

'If it *is* her writing,' Crafty said.

The writing was very small and spidery, and almost impossible to read. If Crafty hadn't recognized the odd word here and there, he'd have thought that it was either in code or in a foreign language.

But the title at the top of the sheet of paper was printed in capitals, and it was clear enough. It said:

REDRAFT ONE

And there was another just legible word that appeared in almost every other line:

aberrations

'Those are creatures or humans that have been changed by the Shole, aren't they?' Crafty asked.

Lucky nodded. 'Yes. Even though we rescued the Duke's son, he's still an aberration – and he's not the first to suffer that kind of transformation.'

'Other people have partially been turned into plants? What happened to them?'

'Same as happens to all aberrations. If they're dead, they end up in the Relic Room. If they survive, they find them a place in the Menagerie – that's where they keep live specimens.'

'Do you think that's where the Duke's son will be?'

Lucky shrugged. 'That would be up to the Duke, but I've heard all sorts of rumours. Some of them are pretty horrible. At least he was only changed from the waist down. I heard the reverse once happened. This poor man was running around, but his head and chest were just branches and leaves. Only his legs from the knee down were still flesh and blood.'

'Then maybe he was no longer aware of what had happened to him?' Crafty suggested.

'Let's hope so,' Lucky said. 'According to the story, they put him in the Menagerie and he just slowly died. He couldn't eat, you see, and they worked out later that he needed sunlight – like a real plant. But the Menagerie is underground, so he just withered and died. I don't think that would happen today. We know more about aberrations. Things have moved on.'

But Crafty couldn't help thinking that Lucky looked a little doubtful. After all, they'd both heard the screams in the night.

He decided to change the subject. 'Crompton-Smythe must be studying aberrations. I'd better put this piece of paper back on the floor for her to find. I don't suppose she'd be very pleased if she knew we were reading it,' he said, walking across and carefully setting it down on the floor again.

No sooner had he done so than the far door opened and she came back into the Waiting Room. He was still standing by her chair, and she stared hard at him. Then her gaze dropped to the piece of paper on the floor. She strode past him, her eyes blazing with anger, her face turning red. She picked it up and looked at it closely.

'You've been reading this, haven't you?' she said, sniffing it. 'I can smell your dirty greasy fingers on it,' she thundered, 'so don't deny it!'

That was really strange behaviour, Crafty thought. How could she smell his fingers? Was it one of her Fey abilities? But there was no point in contradicting her, so he told her part of the truth. 'I picked it up – I thought you'd dropped it – but then I realized that, even though I was trying to help, you'd be angry. So I put it back on the floor.'

'And did you read it?' the girl snapped, her jaw jutting forward,

'We tried,' Lucky said with a grin, 'but your writing's terrible – most of the words were illegible. But we did work out that you're interested in aberrations.'

Crafty winced. Why couldn't Lucky keep his mouth shut? The girl would be even more furious now! he thought.

'You had *no right*!' she yelled. 'Have you no respect for other people's privacy?'

'I'm sorry. We shouldn't have read your notes,' Crafty admitted, trying to calm her down. 'But where did you get your book from? The castle has a library, doesn't it? The Grey Library? I'd like to go in there and read up on stuff about the Shole.'

The girl was just about to answer when the door opened again; Viper stalked into the room and glared at Crafty.

'Come with me, Benson. I have a job for you!' he spat.

Crafty hardly had time to be afraid. He snatched up his coat and followed Viper, feeling the girl's eyes still blazing into his back. No doubt she'd carry on yelling at Lucky after he'd left.

When they got to his study, Viper took a seat behind his desk and pointed to the chair opposite him.

'We have an important task today, a snatch, so you won't need your coat – you have to be able to move freely and to use the gauntlets. It will be a difficult mission, so I want you alert and at your best.' He paused.

'By the way . . . take no notice of what I said yesterday. I was angry at your impertinence and the way you'd sneaked off to complain to the Chief Mancer behind my back. But I've decided to behave as if it never happened. We have to work together. I truly mean you no harm, so shall we agree to put all that unpleasantness behind us?'

Crafty looked at him in astonishment. The man *seemed* sincere. There was nothing sly about his manner – no trace of his usual smirk. He still didn't trust Viper, but there was no point in saying so to his face.

'Yes, sir,' he replied cautiously.

'Good! Excellent. Well, our task today is to snatch a creature that exists in an area that is a geographical aberration.'

Crafty wondered what a 'geographical aberration' was. Had it been Ginger Bob, he would have asked.

Viper opened a drawer in his desk, took out a little wooden box and pushed it across the polished surface towards Crafty. 'Open the box and take out what's inside.'

The sly, gloating expression had returned. Crafty sensed that he wouldn't like whatever he found in the box.

He opened it carefully and stared at what lay inside.

'Well, Benson – pick it up. It won't climb out by itself. Or at least I hope not, ha ha! What are you waiting for?'

With great reluctance Crafty reached into the box and lifted out the object, which was cold and smooth to the touch. It was a finger, probably an index finger from a human hand. It was brown in colour, and shiny – the skin looked more like peat than flesh.

As he examined it, Viper kept talking:

'So, Benson . . . Just over a year ago I sliced that finger off the hand of a dangerous creature we attempted to snatch from a location quite close to your family home. This time I hope to get the rest of it. We have a new lure, which should make the snatch easier.'

Crafty experienced a moment of revulsion – which was quickly overwhelmed by a feeling of sadness for the owner of that finger.

He suddenly knew exactly who that cold dead finger belonged to.

This was the Bog Queen's finger. It hadn't been cut off when Bertha was sacrificed. He'd been wrong about that.

It had been sliced by a guillotine.

Viper wanted him to snatch Bertha.

16

THE BRIGHTEST OF OUR BOFFINS

Crafty's mind raced. How could he do that to Bertha when she was his friend? What would happen to her if he did – what happened when they studied aberrations? He had heard screams which might well have come from the laboratories below. Whatever they did must be very painful.

He couldn't allow that to happen to the Bog Queen. Even if she survived, Bertha would end up in the Menagerie.

Crafty's mind raced. He needed to think of a way to save her – and quickly.

Viper had come to his feet and was pointing towards the chair facing the black curtain. Crafty walked across, gingerly holding the finger in his right hand. In a daze, he watched as Viper strapped him into the chair, then pulled back the curtain to reveal the silver gate.

'Concentrate, Benson. First we'll locate the creature, then we'll fit you with the gauntlets and attempt the snatch.'

Crafty wished he could pretend to fail in his task, but the process seemed to happen automatically. The clouds cleared, and through the gate's frame he could now see an area of flat boggy ground with a few reeds. In places the mud was bubbling gently, with white steam rising as the warmer marsh gas hit the bitter cold above. Apart from the bog itself, nothing was moving.

Looking right, through the gloom of the Shole, Crafty could see three houses. With a pang he realized that the one in the middle was his own home, where he'd once lived happily with his father, mother and two brothers. How strange to be back here now . . .

'So – where is the creature, Benson?' Viper demanded. 'It seems you have failed to locate it.'

'Perhaps she's close by, under the mud?' he suggested. He certainly hoped so – it was through the earth that Bertha had always visited him in the cellar. She was in her element below ground, and if she stayed there, perhaps she'd be safe.

'*She?*' snapped Viper. 'How do you know it's female, Benson?'

'Just intuition, sir,' he said quickly, cursing himself for slipping up. 'Is it a she?'

Viper didn't reply. He just glared and held out his hand for the finger before popping it back into the little box. Then he offered Crafty the gauntlets, and Crafty took them and eased them on to his hands, tugging them right up as far as his elbows.

With a click, Viper released the lock on the pedal that worked the guillotine.

Suddenly Crafty was scared again. What if he tried to snatch Bertha, and Viper killed them both?

'Get ready, Benson. I'm using the lure now!'

Crafty wondered what the lure was this time – an image of meat dripping with blood, as it had been for the other aberration he'd snatched? Somehow he didn't think it would work with Bertha. He hoped that she stayed deep under the mud.

For a while nothing happened. Then the surface of the bog began to ripple. It was as if a storm was driving it into turmoil. There were waves on the surface; undulations that deepened into a swell. It was behaving more like an ocean than a bog.

Viper clearly knew what was going on. Seeing Crafty's alarm, he told him, 'What you're seeing is what we term a "geographical aberration", Benson, because the ground itself, the landscape, has been affected by the Shole. This surface agitation is predictable behaviour.'

Viper certainly hadn't predicted what happened next.

With a great belching, squishing, slurping sound, mud suddenly sprayed up out of the bog like a fountain. It spurted through the silver gate, somehow missing Crafty but splattering across Viper's white shirt and face. He cursed furiously and turned away from the gate, wiping his eyes.

Not waiting to see what had caused the explosion of mud – though he thought he might know – Crafty concentrated, focusing on the image of swirling clouds.

They instantly returned to the surface of the gate, obscuring what was beneath.

Viper turned round again and stared at him angrily, as if this was all his fault. His face and shirt were covered with mud. He smelled of loam, peat and rotting vegetation. If he noticed that Crafty was untouched by the mud, he didn't comment.

'Get back to the Waiting Room, Benson,' he snarled, unfastening Crafty's straps. 'That's all for now.'

Crafty quickly pulled off the gauntlets. He was only too glad to get away from Viper. After that humiliation he'd be in an even more dangerous mood than usual.

When Crafty got back to the Waiting Room, Lucky was gone, but the girl – Crompton-Smythe, he reminded himself – was reading her book. The piece of paper lay on the table next to her, and she was frowning as she took notes with a pencil.

Crafty didn't bother speaking to her. He was in no mood for her insults. He hung his greatcoat on the back of his chair and thought through what had happened.

The bog had only become agitated when Viper had deployed the lure.

Was it that which had caused the eruption? Or was it something else, as he suspected – Bertha herself, maybe?

Then he realized something else. When Crafty had snatched the aberration from the orphanage, Ginger Bob had first summoned the guards. They had brought a cage to contain it. But Viper hadn't bothered with that . . .

There could be only one reason: he'd had no intention of snatching Bertha. Either he'd hoped that the so-called bog creature would drag Crafty through the gate into the Shole, or he'd intended to kill them both with the guillotine.

Crafty couldn't have been sitting there for much more than ten minutes when the far door opened and once again Viper strode into the room.

He was wearing a clean white shirt and his face was full of purpose. Crafty groaned inside. Surely he couldn't want him again so soon!

But instead, without saying a word, Viper beckoned to Crompton-Smythe, who followed him through the doorway, taking her book, notes and pencil with her.

Lucky returned just before noon.

'How did it go?' Crafty asked him, glad to have someone to talk to.

'Ginger Bob wanted me to find your father and the other couriers who were carrying that sedan chair,' Lucky said.

Full of hope, Crafty lurched to his feet. Was there finally to be news of his father?

'Don't get your hopes up, Crafty – we still don't know what went wrong with the mission, or why they left the chair and the Duke's son behind. He's still too traumatized to tell us what happened. I followed their tracks from the chair to the edge of the gardens, but Ginger Bob said it was too dangerous a venture to go beyond the wall. How about you? What did Viper want you to do?'

Crafty told Lucky what had happened, and they both laughed about Viper's shirt and face getting splattered with mud. But Lucky was suspicious of the mancer's claim that he bore no ill will and that Crafty could trust him.

Then Crafty told him his theory about the absence of guards or a cage and what it meant.

'I think you're right,' Lucky agreed. 'He's very sly. He still intends to kill you – make no mistake about that. Nothing has changed.'

'I don't trust him an inch,' Crafty reassured him. 'You should have seen the gloating expression on his face when he made me pick up the finger. He was definitely enjoying my discomfort.'

'So you really think the finger belongs to the mud girl who used to visit you in your cellar?'

'I'm sure of it. It was fortunate that I couldn't find her. Soon after I came back he took Crompton-Smythe on a job. Surely he can't have returned to the bog?'

Before Lucky could answer, their juice and sandwiches were brought into the Waiting Room by one of the kitchen servers. They were ravenous, and tucked in. They had just finished when the Chief Mancer thrust his head in through the far doorway, not even bothering to enter the room.

'Both of you! Come down to my room, now!' he shouted. 'It's urgent. Bring your coats.'

They scrambled to their feet.

'Maybe it's a combined op?' Lucky whispered. 'This could be our chance to deal with Viper!'

If it was, there should have been another mancer, Crafty thought. But then, why else would Ginger Bob want to talk to them together?

When they entered his office, he gestured that they should sit down, then went behind his desk and stood facing them.

'There has been an unfortunate occurrence,' he said. 'What I am about to tell you is strictly confidential. Have I your word that you won't tell another soul?'

'Yes, sir!' the boys said dutifully in unison, though Crafty wondered who he could tell.

Ginger Bob eyed them both severely, then began to speak.

'Mr Vipton took Miss Crompton-Smythe to the location that you, Benson, visited with him earlier today. They were hunting the same dangerous creature, the one which frequents the geographical aberration. It attacked them with great violence. Consequently Mr Vipton was badly slashed on the face and Miss Crompton-Smythe was dragged through the gate and into the Shole. She is now missing.'

'Why wasn't she strapped into the chair?' Lucky interjected. Crafty had been thinking the same thing. This was typical of Viper.

'Don't interrupt, Proudfoot!' the Chief Mancer said angrily. 'There is no time for questions. We must do our very best to retrieve Miss Crompton-Smythe as soon as possible. It is vital to the well-being of the whole Palatine of Lancashire.' He paused and looked up at the ceiling as if gathering himself to say something momentous.

Crafty felt annoyed. What was so special about *her*? he wondered. The short time he'd spent here, working from the castle, had shown him that gate grubs were considered two a penny. How could the fact that she was missing affect the entire county?

Finally Ginger Bob went on. 'Miss Crompton-Smythe has been working as a gate grub in order to better appreciate the nature of Shole aberrations. The bog area and the dangerous creature that inhabits it are of particular interest to her . . .'

The mancer reached into a desk drawer and got out a book, which he placed before them. It was the one the girl had been reading every day. There were still fragments of brown paper clinging to it, but most of it had been ripped away to reveal the cover and the title:

TOWARDS AN UNDERSTANDING
OF SHOLE ABERRATIONS
by
Leticia Crompton-Smythe

'Leticia is an extremely clever young lady,' Ginger Bob continued. 'In fact, to say that she is a genius would hardly do her justice. She is at present revising and extending her own book in the light of new knowledge that she is gaining from her present investigations. I cannot overemphasize how important it is that we find and rescue her.' His face was flushed pink and his left eye kept twitching. Crafty stared at him. He was clearly very worried.

The Chief Mancer coughed and cleared his throat before continuing. 'Leticia is a prodigy – she is one of the brightest of our boffins and the daughter of Myra Crompton-Smythe, who invented the silver gate. Sadly, her mother is no longer with us, but Leticia is following in her footsteps. It was Leticia who developed the impervious material that covered the sedan chair, making it possible to bring the Duke's son through the Shole. If she still lives, we must get her back and save her from that dangerous bog creature.'

Crafty felt a flare of annoyance at that final comment. He felt sure that Bertha wouldn't harm anyone, but if he tried to tell Ginger Bob about her, he knew he wouldn't be believed. After all, he hadn't been believed about Viper. He wondered what had really happened to Viper and Crompton-Smythe; was there any chance that, being Fey, Leticia could survive in the Shole?

Unless Viper had already killed her . . .

Lucky repeated the question he'd tried to ask earlier. 'Why wasn't she strapped into the chair? Isn't that a routine safety procedure, sir?' he asked, with an edge to his voice. Crafty knew that he wanted Ginger Bob to acknowledge that Viper had once again been reckless.

For a moment anger flickered across the mancer's face; then he gave a deep sigh. 'I was the only one who knew Miss Crompton-Smythe's real identity. That was because *she* wanted it that way.'

Crafty wondered why she'd decided to keep it secret. He was going to ask, but Ginger Bob quickly continued.

'Mr Vipton thought she was just an ordinary gate grub. Unfortunately, Miss Crompton-Smythe can be somewhat highly strung and wilful – I believe that is often the case with those who have brilliant minds. It seems that there was a minor altercation between her and Mr Vipton. He was going to strap her into the chair. She refused. And while they were arguing, that dangerous aberration from the bog attacked them both.'

Crafty glanced at Lucky. Was he thinking the same thing – that there was something fishy here? Why would Crompton-Smythe refuse to be strapped into the chair? She knew the dangers of the Shole. It looked like Viper had been up to his old tricks. The girl was rude and annoying, they both knew that. Perhaps she had simply annoyed Viper so much that he'd pushed her through the gate! After all, in his eyes she was expendable.

'I'd had it in mind to conduct this as a combined field operation but, on reflection, I think that's unwise,' Ginger Bob continued. 'We cannot risk you both, so you, Benson, report to Mr Vipton's room immediately. In spite of his injuries, he has bravely decided to attempt to rescue Miss Crompton-Smythe. He now knows who she really is, and he is determined to bring her back.'

Crafty reluctantly came to his feet, pulled on his greatcoat and started to button it up.

'Let *me* go, sir,' Lucky pleaded suddenly. 'I have more experience than Benson – I can find her quicker.'

No doubt Lucky was volunteering because he was worried about the danger Viper posed to Crafty. *He's a good friend*, Crafty thought. *I'm lucky to have him, in spite of all this.*

'Mr Vipton has specifically asked for Benson,' the mancer replied. 'Besides, Proudfoot, we must hold you in reserve precisely *because* you are the more experienced of the two. You cannot be risked. Here, Benson, take Miss Crompton-Smythe's book – it will help you to locate her.'

Without a word, Crafty took it and left the room, his mind awhirl. Why had Viper asked for him? He could think of only one reason. He planned the same for him as he had for Crompton-Smythe.

Bertha would be his excuse for killing them both.

17

STUPID QUESTIONS

Crafty made his way to Viper's room, the book in his hand, his stomach churning with anxiety. But what could he do – refuse to go? Run away? If he did so, the Chief Mancer would surely send him straight back into the Shole. If that happened, he might never find his father. And without the help of his father, there was no way he'd survive out there.

Crafty's mind whirred as he tried to think what to do next. If Viper tried to push him through the gate, he wouldn't be able to stop him. Viper was bigger than Crafty – he'd most likely win in a struggle. And even if Crafty successfully resisted him, it didn't take much imagination to predict what the Chief Mancer's reaction would be. He would always believe Viper's version of events over Crafty's, and no doubt Viper would try to make out that Crafty had attacked him. So it seemed Crafty had no choice but to accept his fate.

The moment he saw Viper, he realized that he was right to be scared. The mancer had four deep scratches on his right cheek, and his white shirt was ripped and streaked with blood. This puzzled Crafty. Viper was usually very fussy about his appearance, so why hadn't he changed? But his thoughts were interrupted by a barked command.

'Sit!'

Crafty slowly made his way to the chair facing the silver gate, and sat down, reluctantly staring into the dark swirling cloud.

'This is a field operation, Benson. We are going to a fixed location, but not the one in the bog. Miss Leticia Crompton-Smythe was far better at seeking than you, poor girl. She found the creature I asked you to locate in a wood near the western edge of the marsh. Unfortunately, it launched a ferocious attack and, after injuring me, carried her off. So we are going to the scene of the attack. The creature will have left tracks. I want you to follow them.'

Crafty looked at him defiantly, knowing that he was lying. 'I don't need to follow her tracks. I can use this book to find her and save precious time,' he said. 'That's why the Chief Mancer gave it to me.'

But Viper snatched the book away, his face livid with anger.

'We'll do it *my* way, Benson!' His voice was dripping with poison. He stared at Crafty and pointed to the gate. 'Look!' he shouted.

For a moment Crafty hesitated. Then Viper's gaze shifted to the gate, as if it had already cleared – and, on instinct,

Crafty glanced over to see what had happened. But the moment he turned away he felt a terrible blow to his left temple, and doubled over.

Tricked! he thought through the haze of pain. *I need to get out of here . . .*

But as he tried to stand, Viper hit him again in exactly the same place. Crafty's mind whirled; he felt numb and sick to his stomach.

He must have lost consciousness for a few seconds, as the next thing he knew he was being dragged out of the chair.

Then there was cold air on his face, and he found himself lying on his back on the grass; he had passed through the gate. He managed to clear his head, and struggled into a sitting position, staring back at the gate. He saw the usual shimmering blue circle; within it, Viper was staring out at him. The mancer looked pale but satisfied; his usual sneer had returned.

Then he threw something through the gate after Crafty, and the blue circle winked out.

Crafty saw that it was the book. Now Lucky wouldn't be able to use it to find the girl either. *That man is such a snake,* thought Crafty, and he wondered what Viper's story would be this time. He'd probably failed to change out of his blood-stained shirt to make his account more convincing; he'd simply add some rips to fake another encounter with the Bog Queen.

Crafty staggered to his feet and looked about him. He was standing on a slope, surrounded by trees. Could this be the wood at the edge of the marsh that Viper had talked about? Did that mean he was close to home?

It was gloomy in the Shole, but it wasn't yet dark, so Crafty hoped that he was in no immediate danger from the aberrations. The cat-like beasts in Winckley Square had only appeared at night, but there might be other aberrations that were active earlier. Nothing was certain here.

More than ever, Crafty wished he knew more about the Shole. His lack of knowledge was probably going to cost him his life.

What would Father do now? he wondered.

Unfortunately his father hadn't talked about the Shole very much – it was as if he wanted to keep that part of his life away from his family. And then, when the Shole had engulfed their house, he'd worked alone, not sharing with Crafty and his brothers the secrets of the magic he'd used to protect the cellar. It was guild knowledge, he had explained, and he couldn't divulge it even to his own children.

Viper obviously wasn't going to open the gate for him – so how long could Crafty hope to survive here? Certainly not through a whole night. Would Ginger Bob use Lucky to try to effect a rescue – if not of Crafty, then of the important Crompton-Smythe? He glanced at the book. Now that they couldn't use it to find her, it was useless. He might as well chuck it away.

Then something occurred to him. Crafty quickly flicked through the pages, but the notes were no longer inside. That gave him a little surge of hope. Had she been wearing her coat when she went through the gate? If so, they might just be in her pocket, in which case they were at a dead end again. But if they weren't, there was a chance Ginger Bob might have them – and if so, they could surely use them to find her again.

Which meant that Crafty had to be with the girl when they found her. That way they would find him too. He had to find her first.

But his hopes were dashed again when he realized that he didn't even know if this really *was* where Viper had abandoned her. Viper could well have been lying – Crafty could be miles from anywhere.

He looked around for footprints to follow. He wandered to and fro, studying the ground, but soon saw that this wasn't like the muddy area where they'd found the sedan chair. This was grass and it was quite short, in places just moss. There was no detectable trail.

Think, Crafty! he told himself. *Where might she go?*

He thought about it carefully, trying to be logical. Crompton-Smythe was feisty and strong-willed. She wouldn't just sit down and wait to die. She was also a researcher and, given what Ginger Bob had said about her, she probably wouldn't be able to resist seeing at first-hand one of the aberrations that so interested her. She would head straight for the bog.

How would she find it? he wondered. How could *he* find it – even if he was where he thought he was? Crafty got to thinking again, and then realized that it would probably lie downhill from him – where enough water could pool to soften the ground and form a bog.

So, with nothing to lose, he began heading down the slope.

After a few minutes of careful walking – always keeping his ears open for the sound of potential predators – Crafty was relieved to see that the trees were giving way to soft ground covered in tussocks of grass. Water began to squelch under his boots. He was approaching the bog!

At least that's something, he thought. Perhaps he'd find Crompton-Smythe, and they could formulate a plan together.

As he walked, Crafty passed heaps of bones. Some were those of small animals, probably rabbits and hares. Others were larger, from cattle or deer. He tried not to look too closely at the ones that might have been human.

It was strange how the Shole killed some creatures yet changed others, Crafty thought. It also brought some back to life, like Bertha. What was the reason for those different outcomes?

He wondered if Crompton-Smythe knew the answer. How much did the castle boffins *really* know? He was certain there were many things that were kept secret from ordinary people; things that would cause panic if they got out. But were the boffins also struggling? Did they also have more questions than answers?

When he finally reached the bog, it didn't take him long to spot the girl. She was sitting on a grassy bank, staring intently into the bog, which was bubbling gently and giving the occasional faint belching sound, as if struggling to digest a meal that had disagreed with it.

She looked up as Crafty approached. 'You took your time. Where's the gate?' she demanded.

Unbelievable. Despite their situation, she hadn't changed one iota, he thought.

'Took my time about what, exactly?' he asked, sitting down on the same bank, but not too close to her.

'Coming to get me after that madman pushed me through the gate.'

'I'm not here to get you. He did the same thing to me,' Crafty replied.

She stared at him hard – but she didn't seem quite as unfriendly as before. Maybe the time she'd spent alone in the Shole had made her think about how she'd behaved – or maybe she was capable of sympathy, now that they were in the same boat.

'You've got a red lump on your temple. Did he do that?' she asked.

'Yes. He hit me and then pushed me through the gate. The Chief Mancer gave me your book to help me find you, but Viper wouldn't let me use it. And he threw it out after me so that no one else could use it,' Crafty said, handing it over.

The girl turned the book over and over in her hands as if it was some oddity that she'd never seen before.

'But I was thinking – the piece of paper with your notes on it isn't here. If Ginger Bob still has that, it would be just as good as the book for finding you . . .' he began, but trailed off as the girl reached into her coat pocket and pulled out the piece of paper. She held it towards him, shrugged and then stuffed it back in.

There was nothing to be said. That was their last hope gone.

They sat in silence for a while, then the girl spoke. 'This used to be a sea marsh. Then the geographical aberration began. It was small at first, just a bubbling muddy hole – but it started to grow, and then there were the first sightings of the bog beast.'

Crafty bristled. 'I know who you're talking about, and she's not a beast. Her name is Bertha – she's my friend and she means no harm. I was trapped in the Shole, sheltering in the cellar of my house for almost a year. I was alone for weeks at a time. She kept me company. She kept me sane. I owe her a lot.'

Then he told an astonished Crompton-Smythe how Bertha had been sacrificed by her tribe, and how the Shole had brought her back to life – and also how Viper was telling people that Bertha had attacked them.

The mud was calm now, but for the ripples caused by the breeze. Even the bubbles had ceased. They both stared at it in silence.

'I was the one who scratched his face,' Crompton-Smythe told Crafty. 'Believe me, he deserved it.'

'What did he do?'

She scowled. 'Let's just say that our working relationship was less than cordial. We had a disagreement, and then he became so violent that I scratched his face. I only acted in self-defence. But he was stronger than me. He pushed me through the gate and told me he was leaving me in the Shole to die.' Her voice was shaking with rage.

Crafty nodded sympathetically. 'He wouldn't have dared do that if he'd known who you really were. The Chief Mancer told us all about you – that you're a boffin.'

She nodded and angrily thrust her book into the same pocket as the piece of paper. 'It was important that the Chief Mancer was the only one who knew. That way I could get on with my work without people asking a lot of stupid questions or trying to interfere. My research is *very* important – I wanted to avoid any distractions. And I was interested to see what it was like to be a gate grub. Well, now I know . . . It's dangerous and miserable.'

'It is,' Crafty agreed. 'You've seen why grubs don't live long. We don't get any proper training and we are given no weapons to defend ourselves with. The only way we learn anything is by asking "stupid questions" when we get a chance. Having a gate mancer like Viper makes it ten times worse – did you know that we're not the first grubs he's tried to kill? He sliced three with the guillotine, and two others were abandoned in the Shole. I tried complaining about him to the Chief Mancer but I got nowhere. I was thrown into a stinking dungeon for my pains.'

Crompton-Smythe grimaced. 'Mr Wainwright has a good heart,' she said, 'but he's a real stickler for the rules, and won't accept that his colleagues don't always maintain the same high standards as he does. But if we get back to the castle, I'll put him right about that odious Mr Vipton, you can be sure of that.'

Crafty smiled at her. 'Thank you. Things here may not be completely hopeless, you know. They may well try to find you and the Bog Queen. That means coming here,' he said, gesturing at the bog, which was starting to bubble again.

'It depends on what that sly Vipton tells the Chief Mancer,' the girl said. 'He might say he saw both our bodies and that we're definitely dead, killed by the so-called beast from the bog. Then they might well feel that it's too dangerous to come here again. That boy you call Lucky is the only gate grub they have at the moment. Until someone else passes the test they might not want to risk using him.'

'Why are there so few?' Crafty asked, surprised by this news.

'At one time there was a fully operational team, with over a dozen grubs. But we Fey form a very small proportion of the county population. Most families won't allow their children to do such dangerous work, so the gate mancers are having to recruit orphans or children from families made desperate through poverty. There's even talk that the Duke might sign a declaration making it mandatory for Fey children to serve as gate grubs. I know that doesn't seem fair, but things are desperate. We're talking about survival here – it's us against the Shole.'

On that depressing note they lapsed into silence. Night was approaching and they both knew that their chances of surviving it were slim.

Then, to Crafty's horror, there were noises coming from further up the slope within the darkness of the trees. He'd expected the first warnings of an attack to be the howls and cries of predatory aberrations.

He was wrong. This was worse. The sound was so creepy that it made the hairs on the back of his neck stand up, and his hands start to shake.

Crafty could hear a slithering and sliding noise as, hidden by darkness, things began to emerge from the trees above them.

THE LADY OF THE BOG

They jumped to their feet.

'There's something up there,' Crompton-Smythe said, her voice shaking. 'Whatever they are, there are a lot of them and they're moving down the slope towards us.'

Yes, that was obvious, Crafty thought, and wondered whether she'd ever spent any time in the Shole, even though she'd researched it thoroughly and written a book about it. If she'd never actually experienced it, she might be even more scared than he was.

'Don't worry,' he said, trying to be reassuring. 'It's probably just the breeze.'

'Don't be stupid!' she spat, back to her old charming self.

Crafty didn't reply. He knew she'd snapped at him because she was afraid. He was afraid too.

The slithering noises were getting louder. Now there was something directly above them, and to either side. Crafty had been going to suggest making a run for it along the edge of the bog, but now it was too late. It seemed that any escape routes had already been cut off.

Crompton-Smythe slowly shifted position. In the dark of the Shole she was just a silhouette, but Crafty felt her reach into her left-hand coat pocket.

'We might as well find out how bad things really are,' she said. 'Besides, those things won't like a bright light.'

With that, she tossed something high into the air. There was a flash of intense light, which immediately dimmed to a steady glow. It was a floating orb, and it bathed the surrounding area in white light as bright as that of the Daylight World. What was it? Crafty had never seen anything like it.

Whatever it was, it showed them the threat they faced. He'd expected to see a horde of hungry aberrations advancing on them.

He was wrong.

There was only one creature – but it was truly monstrous.

At first glance, it looked as if five fat white snakes were slithering towards them down the hill. But, looking up, Crafty saw that they were all joined together. They were more like long necks protruding from the large, shapeless white mass of the body; they were what the Chief Mancer would no doubt have called 'appendages'. But whereas necks were usually on top of a body, these were flat on the ground, and each was supported by hundreds of legs. They looked like monstrous millipedes.

At that moment Crafty wished for a giant guillotine to come scything down. He would have used it to chop off those appendages one by one.

Each of these five appendages ended in an elongated head with wide jaws and the three rows of slanted teeth that Crafty had already seen in carnivores in the Shole. The bulbous eyes were pink and without lids, like an albino's – and clearly very sensitive to light. All five mouths were uttering cries of pain, the heads twitching away from the glowing orb that hovered above Crompton-Smythe.

'It won't last long,' she said, 'and I only have one left.'

Already the heads were no longer screaming as loudly. The light was beginning to fade.

All at once Crafty heard a sound from the bog. The girl must have heard it too, because despite the threat from above she turned towards it a moment after him.

About six feet from the edge, something was emerging from the bubbling surface. It looked like a pointed stick – but then Crafty saw that it was a short blade, and that a hand was gripping the hilt. As the blade rose higher, first a slender forearm then an elbow was revealed.

It was like something from a story he'd once read – a legend from the distant past. But instead of a shining sword glittering in the moonlight, this was a muddy dagger grasped by an even muddier arm. Then a head burst out of the bog like a demented toadstool, and the big green eyes of the aberration opened very wide.

'What on earth is that?' shrieked Crompton-Smythe, clearly alarmed by what she saw as another threat.

'It's Bertha!' yelled an overjoyed Crafty. 'It's the Bog Queen!'

He eagerly ran forward, splashing through the bog towards her. He was immediately knee-deep in mud, but Bertha held the dagger firmly out to him, and he took it gratefully.

But before he could even thank her, she sank back into the bog and was lost from sight. Crafty turned and floundered his way back to solid ground.

The girl was staring at him with wild eyes, her expression halfway between a grin and a grimace. But there was no time to explain: the light from the orb was almost gone now, and those five murderous jaws were slithering towards them once again.

Crafty pointed upwards. 'Throw up the last of those orbs, and then we'll run that way!' he said, pointing to their left, where just one fat slithery 'neck' lay between them and escape.

Crompton-Smythe reached into her pocket and tossed another of the orbs high into the air. Again there was the dazzling flash, and then the steady white glare that halted the creature in its tracks and made its five long necks shrink away again, screaming as if in agony.

Gripping the muddy dagger in his right hand, Crafty ran straight towards the writhing neck on his left. The head was averted from the white light and it didn't see the danger until it was too late.

Crafty buried the dagger up to the hilt in its left eye. The eyeball burst like a boil, and the snake-like neck reared up into the air, almost tugging the dagger out of his grasp. Somehow he held on. The neck was twisting and convulsing – its hundreds of legs writhing as it did so.

He yanked the dagger free, then they ducked beneath the neck and ran.

They stopped at the western edge of the wood, and sat with their backs to the broad trunk of an oak tree, shoulders touching. Given her rudeness, this was nearer than Crafty really wanted to be to Miss Crompton-Smythe, but she'd chosen to sit close to him, and there were probably hundreds of aberrations out there who wanted to eat them. They had to stick together.

'Maybe we should try to climb a tree,' she suggested. 'That could be relatively safe.'

'It could be, but there might be things that can climb better than us,' Crafty pointed out.

'Actually you're right. There are,' she replied. 'There's a sort of squirrel with four arms, but it doesn't eat nuts; it eats other creatures – though not straight away. It tears strips of flesh off its victims, then hangs these out on a branch to dry. It doesn't like blood – just the meat. The good news is that there aren't that many of them.'

Crafty wasn't sure anything counted as 'good news' out here, and said so. 'We might get unlucky and climb the wrong tree.'

'True. Well, if we survive the night, we could try heading for the Daylight World,' she suggested. 'I reckon the castle is about three miles north of here – we might make it.'

Crafty nodded. He had travelled the same route with his father when he'd finally left his cellar. He'd been hooded at the time, but he thought he'd probably remember the way from before, when his village was a part of the Daylight World. Maybe they really could get out alive.

'Have you spent much time in the Shole?' Crafty asked the girl.

'I've visited it more times than I care to remember,' she told him, in such a matter-of-fact way that he immediately changed his opinion of her. It seemed that she wasn't someone who'd simply carried out research from a distance, trawling through the evidence of people who'd actually risked their lives.

'You know a lot about the Shole, don't you? I wish I knew more,' Crafty said wistfully.

'Knowledge is what I do, Crafty. I'm a boffin, and my speciality is aberrations – especially new ones like the Bog Queen. Now that I've seen her, Bertha will be my priority. I'd like to find out as much about her as possible.'

Crafty nodded. 'The Chief Mancer told us that you also invented the material covering the sedan chair.'

Crompton-Smythe actually smiled. 'I know a bit about you too. Mr Wainwright gave me your details – you and Proudfoot. He said that your father is a courier who's currently missing, and he told me about you sheltering in the cellar. I understand that your house is close to the bog. Wouldn't we be safer in that cellar?'

'I'm not sure,' replied Crafty. 'My father used elements of courier craft, a type of Fey magic, to protect us. He installed silver-alloy steps, but the three candles he brought for me burned out – their protective magic is gone. I don't think it would be safe any longer. Something dangerous might have moved in since I left.'

They agreed to stay where they were.

Crafty was disturbed by the talk of his father. He'd been trying not to think about him; after all, he had his own survival to worry about. Now he felt tears pricking behind his eyes.

If I survive this, Father, he swore, *I promise I'll do everything I can to find you.*

Dawn took a long time to arrive; it was probably at least three hours after sunrise in the Daylight World. They took turns to sleep while the other stayed on guard, but the fear of what might be out there kept them on edge, and neither got much rest. Eventually the darkness gave way to twilight, and they set off north, heading for Lancaster.

They avoided the houses. Who knew what might be sleeping inside? Instead, they stayed out in the open as much as possible, so that, even in the gloom, they could see danger approaching: some aberrations were at large even during the day and they didn't want to meet them. Mostly they walked in silence, side by side, listening for danger. After a while Crompton-Smythe suddenly spoke, surprising Crafty.

'I told you that I didn't like boys much,' she said. 'But I'm going to make an exception in your case. You can call me by my first name. It's Leticia.'

Thanks to Ginger Bob, Crafty already knew this, but he certainly hadn't expected her to volunteer the information herself.

'Leticia's a nice name,' he offered.

She shook her head. 'No it's not. It sounds too formal. It's the sort of name the Chief Mancer would have given his daughter, had some poor woman been daft enough to marry him in the first place. In fact, I've changed my mind. If I had any friends, they'd call me Lick,' she said – almost shyly, Crafty thought. 'You can use that.'

'Lick?' he said, trying it out. The sound brought a smile to his face.

'What's so funny?' demanded the girl, suddenly scowling again.

'Nothing! I like it. I'll gladly call you Lick.'

'It's no worse than Lucky or Crafty,' she said, still defensive.

'Exactly!' he agreed. 'They're all good names.'

'They certainly are.' She seemed mollified. 'Viper is a good name too. It fits him perfectly – far better than Vipton. That's what I'll call him from now on. When I get back, he won't have a job any more. Mr Wainwright always listens to what I say. That Viper will end up in a dungeon if I have my way.'

She was frowning again, so Crafty tried to lighten the mood.

'Do you mind if I ask why you call yourself Lick?' he asked. 'It's not really a shortening of Leticia.'

She grinned at him. 'Given time, there's no problem I can't lick. There's no opponent I can't lick at chess. My brain moves at a pretty fast lick. Eventually I'll find a way to lick the Shole itself. I really believe that. There's more – want me to go on?'

Crafty shook his head and grinned back at her. She was certainly full of herself, but why not? he thought. This was certainly no ordinary girl walking beside him. Yes, he could call her Lick!

He also remembered her saying, *If I had any friends* ... Perhaps she was lonely? He could understand that.

The pair walked on in silence, and Crafty's thoughts turned to Viper again. There was definitely a part of him that would have liked to drag Viper into the Shole and leave him there, as Lucky had suggested. But, realistically, Crafty knew that Lick's solution was better – and legal too; he and Lucky wouldn't get into trouble. Her account of what had happened would surely get Viper sacked – maybe even sent to jail.

First, however, they had to reach the Daylight World.

At last they found themselves on the main road that Crafty knew led to the northern edge of the Shole, and the canal beyond.

They probably had only about a mile to go when they saw the familiar blue circle of a gate directly ahead of them.

They grinned at each other – they were indeed being rescued! They could see Ginger Bob gazing out at them through the gate. Eagerly they ran towards it, and then Crafty stepped back politely to let Lick go first. She gave a little laugh, no doubt relieved to be safe, and scrambled through.

Crafty didn't waste any time following her. He wanted to see Ginger Bob's face when Lick told him the truth about Viper –

It happened so fast that Crafty had no chance of helping her, no chance of stopping what happened next.

He heard Lick scream, then shout out four words: 'He's used a lure!'

It didn't make any sense until Crafty was through the gate too.

Then, all at once, he realized that it wasn't Ginger Bob's gate. It was Viper's! He'd used a lure to deceive them into thinking they were being rescued.

Crafty took in the scene before him with horror. Viper, still in his blood-stained shirt, was holding a big wooden club in both hands; he swung it at Lick.

Crafty had no time to get between them; no time to try and save her.

The club came down on Lick's temple with a terrible blow. Blood splattered out in all directions. She gave a little cry, and fell forward on to her face.

Crafty leaped towards her, his heart in his mouth. He knew that a blow like that could have killed her. He saw that she wasn't moving – but was she dead?

Meanwhile Viper had immediately turned his attention from the stricken girl to Crafty.

'You're next!' he said, shoving him backwards and waving the club in his face. 'I'll say one thing for you, Benson, you're a survivor. Which is exactly why I thought it was worth putting in a bit of observation time just in case. There are fixed locations all along that road, and I knew that, if you survived, you'd pass this way. Can't have you telling tales again, Benson, so we're off to another location – one I believe you've visited before. The one where you made your first snatch.'

Keeping one eye on Crafty, and still brandishing the club, Viper reached forward and adjusted the gate's ratchet-dial.

Click! Click! Click!

The dark clouds swirled briefly, and then, through the gate, Crafty saw once again the grim stone building of the orphanage, its front door still hanging off its hinges.

'I'm using another lure now,' Viper said. 'This time it'll be raw meat dripping with blood. That'll bring those sharp-toothed monsters running! And this time they won't be disappointed. They'll have plenty of real flesh and blood to satisfy them – yours and the girl's! There'll be no trace of you remaining.'

'You're mad,' gasped Crafty. 'What on earth have we ever done to hurt you?'

Viper shook his head as if in pity. 'You really don't know, do you? You haven't a clue what this is all about . . .'

'No, I don't understand. What do you mean?' Crafty asked, keeping one wary eye on the club in Viper's hands.

'You're just like the rest of the fools in this castle – running around like idiots, attempting to fight a battle you'll never win. Eventually the Shole will take over the whole world and, once it's done that, things will be far better. People will come back from the dead. We'll be immortal.'

'You think *we're* idiotic? Step through that gate and you'll be dead or changed. That's what the Shole will do to *you*!'

'Not true! We chosen ones don't die. We're changed, yes, but for the better. We will rule the world, but first we have to eliminate those who oppose us – particularly the Fey. *You* are the biggest threat to our aims.'

Crafty suddenly realized who the 'chosen ones' were. 'You're a member of the cult? One of the Grey Hoods?'

'Of course I am – and I'm not the only one working in the castle. Where better to fight those who threaten the Shole? And today I'm truly fortunate. I get to kill one of the last remaining grubs and the brightest castle boffin – two little birds with one stone!'

Viper advanced towards him, and Crafty retreated a couple of steps, keeping his back to the gate. The mancer was holding the club in his right hand, tapping it rhythmically into the palm of his left. Crafty readied himself to spring out of the way the minute Viper attacked.

Then he saw a sly expression come over the mancer's face.

Viper pointed at the gate behind Crafty. 'Here they come, Benson – lots of the horrible little aberrations – and they're right behind you, waiting to tear you limb from limb.'

But Crafty wasn't called Crafty for nothing. He'd been fooled by Viper once before; he wouldn't fall for that trick again.

He made to look over his shoulder to where Viper was pointing – and then he ducked.

As predicted, Viper swung at him with the club. But, thanks to Crafty's dive, he missed and overbalanced, his momentum carrying him tumbling towards the gate. All he needed was a little push. But Crafty pushed him really hard, just to make sure.

Viper screamed as he fell through, but the scream was abruptly cut off as Crafty closed the gate on him. Once more it was filled only with swirling clouds.

He stood there panting for a moment, coming to terms with what he'd just done. He'd killed someone – a madman, yes, and in self-defence, but a person all the same.

For what felt like the millionth time since he'd arrived at the castle, Crafty wished beyond anything that his father was there.

But there was no time to waste. He ran over to check on Lick.

She was alive, but her breathing was shallow. Blood was beginning to form a puddle under her head. She urgently needed help, so Crafty sprinted out of the door and along the corridor to the Chief Mancer's office. Lucky was outside the door, probably waiting to be admitted, but Crafty didn't even have time to nod to him.

He burst through the door and, before Ginger Bob could say anything, told him what had happened. The Chief

Mancer leaped to his feet, but as they raced back to Viper's office, Crafty noticed that the Chief Mancer kept glancing at the blood on Crafty's hands and the red footprints left by his boots.

Surely he can't be worrying about the mess I'm making at a time like this! thought Crafty.

After the alarm had been raised, and Lick had been taken away by the doctor, the Chief Mancer questioned Crafty at length.

Finally he delivered his verdict.

'You're a liar, Benson! You're a liar and a murderer!'

THE TRIAL

Crafty had expected to be given a proper trial – perhaps in a courtroom with a judge seated behind a high desk. The Chief Mancer would be a witness, and someone would prosecute him and someone else would defend him. Maybe there'd also be an audience who'd come to see justice being done.

But when – several days after he'd pushed Viper through the gate – the guard brought Crafty up from his deep, dark, dank cell and marched him into a small wood-panelled room, there was just one person waiting there: a black-gowned judge seated behind a small desk.

Crafty's eye was immediately drawn to the black cap just to the left of the judge's notepad. A judge only put that on when he was pronouncing the death sentence. The sight of it made Crafty's mouth become very dry.

The judge was a big man with white hair and a deep' lined face, who must surely have been a judge for ·

years. Crafty suddenly wondered how many prisoners he'd sentenced to death.

The man spoke. 'You are Colin Benson, son of Brian Benson?'

'Yes, sir.'

'You are charged with the murder of the gate mancer Mr S.W. Vipton. You have confessed that you pushed him through a gate and into the Shole, deliberately leaving him there. Whether consequently changed or dead, the result is the same: he is now dead to this world. How do you plead?'

Crafty's heart hammered in his chest. 'Not guilty, sir. I acted in self-defence. What happened was –'

'Silence!' cried the judge, interrupting him. He was staring at a point just above Crafty's head. He never once looked into his eyes. 'Your plea is duly noted, but there is no arguing against the evidence. You confessed to the crime, for goodness' sake.' He tutted, as if annoyed that Crafty should be wasting his time.

Crafty tried to speak again, desperate to argue his case, but the guard gave him a hard shove to silence him. The judge picked up the black cap and placed it on his head. Then, although Crafty could scarcely believe it, he began to pronounce his sentence, speaking low and sonorously.

'The judgment of this court is that you are guilty as charged. You will be taken from here to the death cell, where you may gaze upon the Daylight World for the last time. You will be kept in confinement until you are taken to Execution Square, and there you will be hanged by the neck until you are dead. Afterwards your body will be cast into a lime pit. May God have mercy upon your soul.'

And that was it. Crafty hadn't been able to say a word in his defence, and now he was sentenced to death.

The guard didn't take him back to his previous cell. Instead, after climbing several flights of stone steps, he was shoved into a cell with a barred window. A shaft of sunlight came through it and lit up the opposite wall. It was a huge improvement on the stinking underground dungeon where he'd spent the previous week. But it was still the 'death cell'.

'That wasn't a fair trial,' he complained to the guard as he unfastened the iron manacles from around his wrists. 'I never got a chance to speak, and there was nobody there to defend me.'

'That's the way things are now, boy,' the man replied – not unsympathetically, Crafty thought. 'The Shole threatens our very existence and it's more difficult for everyone – even the innocent. There's neither the time nor the resources to keep the old ways going. At least you won't have to listen to them building your scaffold,' he said with a grin, gesturing towards the window, 'seeing as it's already been built.'

Crafty suddenly recognized this man – he was the same red-faced guard who'd tried to scare him, Lucky and Donna when they went to see Old Nell. The guard clearly had a black sense of humour.

'Enjoy the view from the window! What you can see ' Execution Square!'

When he'd gone, Crafty looked out on to the small flagged courtyard below. At its centre, and taking up most of the space, was a platform and a gibbet very similar to the one where Old Nell had met her end. A vivid image came into his mind of her swinging at the end of the rope, her body spinning, her legs jerking in that final painful dance of death. That was going to happen to him.

But when? he wondered. The judge hadn't named the day when he'd be hanged. It could be weeks from now; it could be tomorrow. Tonight might be his last on earth.

Crafty spent the night tossing and turning. He had been hoping that his father might somehow have survived in the Shole but, with his own impending death, he realized that he might never see him again. He kept going over and over what had happened in the courtroom, and the injustice of it all – including Ginger Bob's refusal to believe him. The Chief Mancer hadn't even listened to his explanations.

Lucky had been kept waiting outside and must have overheard their dispute. He'd suddenly rapped on the door of Ginger Bob's office and walked in without an invitation. Then he'd pointed out that Viper's claim that Lick had been dragged away by Bertha didn't make any sense – after all, here she was, having clearly been hurt on *this* side of the gate.

But the Chief Mancer had just looked at the blood on Crafty's hands and boots, shaken his head and then suggested that *he* had hurt Lick after Viper had rescued her.

When Crafty protested that he had no reason to hurt Lick, Ginger Bob had simply shaken his head. So then Crafty told him that Viper had admitted to being a member of the Grey Hoods – and that had unleashed a torrent of angry words.

'How dare you make such allegations! You are beyond belief, and will clearly say *anything*, no matter how preposterous, in an attempt to save your own skin. You are maligning a valued member of our guild. Do you not realize that any new recruits are carefully vetted? It is unthinkable that Mr Vipton should have been a member of that evil cult.'

In the end he could focus on nothing but the fact that Crafty had pushed Viper out into the Shole; that he'd dared to lay hands on a gate mancer, and had brought about the end of Viper's life.

Crafty's only hope was that Lick would recover in time to explain what had really happened. He was hoping that this was still possible, even though her injury had been serious and there was a danger that she would die. Crafty had repeatedly asked for news of her, but each time had received an angry glare and stony silence.

Wake up, Lick, he willed in the darkness of the night.

The following morning the guard came in and handed him breakfast – a bowl of cold porridge. 'You've got three more days to live,' he announced cheerfully. 'You'll hang on Monday at three in the afternoon. Any last requests?'

The news was like a punch in the stomach.

There was nobody Crafty could ask for help – except Lick, and for all he knew she was already dead. But there was one person he desperately wanted to see. Somebody who would still care about him, in spite of what he'd done.

'My father is Brian Benson – he's a courier. He's missing in the Shole. Has there been any news about him? He's been missing for over two weeks, but the Chief Mancer promised me that he was looking for him. I'd also like to find out how Miss Leticia Crompton-Smythe is doing. She has a head injury. She's my friend,' Crafty said, realizing that it was true.

The guard huffed in disbelief. 'Word has it, boy, that her head injury was *your* doing. Some friend.'

Crafty tried to protest, to tell him what had really happened, but, like the Chief Mancer and the judge, the guard refused to listen, and silenced Crafty with a gesture.

'I'll see what can be done,' he muttered, locking the door and leaving him alone with too much time to think.

Later, just as it was getting dark, his cell door was unlocked and opened a crack. The guard didn't bother to come in; he just put Crafty's supper on the floor and told him the bad news.

'Miss Crompton-Smythe is still unconscious. It's not looking good. And your father is still missing in the Shole. No courier has ever returned after being missing for so long.'

With that, he clanged the cell door shut again.

Crafty's heart plummeted. He was heartbroken about his father, and the news about Lick was terrible too. If only she could wake up and tell the truth about Viper!

But maybe she'd never wake up . . .

Crafty was running out of time.

The days and nights passed all too quickly as the hour of his execution drew nearer. Of course he was afraid of being hanged – of choking and being unable to breathe. But he was even more terrified of what awaited him beyond death. Would he be punished for what he'd done to Viper? The Church said that murderers went to Hell for all eternity, and were tortured there by devils and demons. Was that to be his fate?

Was this what you meant by me 'getting what I deserved', Old Nell? he wondered.

Then, early in the morning of the day Crafty was to be hanged, the guard brought him what he evidently considered to be good news.

'Cheer up, boy!' he said, handing him his usual unappetizing breakfast of cold porridge. 'It seems you won't die for another week. The Duke fell off his horse while out hunting yesterday and broke his neck. He's as dead as a doornail, so there'll be several days of mourning. Folks have too much fun at hangings, so there won't be any until the mourning's over!'

It hardly seemed like good news to Crafty. A week would soon pass, and now the torture of anticipation would be stretched out, after which they'd stretch his neck.

Then he realized that the longer the hanging was delayed, the more time Lick had to recover and speak up for him.

Crafty suddenly remembered all those mysterious rooms on the ground floor of the castle – the ones with strange names like the Pessimists' and the Optimists' Rooms – and gave a bitter laugh. It seemed that he suddenly found himself belonging in the latter.

20

ROOTS

The final week was dragging on torturously. Crafty's thoughts churned constantly – he switched between worrying about his father to worrying about Lick dying. He often pondered on Old Nell's curse too – was this *really* what he deserved? Maybe it was. After all, he had killed a man. But he'd wanted to rescue Lick, and it didn't seem fair that he should be punished for that.

Finally, the morning before he was due to be hanged, the guard arrived without bringing him any breakfast.

'Come with me, boy!' he ordered, and marched Crafty out of the cell with a heavy hand on his shoulder.

Crafty's heart began hammering. Was he being taken to be hanged now, before the designated day? He was too scared to ask.

They went down a flight of steps, and the guard opened another door before pushing him through.

'You've got ten minutes,' he said. 'Get yourself cleaned up.'

The room was small, and empty but for a pail of water and a wooden chair. Crafty gazed at the chair in amazement – or rather, at what was on it. A towel was draped over the back, and folded upon the seat was a clean gate-grub uniform. On top of the shirt there was a bar of soap.

He eagerly stripped off his dirty clothes and started to wash himself. The water was freezing and made Crafty gasp, but he gave himself a thorough wash, glad to be free of the grime and stink. Once he'd towelled himself dry, he got dressed in the clean uniform.

Surely they wouldn't hang me in my uniform? he thought, and a sliver of hope began to creep into his heart.

He was only just ready when the guard opened the door and beckoned to him.

'Come along, lad!' he bellowed. 'It doesn't do to keep the Duke waiting.'

Astonished, Crafty followed him down the corridor. Had he really said 'the Duke'? But the Duke was dead . . . Then he realized that he must be talking about the *new* Duke of Lancaster, one of the dead Duke's sons. He had two, didn't he? Or was it three? Crafty wondered absently if the one they'd rescued was still alive, or had been totally changed into wood.

Instead of climbing the stairs which Crafty knew led to the Duke's rooms, right at the top of the castle – the fancy quarters where he stayed when in residence – he was taken to the ground floor – the Pessimists' Room ... although there was a new brass plaque on the door. It read:

THE DUCAL CHAMBERS

Two armed guards dressed in full ceremonial uniform stood outside. As Crafty and his escort approached, they crossed their long spears to bar them from entering, but now his own guard called out in a loud voice: 'Master Colin Benson to see the Duke!'

As if by magic, the two men moved their spears into a vertical position, the doors opened and Crafty followed his guard into a vast room. There was a red carpet down the middle, leading up to a set of shallow steps, and they walked along it until he found himself looking up at the new Duke.

It was the young man they'd rescued from the Shole!

The Duke was dressed in a green shirt with gold buttons. His face was ruddy with health and his blond beard had grown a little and thickened out. He smiled at Crafty, who wondered if he did in fact recognize him, or whether he was just kind.

'Bow to the Duke!' the guard hissed into his ear.

Crafty bowed clumsily and then looked up at the Duke again, trying to keep his eyes on his face. But he felt his gaze wandering down to the lower part of the man's body – or, rather, where it would have been had it not been covered.

The Duke appeared to be sitting in a huge cylindrical container, with three sets of steps leading up to it; one at the front, and one at each side. Knowing what he did, Crafty guessed that it was filled with soil, but you couldn't see that or any of the roots that now formed the young man's lower body. A rich purple cloth enclosed his waist and flowed across the container and down to the floor so that not one inch of it was visible. He looked as if he was wearing an enormous skirt!

Crafty had a sudden urge to giggle, and bit his lower lip hard. To laugh at the Duke would have been disastrous. And he knew that it wasn't really funny. The Duke was in effect planted in a giant pot – a sad and horrific fate. His lower body had been transformed into woody roots, and he was fixed in this position for the rest of his life. He would never walk again. Crafty knew that the purple cloth was an attempt to afford the Duke some measure of dignity.

'You may leave!' the Duke commanded the guard, and waited in silence as the man left the chamber and the large doors closed behind him.

'You may wonder why you are here,' he said to Crafty. 'I will explain everything in due course, but first I am happy to put your mind at rest. You will not be hanged.'

The sense of relief spread through Crafty's body. He began to tremble, and let out a big sigh before he could contain it.

The Duke gave Crafty another kind smile. 'The roots of trees are very sensitive,' he said. 'It seems that mine are particularly so. For example, my roots enable me to hear things from afar. There are so many different voices; a babble that can be overwhelming. I am gradually learning to be selective and to focus upon individual conversations. I can hear the pessimists in the distance wallowing in doom and gloom, complaining about being evicted from this room and making plans they are convinced will fail. I can also hear the giggling of the servant girls as they wash the pots and pans in the kitchen, and make eyes at the sous chefs. And you too, Crafty – I heard what you said . . .'

He stared at Crafty, no longer smiling, and Crafty felt himself glow red with embarrassment.

'When, sir? And what did I say?' he asked, wondering what the Duke could possibly have overheard recently. Did he talk in his sleep? Had he said something treasonable?

Then he realized that the Duke had used his nickname – *Crafty*. Surely he wouldn't do that if he was angry with him?

'I heard what you said before you rescued me from the Shole,' the Duke replied. 'You knew about trees and plants. You knew that to cut through my roots or dig me out too roughly would cause me agonizing pain. You knew that to sever my taproot would mean death. By taking charge and guiding the others, you undoubtedly saved my life.'

'I just tried to do my best for you, sir,' Crafty told him.

'Well then, I will now do my best for you. I believe you have been found guilty of murder and sentenced to death. Instead, I grant you an immediate pardon and restore your freedom to you.'

Crafty was amazed and delighted. He wondered how the Duke had come to hear of his fate. But before he could wonder too much, the Duke went on.

'Although I am pleased to grant you such a pardon, you will be relieved to know that it is because the facts of the incident with Mr Vipton have now come to light. And, indeed, it seems that were Mr Vipton still alive, *he* would be the one facing execution. Come closer . . .'

The Duke beckoned him up the steps in front of him, and Crafty climbed until he was level with him. Then the Duke reached behind his back, retrieved something, and held it out to Crafty with both hands.

'Take it!' he commanded. 'Yours is a dangerous job. You need go unarmed into the Shole no longer. I believe it belongs to you anyway.'

It was the dagger that Bertha, the Bog Queen, had given him. It had been taken from Crafty immediately after his arrest.

He looked up at the Duke and grinned. 'Thank you, sir. Thank you very much!' Then he remembered something important. 'Sir, have you been told what Mr Vipton claimed to be? That he said that he was a member of the Grey Hoods?'

The Duke looked astonished. 'No, that has not been reported to me. What else did he say?'

Crafty realized that the Chief Mancer had probably kept this information quiet. It reflected badly on his guild that they had allowed an enemy to join their ranks.

'He said that other members of the cult were secretly working in the castle and trying to hinder our efforts to fight the Shole. They want the Shole to engulf the whole world.'

The Duke stared at him until Crafty could no longer hold his gaze. As he bowed his head, the Duke finally spoke.

'I want you to give me your word that you'll not mention this to anyone – neither to friends nor to colleagues. Do you promise?'

'Yes, sir.'

'I assume that you reported it to the Chief Mancer – although he did not see fit to pass the information on?'

'Yes, sir, but he didn't believe me anyway . . .'

'Let me worry about that, Crafty. I need to think carefully about this, but I can tell you one thing – there will eventually be very big changes here. Just keep your word and you'll have nothing to worry about.'

Although Crafty had no intention of breaking his promise, he did feel a little uncomfortable. He didn't like keeping such a secret from his friends – and he wondered what it might mean for Ginger Bob.

It was only after he'd left that Crafty realized he hadn't asked the Duke about Lick. So, as the guard escorted him back to his old room in the tower, he asked him instead.

'She's made a full recovery,' he was told. 'But I regret to say that your father's still missing.'

Crafty felt a strange mixture of emotions – he was sad about his father, but very relieved to hear that Lick was better now. He guessed it was she who'd given the 'facts of the incident with Mr Vipton' to the Duke. He could only hope that his lucky spell would continue, and that his father would soon be found.

He'd hardly been back in his room five minutes when his breakfast was delivered by a kitchen server. It was bacon, eggs, tomatoes, mushrooms and fried bread, all fresh, hot and delicious – certainly an improvement on the cold porridge he'd been served in his cell. He wolfed it down.

After he'd wiped his plate clean with the last piece of bread, Crafty washed his hands. He picked up the dagger he'd been given and examined it carefully. There wasn't a trace of mud on it. Someone must have given it a good wash. The narrow blade was about five inches long, but the hilt added perhaps another four to that.

All at once something caught his eye. On the hilt was an embossed green shape that looked like a snake coiled into a spiral, with its head at the centre. He looked more closely and saw that the last section of tail crossed the spiral and was in the snake's mouth. It was eating its own tail! That was weird. If he ever saw Bertha again, Crafty decided, he would ask her about it.

He pushed the knife into his coat pocket and reported to the Waiting Room. It was very strange – all those days stuck in a cell had made him keen to get back to the job, and to see his friends. He wanted to thank Lick – he realized he hadn't asked if she was well enough to resume work yet – and he couldn't wait to see Lucky.

Lucky was sitting in his usual place. Crafty smiled broadly at him. '*May* I sit down?' he joked.

'It's good to see you back, Crafty!' Lucky leaped to his feet and clapped him on the back, grinning. 'And I'm really sorry I didn't manage to come and see you. I tried, but they said you were being kept in solitary confinement and no visitors were allowed. But last night Ginger Bob told me that you were going to be pardoned.'

They'd a lot of catching up to do, but just then the far door opened and the Chief Mancer strode in.

'I have a job for you, Proudfoot,' he said, appearing to ignore Crafty.

Lucky shot him a look, then came to his feet and headed for the door. But as they were about to leave, Ginger Bob suddenly turned and fixed Crafty with his stern gaze. Crafty wondered if he was still angry with him because of what had happened to Viper. Did he still feel some loyalty to his colleague, even though the Duke now considered Viper to be guilty?

Eventually the mancer spoke. 'Welcome back, Benson. We have had to reorganize work allocations in your absence. From today you will be working with a new gate mancer . . .' He paused. 'Everything will be explained later.'

Then he and Lucky were gone, leaving Crafty to wonder what he'd meant.

It wasn't long before he found out. Five minutes later the door opened again and the new mancer entered, giving him a look stern enough to rival Ginger Bob's.

'I have a job for you, Benson. Come with me and bring your coat!' she commanded.

It was Leticia Crompton-Smythe.

Crafty wondered if he was still allowed to call her Lick.

21

ANYTHING THAT BLEEDS

Miss Crompton-Smythe – as Crafty supposed he'd have to call her again – led him to the door of Viper's old office in silence, with no hint of their former friendliness. A brass plaque with her name on it had now replaced Viper's.

Once inside she sat behind her new desk and pointed Crafty to the chair opposite. Looking around, he saw that the room had changed. There were three large bookcases filled to capacity, and Viper's white shirts had gone. Even the walls had been painted a tasteful pale green.

Suddenly Lick's expression softened and she smiled at him, and Crafty found himself smiling back. Perhaps they were to be friends after all?

'Thank you for saving my life, Crafty,' she said. There was a large bruise over her left temple, but it was fading. 'Thanks for bringing me out of the Shole alive, and for trying to help me after Viper hit me. I'm so sorry for what you've been through. I only woke up two days ago, and for a while I didn't even know who I was or what had happened to me.'

'I'm glad I could help,' he said. 'I'm just sorry that I couldn't prevent Viper from hitting you. But things seem to have moved fast since you woke up,' he said. 'Why have they appointed you a gate mancer? I thought you were a boffin?'

'As a boffin, I'm qualified and trained to do all sorts of other jobs, such as gate grub, mancer, and roles you've probably never even heard of. Boffins are researchers and inventors who are vital to the fight against the Shole; we are allowed to work within a variety of different guilds. Although, as you can imagine, we're sometimes far from welcome! It was my idea to become a gate mancer for a while, so we'll be working together from now on.'

'But you don't really need a gate grub, do you?' Crafty interrupted. 'You're Fey, so you can operate the gate and find new locations by yourself.'

Lick nodded and smiled. 'That's true, Crafty, but it's better with two of us working as a team. In any case, I couldn't go out and leave the gate unguarded. Anyway, most of the time we won't be working for the Chief Mancer, although we'll consult him as a courtesy. We'll be reporting back to the Duke himself. It's not for nothing that he's chosen to take up residence in what was the Pessimists' Room, ousting its gloomy inhabitants. His father was very conservative in his methods of governance, but the new Duke has shown himself to be radical and innovative.'

Crafty didn't understand. What she was saying didn't make sense – if the Duke was a pessimist, then surely he'd be more likely to be cautious like his father?

'But then, why is he a pessimist?' he asked. 'Does the Duke think we're going to lose our fight against the Shole?'

'No, Crafty. We're going to carry on the fight in ways never attempted before – we're going to take risks. The Duke is pessimistic in just one regard. He thinks that things will get a lot worse before they get better. He believes that the castle will soon be engulfed by the Shole. But some of us won't abandon it. We're going to stay and fight from within the Shole to find out exactly what it is and why it began. Eventually we *will* win!'

Crafty grinned at her, encouraged by her passion. Maybe one day they really *could* destroy the Shole! Then he had a crafty idea. If Lick was feeling grateful, perhaps she'd let him look for his father . . .

'So what are we going to do first? I know that research is our key priority, but . . . I was hoping we could search for the three missing couriers? You'll remember that one of them is my father . . . Could we search for them at the same time, Lick – I mean, Miss Crompton-Smythe?' he asked eagerly.

She nodded. 'We certainly will – and please do still call me Lick. I promise we'll make a start on our search before the day is out, but first I'd like to talk to that aberration from the bog – the girl who gave you the dagger.'

Crafty was wary. 'We could find her and see if she's happy to talk to you, but I won't try to snatch her,' he said firmly.

'How can you even say that to me, Crafty!' Lick snapped, giving him one of her scowls. 'I wouldn't dream of trying to snatch Bertha. If she hadn't given you the knife, we probably wouldn't have survived. There are enough deadly aberrations in the Shole. We need allies there too.'

'Sorry . . . you're right,' he said, embarrassed.

Lick nodded, forgiving him. 'Can I have a look at that dagger?' she asked.

He pulled it out of his coat pocket and handed it to her. She turned it over and over in her hands before pointing to the image on the hilt.

'Have you looked closely at this?' she asked.

Crafty nodded. 'Yes, it looks like a snake eating its own tail.'

'It represents more than a snake, Crafty. It's the great serpent called Ouroborus. It's sometimes called the Earth Dragon, and the fact that its head is joined to its tail is a symbol of rebirth. It would no doubt have been important to ancient tribes like the Segantii. It's interesting when you think that, in a way, Bertha has herself been reborn!'

She smiled and handed him back the dagger before reaching into her desk to pull out a little box.

Crafty already knew what it contained. He picked up Bertha's cold brown finger and went across to the chair while Lick drew back the black curtain to reveal the silver gate.

As he sat down, he realized that he might finally get an answer to some of his questions. 'Do they really mix the ground-up bones of grubs into the silver frame?' he asked.

Lick nodded grimly. 'I'm afraid so. That's part of the Fey magic. Without that, the gates wouldn't work.'

Crafty felt sick, and could hardly bear to ask his next question. 'There was a gate grub called Donna – a friend of mine and Lucky's. She was killed very recently. Will . . . will they use her bones for a new gate?'

Lick shook her head and began fiddling with the ratchet-dial. 'They only need a very small amount of bone. Usually they take just the end of the little finger of the left hand. After that, the bodies of most gate grubs are taken to a special experimental graveyard inside the Shole – in the hope that one day the Shole will bring them back to life, as it did with your friend Bertha. We could learn more about life, death and the Shole, and even gain new allies. Why do you think your father buried your brothers in the cellar?'

'I have no idea. I don't even know how they died. And why was my father allowed to bury them in our cellar rather than the graveyard?' Crafty asked.

'Your father is a well-respected courier, and he made a special plea to the previous Duke. He wanted to keep his family together, even in death. In view of what happened to your mother – yes, I know all about her, and I'm sorry, Crafty – the Duke decided to allow it. Of course, your father hopes that one day your brothers might live again . . .'

This was what Crafty had always wanted. Their whispering had made them seem close – almost close enough to return at any time. He knew that Bertha had been returned from the dead – but might Donna one day come back to life too, along with his brothers? He hardly dared to hope.

But Lick was as brisk and businesslike as ever. 'Now – let's concentrate on finding Bertha,' she said.

Crafty settled himself further into the chair, then pointed up at the sharp blade of the guillotine. 'That thing still makes me nervous,' he told her. 'You're a boffin. Couldn't you come up with something better and safer for gate grubs?'

Lick gave a small sigh of annoyance, or perhaps just of impatience. 'I'm not Viper, so at least *try* to trust me, Crafty. And yes, I will put my mind to finding a better defensive system, but for now we'll have to put up with what we have. We have other priorities.'

Crafty nodded and began to stare into the dark swirling clouds inside the circular frame of the gate. He concentrated, and moments later he was looking at the edge of the bog. The light was dim, but in the distance the three houses, with his house in the middle, were just visible through the gloom.

So where was Bertha? Would she come out, or would the presence of the gate put her off?

Crafty stared at the surface of the bog. It was bubbling gently and steam was rising from it. There was no sign of the Bog Queen. Would she know that he was here? he wondered. She must have known who he was when she gave him the dagger – he had to hope that she'd sense him again.

'Maybe Bertha won't come near the gate?' he suggested. 'Viper tried to snatch her before and the guillotine chopped off her finger. She's probably wary.'

'You could be right, Crafty,' agreed Lick. 'Give me back her finger, then go through the gate – but stay in sight. And head straight back at the very first hint of danger.'

While Crafty pulled on his greatcoat, Lick replaced the finger in the box. Then he clambered through the gate into the Shole.

The air was chilly and damp. He walked slowly along the sloping edge of the bog, moving in a clockwise direction towards the house where he'd once lived. He glanced back at the shimmering blue circle. It was a lot better working with Lick, he thought. She wouldn't play stupid tricks or abandon him. And later he'd get to search for his father. How his prospects had changed in the space of only a few hours!

Crafty had taken only twenty steps when there was a disturbance on the surface of the mud to his right. Seconds later the crowned top of Bertha's head broke through, as far as her nose. Her green eyes stared up at him without blinking.

Crafty smiled at her, and held up his hands to show her that she could trust him.

Her head rose up further until her mouth was clear of the mud. 'Why have you come here again?' she asked, her voice low and soft.

'I've come to thank you for giving me the knife, Bertha. Without that I would never have escaped. I'd be dead.'

She didn't seem to hear him. 'It's dangerous here,' she warned. 'You must stay away.'

'But I can't stay away, Bertha. It's my job to come through the gate and find out as much as I can about the Shole. My people are suffering, and we have to find a way to defeat it. I'm with a friend, a girl called Lick. She's a gate mancer,' Crafty said, pointing back towards the blue circle. 'You saved her life too. She'd just like to ask you some questions. Will you help us?'

Bertha's face remained as impassive as ever, but her tone took on a harder edge as she spoke. 'I trust you, Crafty. I know you. But how can I trust a gate mancer? Those people are cruel. They tried to drag me away. They cut off my finger too.'

'Some mancers *are* cruel – that's true. Some have been very cruel to me. But this one is different.'

'Different how? Will she give me back my finger?'

Crafty hesitated. Lick was pretty reasonable, but he suspected that she'd be reluctant to simply hand the finger back.

'I'll ask her.'

Bertha gave the slightest nod of her head. 'If she returns it, I will talk to her – but I won't approach that gate. *She* must come to *me*. I know she's Fey, like you and your father, and the Shole itself won't harm her. I'll warn you both if danger approaches.'

With that, Bertha sank back down a few inches into the bog, and Crafty returned to the gate, where Lick was staring out at him. He told her what Bertha had said.

Lick frowned. 'That presents me with two serious problems. The finger is the property of the Relic Room, and the curators won't like me going back without it.'

'No,' Crafty said, frowning back at her, 'it's the property of Bertha. It's *her* finger! And it's of no use to us. We don't need it to find her – she finds us – and we know she only shows herself if she wants to. And surely the Relic people must have finished studying it by now?'

'You're right, Crafty, but the curators might not see it that way. They don't only store and conserve artefacts. As new knowledge comes to light, their specialists re-examine the specimens. Research is continuing all the time.'

Lick paused and sighed, then went on. 'And there's something else for us to worry about. A mancer isn't supposed to leave the gate unattended. Most can't anyway – they cannot risk going into the Shole. Of course, I can, but I'd be leaving the gate in a very vulnerable position. What if something got through into the castle – some dangerous aberration that might kill people? I'd be responsible.'

'I agree that it's a risk, but I could stand behind you, near the gate, in case there's any threat,' Crafty said, pointing to the hilt of the dagger protruding from his greatcoat pocket.

For a moment Lick covered her face with her hands, clearly wrestling with her conscience. Then she dropped them and, with a look of determination, silently picked up the box containing Bertha's finger and climbed through the gate to join Crafty.

He gave her a pat on the back, glad that she'd seen sense.

'Don't you get too familiar!' she warned, but then she smiled and winked at him, and marched off towards Bertha.

Keeping his distance, Crafty followed her. He saw that Bertha was now standing up in the bog. He halted, carefully positioning himself so that he could just hear what was being said, but could also run back to defend the gate if anything happened.

The gloom of the Shole seemed thicker today. The blue of the gate was dim, and the outlines of Bertha and Lick indistinct.

First Lick held out the box and Bertha accepted it. Then, wasting no time, Lick asked her first question:

'Where do you live? Have you a shelter, a place of refuge?'

Bertha pointed to the bog. 'I live in the bog. Deep within it there is a chamber where I spend time. My things are there.'

'What things?'

'Some are things that belong to my own time; things that were buried with me. Others are objects I have found – in the bog and elsewhere: weapons, brooches and amulets that contain magic.'

Lick was busily scribbling all this down. 'And what do you eat, Bertha?' she asked.

'Anything that bleeds. Mostly small creatures that swim through the bog. I might eat you, if you were not a friend of Crafty,' she said calmly.

Crafty was shocked by that. Bertha had always seemed so gentle, kind and friendly. He'd never thought about what she ate. But he supposed that violence and blood-lust were part of the reality of being a creature of the Shole. She was simply telling them the truth.

Lick glanced warily back at Crafty before continuing with her questions. She looked just a shade nervous. 'Do things hunt *you*, Bertha?'

'Yes – many things, big and small. It is kill or be killed here. Always keep moving. Be alert or die.'

'Crafty's father and two other couriers have disappeared as well. Do you know what's happened to them?'

'I have already searched for Brian Benson because Crafty is my friend. I cannot find him and do not know where he is. Something as yet unknown has taken the couriers.'

Crafty felt his heart contract with fear and pain. What did she mean 'something as yet unknown' had taken them? What had happened to his father? They had to try and rescue him as soon as possible.

Perhaps knowing that he'd be upset by this news, Lick decided that it was time to go.

'Could I return later to ask you more questions?' she asked Bertha.

'Yes. Come back to this same place, close to the bog. I will know when you are here. We will talk again.'

With that, Bertha sank down again, and Lick jogged back over to Crafty. They returned to the gate, and made it safely through, grateful that they'd not encountered any danger.

Sitting at her desk, Lick spent ten minutes making more notes, carefully recording what Bertha had said.

'We'll go back tomorrow and talk to her again,' she told Crafty, placing her notebook in her desk drawer and taking out a pair of scissors. He wondered what they were for.

'Did you learn anything useful?' he asked.

'A little, though the most important thing was to get her to trust me. But you heard what she said. Did you already know that she killed and ate other creatures? And that, if I hadn't been with you, I could have been on the menu?'

This was part of life in the Shole that Crafty had pushed to the back of his mind. Mulling it over, he worried about his brothers. If they returned to life, would they be the same – could they be a threat even to him?

'She's my friend, so perhaps I didn't dwell too closely on how she lived in the Shole. But I suppose you have to survive in any way you can.'

Lick nodded, and then finally shut her notebook.

'Right, Crafty. Let's go and see if we can find your father.'

An Irresistible Summons

'We don't know where he is,' Lick began, 'but you love him, don't you?'

Crafty scowled at her in disbelief. What a question to ask! 'Yes, of course I do!'

She ignored his anger. 'So you must be emotionally close to him. That can often be enough to establish a connection. Now, concentrate! See if you can find him using your mind.'

Crafty eagerly took his seat in front of the gate and concentrated hard. He thought of the last time he'd seen his father – the moment when he'd left Crafty at the castle. He remembered his final words: *I'll be back soon to see how you're getting on* . . .

Nothing happened. The dark clouds still swirled within the gate's frame.

Then he allowed his mind to go further back, and found happy memories from when he was younger. Crafty remembered standing at the garden gate with his mother and two brothers, watching his father set off for work. He was wearing his courier uniform and his big coat. He'd turned and waved. As Crafty remembered that, a lump came into his throat. He'd been so proud, but also afraid for his father, knowing that he was going into danger. Crafty wondered what kind of danger he was in now.

Still nothing happened.

'I can't do it,' he said sadly, staring at the opaque cloud.

'Not to worry, Crafty,' said Lick kindly. 'People with a lot of skill and long experience have tried and failed to find him using many different means. The main problem we face is that because couriers don't live in the castle, or leave any of their possessions there, there is nothing to hand that we Fey could use to locate him. We'll just have to get our thinking caps on and work out another way.'

'Why don't we just go back to the garden where they left the sedan chair? There were footprints: I could follow them.'

'That's already been done, Crafty. Beyond the garden those footprints hit a cobbled road – they can't be followed any further.'

'I'd like to take a look anyway,' he insisted stubbornly.

Lick shrugged. 'It won't help, but if it'll make you feel better . . . fine. I'll take us to the fixed location in Winckley Square, where you found the sedan chair. According to the Duke, the couriers dropped his chair very suddenly and it fell on its side. Then they went off, abandoning him. He shouted out, asking why they were leaving him there, but there was no reply. They just went off without a word of explanation. This suggests to me that they were compelled in some way. Maybe it was some form of malevolent magic?'

Before Crafty could comment, Lick adjusted the ratchet-dial and, seconds later, the clouds in the gate cleared. Through the gloom he could see trees and the wall that enclosed the large central garden. In the foreground was the sedan chair, still lying on its side.

'We're going to try something new,' Lick said, approaching him with the scissors. 'We're in a unique position to experiment – we're both Fey *and* have gate-grub ability. You go through the gate and follow the couriers' footprints. I'll sit in the chair and follow you with the gate – jumping forwards to keep up with you. That way we can stay in contact – and keep you safer – without having to leave the gate unattended. But first I need something to track you with. A bit of hair will do. Keep still. I don't want to nick you.'

She reached out and cut a short length of hair from just above his ear. She clutched it in her left hand, then said, 'Right, off you go, Crafty . . .'

As he stood up and clambered through the gate, Lick sat down in his place.

He approached the sedan chair and looked down at the footprints. He recognized the set that belonged to the youth who was now the Duke. They led off along the path towards the place where he'd been changed by the Shole. There were three other, broader sets of prints, clearly made by the big boots of the couriers, one of them his father. They headed in the opposite direction to the Duke, and Crafty followed their trail up through the trees. At first the prints were clear because of the muddy ground, but as he climbed up the slope approaching the wall, they became less deep, less clearly delineated.

He glanced back. He could still just make out the blue circle of the gate in the distance. Suddenly it winked out.

His heart thudded with fear. Had something gone wrong? Had Lick abandoned him? Crafty suddenly became all too aware of the cat-like beasts sleeping in the houses around the square.

The next second the gate reappeared much closer. Lick calmly waved at him through the circle.

Relief flooded through him. Of course, it would keep disappearing. Lick would have to jump forward to follow him each time; it wasn't possible to follow him smoothly.

He reached the wall. It wasn't very high, but it was topped by an iron railing with sharp pointy spikes. High up Crafty saw a sign that said:

WINCKLEY STREET

But then he saw that there was a gap in the wall, and the footprints led right to it.

On the other side there were no more prints to follow. The road was cobbled, and directly ahead a narrow lane called Winckley Street led out of the square. It was what Crafty had been told to expect, but still his heart plummeted in disappointment. The silver gate wasn't far behind him, so he went back and clambered through to talk to Lick.

'The people who carried out the investigation were right,' he admitted. 'There's no way to follow those tracks across the cobbles.'

'No. But the direction in which they were clearly heading is interesting,' said Lick. 'It's the least likely route any courier would take from here.'

'Why?' he asked.

'Because if you head that way, you're approaching the place where the Shole first began. All our experience and research indicates that this is the most dangerous place of all. Why would three experienced couriers, who know that only too well, head there?'

'And why would those couriers abandon the sedan chair in the first place?' Crafty asked.

'Probably because they were drawn towards that heart of darkness that lies at the centre of the Shole. This is all suggesting that some form of magic was used against them. As I said, it looks like they were compelled by an irresistible summons.'

'Are we going there?' Crafty asked, unable to hide the fear in his voice. 'You could follow me using the gate.'

Lick shook her head. 'I hope that we might soon develop shields and devices that allow us to do so – we're working on them now – but at the moment it's far too dangerous. Unknown things could come through the gate into the Daylight World. The guillotine might not be enough to stop them. It's a risk we are not prepared to take.'

'But if that's where my father is . . .' Crafty protested. 'Am I just supposed to forget about him? He might still be alive!'

'I understand how you feel, Crafty, but you need to obey me. Now is not the time.'

Crafty scowled. He didn't like the way Lick had used the word *obey*. It reminded him that they were by no means equals. She might have allowed him to call her Lick, but nothing had really changed. He was still just a commoner, a lowly gate grub. Suddenly he felt very angry.

'I thought you said that things would be different now that we're working for the new Duke? I thought we were going to carry the fight to the Shole, to take risks? Think of all those people trapped in the Daylight Islands. We could be using sedan chairs to get them out. Why aren't we doing that? Why aren't we doing *something*?'

'Don't be silly, Crafty. Think how long it would take to carry them all to safety! Think of the danger to the couriers – remember what happened to your father. We *are* doing something, but we have to be ready, and that will take time!'

Now Lick was getting cross. Crafty could see the anger in her eyes as she struggled to remain calm and reasonable. But he felt so powerless.

'If he's still alive, my father may not have much time left!' he exclaimed in frustration. 'We should go and try to find him now.'

'We can't, Crafty! Be sensible, and –'

'Sensible?!' he shouted, interrupting her. 'Use a bit of empathy, if you have any. Think how I feel. If it was *your* father, you'd be off trying to save him right now!'

This was clearly too much.

'You know *nothing* about *my* father!' Lick snapped, her voice cold and hard. 'That's enough for today. Return to the Waiting Room immediately.'

'Yes, Miss Crompton-Smythe,' Crafty replied, equally coldly, and then turned and left the room.

The following day was a Sunday, so Crafty headed out into the city with Lucky.

They sat at the edge of the market place listening to the shouting of the vendors, who were desperately trying to attract the few potential customers. Lancaster was getting quieter by the day. More and more people were leaving. And who could blame them? The Shole could surge at any moment. Soon there'd be nobody left but the workers from the castle.

Still, the sun was shining and it was a glorious day – probably one of the last they'd have before autumn came, bringing with it cooler weather and earlier nights.

The conditions in the Shole would be much more dangerous then.

They'd bought bread rolls wrapped around fat beef sausages. Crafty realized that gate grubs didn't get paid much, and a big part of what they earned was deducted to cover the cost of their uniforms and their board at the castle. Those sausage rolls had taken a big chunk of the little money they had left, but they were worth every penny – piping hot and dripping with butter!

For a while they didn't speak, happy to be well-fed and out in the sunshine.

When they'd finished, Crafty brought Lucky up to date, telling him everything that had happened – from Bertha giving him the dagger to Lick's refusal to accompany him along the road to the place where he thought his father might be held prisoner. But, of course, remembering his promise to the Duke, Crafty didn't tell him that Viper had been a member of the Grey Hoods.

'I thought Crompton-Smythe was different from that rude girl we first met in the Waiting Room. Now I'm not so sure,' Crafty said bitterly. 'She still thinks she's better than everybody else.'

'Well, she's a boffin, and we know she's brighter than most. She probably comes from the sort of family that gets invited to castle banquets,' Lucky said, 'so I don't think the likes of you and me could *ever* be her equals. But, tell you something, I wish it was *me* working with her and reporting directly to the new Duke. You've just got to be patient, Crafty. I reckon she knows what she's doing.'

'You're probably right,' he conceded as they started to make their way back to the castle. 'I'll just have to try and make the best of it. At least it's better than working with Viper.'

'It certainly is! Also, what you told me about Donna being buried in the Shole makes me feel better. I thought they'd just grind up her bones and mix them into a new gate. Now it seems that she might eventually be returned to us!'

Crafty smiled and nodded, not sharing his own troubled thoughts on the matter. Would that return – if it happened – mean that Donna would need to kill things in order to eat, just like Bertha? She probably wouldn't be able to tuck into those juicy beef sausages; she'd have to eat her meat raw, even tearing at living flesh with teeth and claws. Under different circumstances, Lick might have been Bertha's prey.

This dark thought led to others; thoughts that he'd always tried to thrust to the back of his mind. What had really happened to his mother? he wondered. When the Shole enveloped her, had she died? They'd never found her body, so it was possible that, as he feared, she had been changed. Maybe his father had found out the truth, but had kept it from him?

He and Lucky were just inside the castle entrance when there was a disturbance somewhere down the hill behind them. Crafty could hear shouts and cries of fear.

Lucky grabbed his arm. 'Something's happening. Let's go and see!'

But before they'd taken two paces, the portcullis had begun to descend and guards were closing the heavy main doors to the courtyard. There was obviously some kind of threat and the castle was being secured against it. A few moments more and they'd have been left outside!

'Let's go up to the battlements and see what's happening,' Crafty suggested.

Lucky nodded and they ran up the nearest staircase. At the top they found a good vantage point looking south down the hill.

In the foreground Crafty could see people hurrying through the streets, and heard the sound of doors banging as everyone rushed indoors. Further down the hill, market traders were hastily packing away their wares.

Then Crafty looked down the slope – and immediately realized what had happened to cause such panic. The sun was still shining, but it no longer reflected off the waters of the canal.

Without warning, the dark wall of the Shole had surged north again.

23
THE KITTEN

'We'd best report to the Waiting Room,' Lucky said. 'When something like this happens, Sundays become working days.'

They both headed back to their rooms. Crafty quickly dressed in his uniform, grabbed his coat and, after checking that the dagger was in the pocket, rushed down to report to the mancers.

He wondered what he and Lucky would be doing. There hadn't been time to ask. But what could anyone do when the Shole advanced like that? The sudden surge had carried it forward about thirty yards, over the canal and towards the castle.

When Crafty entered the Waiting Room, Lucky was already there. Somehow he always got there first, however much Crafty hurried.

'So what's going to happen?' he asked, but before Lucky could reply, the door opened. The Chief Mancer, accompanied by the large and portly Mr Humperton – who Crafty had still not worked with – strode in and approached them. Crafty and Lucky immediately came to their feet.

Crafty peered round the mancers to the far door, but there was no sign of Lick. Where was she? She'd told him that he'd be working with her from now on. Maybe she'd changed her mind? After all, they hadn't parted on the best of terms. He wondered whether the search for his father had once again been abandoned.

'You will no doubt be aware of what has happened,' Ginger Bob began. 'As far as we know at this stage, no occupied houses have been engulfed, but a few people will almost certainly have been taken. The loss of that southern section of the canal will have struck fear into the hearts of the inhabitants.'

He sighed. 'There is no way of predicting when the next advance might take place – it might even swallow the castle itself – but it is your duty to remain calm and carry out your orders. You, Benson, will assist Mr Humperton. Proudfoot, come with me.'

Crafty followed Humperton down the steps to his office. The mancer gestured to a chair and Crafty sat down facing him across the desk. It was clear of papers and books, but in front of Crafty was a black leather case, opened to reveal a green felt lining and a number of small metal rods set in recesses within it.

'We call these "locators",' Humperton said, pointing at the rods. When he spoke, he wheezed a little, and beads of sweat stood out on his forehead. Crafty realized that climbing the stairs to the Waiting Room must be hard work for him.

'Each locator is numbered and is one half of its original length,' Humperton continued. 'The other halves were buried in the ground by the canal in the event that it was engulfed. New sections of the Shole are very unstable and therefore difficult to visit using the gate –'

'Why are they unstable, sir?'

Curiosity had made Crafty blurt out the question, and he thought the gate mancer might be annoyed by his interruption. But instead Humperton paused and answered him patiently.

'This is what our records of previous sudden engulfments show, but we haven't yet determined the reason for such instabilities. Of course, there are theories, but it is vital to go into these areas as soon as possible to learn what we can. As I was about to say, these rods make things easier. We are particularly interested in the changes that take place in the first hours and days following an engulfment. Later, if the opportunity presents itself, we may attempt a snatch. However, we will begin with fieldwork, so put on your coat, Benson – it's likely to be chilly.'

Crafty did so, then seated himself in the chair facing the silver gate. Humperton handed him the first of the small rods, and Crafty began to concentrate. Immediately the clouds cleared and he could see that the rod had worked. He was close to the canal, with the towpath on his right and the grey water on his left.

'I suggest that you go out and take a look around,' Humperton said. 'See if anything is alive out there. Don't worry – it's too soon for anything to have become dangerous. The process will only just be starting. But don't go too far from the gate all the same.'

Crafty had no intention of doing so. Despite Humperton's attempt to reassure him, he was taking no chances.

He clambered out and stood on the towpath, sweeping the area with his eyes, alert for any sign of danger. It was very gloomy and night was fast approaching. It was not a good time to enter the Shole – even if it was a new section and he was close to the edge.

The surface of the canal was perfectly calm. Once, Crafty thought, seventy years earlier, this stretch of water would have been busy with barges making the journey from Preston through Lancaster and on to Kendal. They'd carried coal, wood, ore, furniture, salt and food – anything people wanted and were prepared to pay for. But the Shole had put an end to all that.

To the south Crafty could see trees, with a few isolated buildings in the far distance. He knew that the largest one had once been a warehouse. In the middle distance was a single narrow barge covered with an old tarpaulin. No doubt it had been abandoned.

Suddenly he heard a little cry behind him. He turned and saw a small black-and-white kitten walking towards him across the grass at the edge of the towpath. It rubbed against his leg and made another pleading meow, so he picked it up.

Immediately Crafty realized that this wasn't a wise thing to do. Perhaps the kitten had been changed by the Shole and fancied some of his blood? But, as Humperton had said, it was probably too early after the engulfment for that – and besides, it looked harmless enough. He stroked the kitten gently and it began to purr.

All at once he noticed a movement out of the corner of his eye. Humperton was waving at him from the gate, trying to get his attention. Although a grub could talk to the mancer on the other side from nearby, sound didn't carry very far out into the Shole. Crafty went back, still carrying the kitten, to hear what he had to say.

'That was a foolish thing to do, Benson!' Humperton shouted at him when he reached the blue circle of the gate. '*Never* pick up or touch any living creature in the field unless instructed to do so. You should know that by now!'

'Sorry, sir, but it looked harmless enough –'

'Appearances can be deceptive. But seeing as you already have it, we might as well take it – after all, the Shole hasn't killed it, so the animal is probably undergoing the first phases of change. Here – put it in this,' he instructed, holding open a small leather bag.

Crafty knew that once the kitten was inside, Humperton would tie the string, sealing it in. It would become a sample – to be studied in the Forensics Room or stored in the Menagerie. Crafty knew that it was something that had to be done – how else could they discover more about the Shole? But he couldn't bear the thought of that friendly little kitten being submitted to all sorts of tests – maybe hurt badly enough to make it cry out in the night. He just couldn't do it.

So, as Crafty held it out towards the bag, he pretended to lose his grip, allowing the kitten to slip through his fingers. It dropped on to the towpath, landing safely on all four feet, as cats usually did when they fell.

Crafty realized that he really wasn't suited to this job. He found it very hard to take orders, as gate grubs had to, and he was just too soft-hearted.

'Clumsy boy!' Humperton snapped. 'Pick it up at once!'

To Crafty's dismay, instead of running away, the kitten began to rub itself against his ankles again. However, he was very close to the gate and realized that from where Humperton was standing he wouldn't be able to see his feet, or the cat.

Then Crafty did something that seemed cruel, but he thought it was probably the lesser of two evils. He didn't want that kitten to be caught. So he deliberately trod on its tail.

It squealed and ran off like the Devil himself was after it.

He turned to Humperton and grimaced. 'Sorry, sir,' he said meekly.

The mancer shook his head in exasperation, then put down the leather bag and held out something else towards him. It was a green bottle with a cork in the end.

'Get me a sample of the canal water,' he ordered. 'There might be all sorts of small life forms undergoing change in there.'

Crafty walked about five paces from the gate, knelt at the edge of the canal and eased the cork out. He submerged the bottle, tilting it up. The air surged out in an explosion of bubbles and then it began to fill with murky water. Once it was full, he replaced the cork.

What happened next almost made him drop the bottle – for suddenly he saw something lithe and sinuous moving below the surface of the water; something very big, like a gigantic blue eel. A huge eye stared up at him.

Crafty lurched to his feet in panic, but in an instant the creature was gone.

When he handed back the bottle, Humperton beckoned him back through the gate. Crafty sat down on the chair and told him what he'd seen lurking in the canal.

'Something that big isn't really of interest to us right now,' Humperton remarked. 'Its size probably indicates that it isn't newly changed. It's probably an eel that swam up the canal from Preston. Don't worry about it.'

Don't worry about it?! What a stupid thing to say, Crafty thought. Humperton was beginning to annoy him. He was very casual about it all, but Crafty had been the one in danger. It might have looked like an eel, but it was as big as a shark and no doubt had teeth to match. It could have leaped out of the water and snatched him from the bank in the blink of an eye. Crafty could have been ripped into pieces by now, digesting in its belly.

It was yet another reminder that gate grubs were expendable.

Humperton gave him another of the metal rods to hold, and then Crafty moved the gate to the next location. It wasn't very far away – about fifty yards west, beyond the barge he'd seen previously.

'Take another little walk,' the mancer told Crafty. 'See what you can find. Don't go too far and keep your eyes peeled for danger.'

As if he needed reminding!

It was really gloomy now; within half an hour it would be dark, but there was still enough light to see danger approaching. This time Crafty kept a careful eye on the canal, thinking that it was probably the most dangerous place. Something could lurk in the depths, waiting for him to get near enough to grab; something that would be invisible until it was too late.

As he was thinking this, he spotted a body lying close to the barge. Crafty approached it cautiously, then halted about five paces away.

The dead person looked like an adult and was wearing trousers and a shirt; it must have been a man. As far as Crafty knew, only girl gate grubs wore trousers, and even *they* would never go out into the city dressed like that.

In that moment Crafty learned something new about the Shole. It seemed that people killed by it died instantly and rotted quickly. It was only an hour or so since the surge had engulfed this area, but already the flesh had gone from this body, leaving only the skeleton, with some connective cartilage. The remains were slimy and the clothes were wet. It didn't smell pleasant. Crafty gave it a wide berth.

He turned to look at the gate, and saw that Humperton was beckoning to him again. Crafty went back to see what he wanted.

'What were you staring at? What did you find?' he demanded.

Crafty glanced at the barge. The gloom was deepening and he realized that the skeleton couldn't be seen from here. He quickly told him about the remains of the man.

'Good,' Humperton said, handing him a small sample box. 'Get me a piece of bone to analyse. The body of someone freshly dead should tell us a lot. Here – use these . . . Just snip off a fingertip. Cut through the gristle that connects it to the next bone.'

He gave Crafty a small pair of pliers with sharp blades, and a wooden box. Crafty reluctantly accepted them and walked back to get the sample.

He knelt beside the body, feeling slightly sick. Just an hour ago this had been a person, walking around, going about his business, and now he was reduced to this. He didn't want to touch the wet and slimy remains, but luckily for him one dead hand was lying flat on the ground, palm down. He positioned the blades of the tool on either side of the first knuckle of the little finger, and quickly snipped through the gristle to cut it off. He couldn't suppress a small shudder. This was nasty work, whatever way you looked at it.

He opened the box and slid it along the ground to scoop up the sample of bone, then snapped the lid closed and pushed it into the pocket of his greatcoat before striding back towards the gate as fast as he could. He was only too glad to leave that skeleton behind.

All at once something halted him in his tracks. The little black-and-white kitten was standing on the towpath directly ahead of him. Treading on its tail clearly hadn't been enough to drive it away. It meowed at Crafty plaintively. No doubt it was hungry.

'Go away, you stupid little cat!' he hissed, keeping his voice low so that Humperton wouldn't hear. Crafty could see him staring at him through the gate, though thanks to the gloom he wouldn't be able to see the kitten. If he did, he'd want Crafty to pick it up again – that was for sure. He was just about to chase it away again when –

Maybe it was instinct or some sense Crafty didn't know he had. Whatever it was, he immediately felt that something was wrong, that danger was nearby.

He stepped closer to the kitten, feeling tense and nervous, already gripping the dagger in his pocket.

The hairs on the kitten's back suddenly stood bolt upright and it turned to look at the canal. That was all the warning Crafty needed.

Something big and blue and scaly burst out of the water, murderous jaws open wide.

24

DEAD BEFORE MORNING

The water beast's three rows of sharp teeth were just inches from the kitten's head.

But Crafty was there first. He struck in a rapid arc from right to left, slicing open the creature's forehead just above the eyes. Black blood sprayed up into the air. The aberration gave a scream and fell back into the water with a huge splash.

In an instant it had vanished from sight, but its image was burned into Crafty's memory. At first he'd thought it was like an eel, but now he'd seen that it was covered in blue scales, and had two thin arms projecting from the place where – had it been human – the shoulders would have been. The arms had ended in three long fingers with murderous talons.

But it was the eyes that were the most disturbing thing about it. They had been human. That creature had once been a person.

Nervously eyeing the surface of the canal, Crafty wiped the blade of the dagger on the grass at the edge of the towpath and returned the weapon to his coat. The frightened kitten had dashed away, but now, as he headed towards the gate, it began to follow him again.

'Go away!' he hissed, but it continued to follow closely at his heels. Being nasty to it didn't work.

Crafty reached the gate and handed the sample box through to Humperton, who was impressed.

'That was astonishing, Benson! I have never seen such fast reactions. I think it was a good idea to permit you to bear arms.'

Crafty didn't reply. The kitten was rubbing itself against his leg and meowing. He cringed, knowing that Humperton would hear it.

He did. 'Ah good, the little cat has returned.' He opened the leather bag again, holding it out. 'Put it in here,' he told Crafty.

Although he knew that it would get him into trouble, Crafty still couldn't bear to do it. 'I'm sorry, sir, but I can't,' he told him, shaking his head.

There was an ominous pause. 'What did you just say?' Humperton demanded, raising his voice a little.

'This kitten doesn't deserve to be tested and kept in the Menagerie. It probably saved my life back there! It gave me warning of the attack, sir,' Crafty pleaded.

He knew that this wasn't quite true: the blue-scaled water beast seemed to have been going for the kitten rather than him, but he didn't care. There was no way it was going into that bag.

'A gate grub may neither question nor disobey the legitimate order of a gate mancer!' blustered Humperton. 'Maybe your judgement has been affected by the danger you have just faced. I will give you one more chance, Benson. Collect that sample!'

'No!' Crafty shouted, not bothering to add the 'sir'.

Humperton gave an angry bellow, then demanded that Crafty come back through the gate. Reluctantly he clambered through, afraid of what he was about to face, though relieved that the kitten was finally safe.

The mancer stared down at him, his face flushed and slick with sweat, his breathing rapid.

'I will report you to the Chief Mancer first thing tomorrow morning. You clearly don't belong with us, Benson. This is just the latest in a string of acts of insubordination. Oh, yes,' he said, seeing the look on Crafty's face, 'the Chief Mancer told me all about your lack of regard for professional etiquette. And don't think that because you were pardoned by the Duke and have his ear, it will make any difference. The Duke understands the need for discipline. All employees of the castle must be subject to it – our very survival *depends* on it. Go to your room at once.'

Crafty slumped on his bed, feeling very depressed. The server brought his supper, but he couldn't eat it. The next day Humperton would make his report to Ginger Bob, and Crafty would be dismissed and returned to the Shole.

Without his father's help, he would have no protection against the aberrations.

He wouldn't last long. He'd be killed within hours.

But Humperton never got the chance to make his report. He was dead before morning.

'It is a terrible loss,' the Chief Mancer said. Crafty and Lucky were sitting in his office to receive the bad news. He was evasive, and wouldn't say exactly how he had died; just that 'the security of the gate had been breached' – whatever that meant. Crafty wondered if something had managed to get through the gate to attack him – that was a worrying thought.

He also had mixed feelings about Humperton's death. On the one hand he was saddened by it – he had seemed pretty decent, certainly better than Viper. But on the other hand Crafty felt glad that he wouldn't be able to report him. And then felt guilty about feeling glad.

'Mr Humperton was a first-class gate mancer, with an excellent operational record, and he will be badly missed,' Ginger Bob continued. 'All gate activities are suspended for the day while a full investigation is carried out.'

They were dismissed, so Crafty and Lucky decided to go for a stroll to pass the time. It wasn't much fun: it was typical Lancashire end-of-summer weather – depressing grey clouds, a blustery wind and rain. Not only that, thanks to the sausage rolls bought the day before, they'd already spent their meagre wages for the week – and it was only Monday!

Soon they were walking back up the hill towards the castle.

'Ginger Bob never actually told us how Humperton died,' Crafty pointed out to Lucky. 'Do you think a breach of gate security means that something came through the gate and killed him?'

'Something like that,' Lucky agreed. 'He must have been working without a grub, checking fixed locations. He was a big bloke – carrying all that weight no doubt made him feel tired, so perhaps he sat in the grub's chair. You can't work the guillotine if you're sitting there. He must have been taken by surprise. Maybe his fat bum got *stuck* in the chair,' he added with a grin.

Crafty didn't smile back. Humperton might have been overweight, but he was dead. It didn't seem right to joke about it.

'We could find out, you know,' Lucky continued. 'I know an older lad who works in the Forensics Room. Although they work on aberrations, they also investigate any human deaths and maimings – they'll probably have looked into Humperton's death by now.'

'I thought different departments weren't supposed to talk to each other except through official channels? You said Ginger Bob doesn't like us fraternizing!'

'Guilds have strict guidelines about keeping secrets, and Ginger Bob is obsessed about fraternizing. He's a stickler for the rules. But as long as we don't get caught, it doesn't matter, does it? Don't tell me you don't want to know what happened!'

Crafty did, though he suspected that the truth wouldn't be nice. 'Count me in,' he said.

They couldn't approach the lad from Forensics until his shift was over. It was well after dark by the time the boys walked down into the town again. The lad's name was Doon, and he liked a drink, so Lucky led Crafty to Doon's favourite watering hole – The Pendle Witch.

Crafty and Lucky were too young to be allowed in, but they could see Doon through the window, swigging ale and laughing and joking with a group of men playing dominoes. After a lot of waving Lucky managed to catch his eye, and he came out to talk to them, still clutching his tankard.

Doon was a big ginger-haired lad with an accent from somewhere a long way north of Lancashire. Crafty thought he was probably Scottish.

'And what might you two wee scallywags be wanting?' he asked, before taking another big gulp of ale. 'Oh, let me guess! Ye want the dirt on the demise of poor Fatty Humperton! You and half the castle, lads.'

'Go on, tell us what happened to him, Doon!' Lucky begged. 'Did something come through the gate and kill him before his fat arse could wriggle free of the chair?'

Crafty had expected Doon to laugh at this, but he suddenly looked very serious and shook his head.

'No, and that's why everybody's so worried. No mancer would leave a gate open while he wasn't working there. He was sitting at his desk when he was killed. It was splatted across all four walls of his office.'

'The desk or his blood?' Lucky asked with an evil grin. Crafty looked at him, surprised – where had this bloodthirsty streak come from? He was suddenly reminded of Lucky's surprising venom when they'd gone to see Old Nell being hanged.

'Well, it was no' exactly angels' milk!' replied Doon. He must have been slightly tipsy – he seemed only too happy to talk to them. 'It seems that something came through the gate and butchered him where he sat. There was blood and pieces of him everywhere. Not much flesh though – no doubt that ended up in the aberration's stomach. I don't envy you your job. None of you will be safe now.'

And with that, he staggered back into the pub. The conversation clearly over, the boys made their way back to the castle. Crafty was confused about what Doon had meant by none of them being safe now, but Lucky explained.

'As you know, when a gate isn't being used, it's full of dark swirling cloud and you can see nothing of the Shole from this side,' he said. 'And when nobody's using it, the gate shouldn't be visible from the Shole side, either. Nothing should be able to see the blue circle of the gate or know its location. Humperton was at his desk, so we can assume that the gate wasn't being used. Which means that some aberration from the Shole was somehow able to find and come through it, kill and eat most of him, and then escape back into the Shole. If it happened to Humperton, it could happen to anyone. It looks as though the gates are no longer safe. I don't think we'll be able to use them again. They might even have to be destroyed so as to prevent aberrations from coming directly into the castle and butchering everyone inside!'

Crafty was stunned. If Lucky was right, what did it mean for them?

He'd avoided being reported and sacked. But now he was redundant – without the gates, there'd be no need for gate grubs.

Perhaps he'd be going back to the Shole after all.

That night Crafty found it difficult to sleep; as he tossed and turned, he tried to recall happier times. He remembered that when he was young, he'd wanted to follow in his father's footsteps. His father had always been kind to him, and full of good advice.

'Your mother tells me you have a few worries, Crafty,' he'd said one evening, taking him to the edge of the garden, out of earshot of his two older brothers. Brock and Ben were sitting on the bench against the wall, talking to their mother. Crafty was about eight at the time and his head was full of worries about his future.

'What did she say?' Crafty asked in alarm. He hadn't wanted his father to know in case he laughed at him.

'That's for *you* to tell *me*, son.'

'Promise you won't laugh, Father . . .'

His father patted him on the back and smiled. 'I can't promise that, Crafty. If what you say is funny, I won't be able to stop myself laughing, will I?'

Crafty's face fell but his father grinned and knelt down so that they were eye to eye. 'I'm only having a little joke, Crafty. I already know what your problem is, because your mother told me. We don't keep secrets from each other, so whatever you tell to one, the other will know soon afterwards. When you grow up, you want to be a castle courier like me? Isn't that so?'

Crafty nodded.

'Well, there's nothing wrong with that. It's a dangerous job, but a vital one. But you're worried about something else too – that you won't have the special abilities you need.'

Crafty nodded again, still embarrassed. 'Brock and Ben told me that because Mother isn't Fey, we might not develop *any* gifts when we're older.'

His father looked thoughtful. 'There have been a few marriages between the Fey and non-Fey, and in most cases the children went on to have useful abilities. No, it's nothing to do with your mother. It's just how it is. Nobody can predict what will happen. The best thing you can do is stop thinking too much about the future. Things will take care of themselves.'

'But what if I *don't* have any abilities?'

His father had smiled. 'You will, son, so don't worry about that. And remember this: whatever happens, your mother and I will always take care of you.'

Crafty remembered how reassured he had been by those kind words – as if a heavy weight had been lifted off his shoulders. But now things had changed – he no longer had a father and a mother to look after him.

As for his gifts – he wasn't sure. He must have *some* ability or he wouldn't have been able to find things using the gate. Then there was the whispering of his dead brothers – was that a gift, to be able to hear the dead talking? One day he would ask somebody about it. Hopefully that somebody would be his father.

A VALUABLE RESOURCE

The following morning Crafty and Lucky both reported to the Waiting Room. They weren't supposed to know the truth behind Humperton's death, so they'd have to pretend it was business as usual.

Crafty barely had time to nod good morning to Lucky and sit down before the Chief Mancer came into the room.

'Come with me, Benson! Bring your coat,' he snapped.

It seemed that they weren't redundant after all. Crafty was relieved, but also a little disappointed that Ginger Bob had demanded *his* services. He'd hoped that he would choose Lucky, and that Lick would come for him. Their special partnership hadn't lasted long. So much for working directly for the Duke and helping Crafty to look for his father.

He followed the mancer down to his room, where he was ordered to sit down and face the silver gate. 'Put your coat on. You're going into the field,' he was told.

After Crafty had done so, the Chief Mancer immediately used his foot to flick off the guillotine's safety catch.

Crafty glanced up in dismay at the long sharp blade, and his bad mood was overtaken by nerves. They hadn't used the guillotine when he was out in the Shole with Humperton. Noticing his alarm, the Chief Mancer spoke.

'Calm yourself, Benson. As long as you act with alacrity and obey my every command, all will be well. As you know, there has been a serious breach of gate security. I'm going to take you into my confidence, and hope that in return you will reward me by staying calm. An aberration came through a gate from the Shole and killed poor Mr Humperton – and this was when he was at his desk rather than operating the gate. This is a new kind of security breach. A very disturbing one.'

'Yes, sir,' Crafty said, pretending that he was receiving this information for the first time.

'However, there are two of us and we are working as a team. My guillotine skills are excellent, Benson, so you needn't be afraid. We are going out into the Shole for a very simple, routine exercise – but of course we will be testing to see if it's still possible to use the gate.'

The mancer went back to his desk and opened a leather case, taking out a rod. 'Here – take us to this location,' he said, handing it to Crafty.

Crafty gripped the metal rod and stared into the dark whirling clouds within the frame, concentrating on what he was holding. Instantly the view cleared, and there was the canal bank again. Once again, the towpath was on his right, the grey water on his left, but there was no sign of the barge or the body, so this was a different section of canal. The big abandoned warehouse was much nearer now.

The Chief Mancer handed over a small bottle. 'Let us start with a sample of the canal water,' he said. 'Let's see how microbial life is continuing to change.'

Crafty didn't like the idea of going near the canal again.

'There was a dangerous aberration in the water the last time I came here,' he told the Chief Mancer. 'It leaped up towards me. I cut it with my knife and it fell back. I think the canal is dangerous, sir.'

'I'm sure you're right, Benson. Indeed, the whole of the Shole is dangerous. Be vigilant and no harm will come to you. Now get me that sample!'

Crafty had no choice but to obey, so he handed him the metal rod, took the bottle and clambered through the gate. Staying close by and watching the canal carefully, he knelt on the bank and quickly filled the bottle. He was nervous – but surely, he thought, he'd see the approach of any danger along the canal and be able to make his escape; anything lurking in the dark water was a different matter. After his previous visit, that was what really scared him.

Moments later he was handing the Chief Mancer the corked bottle of canal water. Crafty could see things floating in it – maybe tiny fish, tadpoles or insects – they were far too small for him to be sure. Maybe some were alive. If so, it was exactly what Ginger Bob was looking for – early changes brought about by the Shole.

'Excellent, Benson. That was easy enough, wasn't it? Now for a sample of the fauna on the canal bank,' the mancer said, handing him a small wooden box. 'Try and find me something small – an insect will do . . .'

Crafty had to scour the bank on hands and knees, one eye constantly on the water, to find what he wanted. At last he spotted what looked like a small hairy spider – though on closer inspection he was no longer sure. For one thing, it had too many legs – he counted thirteen – and a strange round head that looked almost human in shape. This was surely something that had started to change. *Imagine if it grew larger,* he thought nervously. *What if it became the size of a dog?*

He slid the sample box along the ground, scooped up the tiny thing and put on the lid to trap it. Thinking of dogs, Crafty wondered what had become of Sandy: was she still alive, and would he ever see her again? He hoped the kitten wouldn't turn up. It had probably begun to change by now, but he knew he still wouldn't be able to take it as a specimen, and refusing to obey an order from the Chief Mancer would certainly spell the end of his time as a gate grub.

When Crafty handed over the box, Ginger Bob gestured for him to come back through the gate.

'That's enough for today, Benson. We have just proved that, in spite of Mr Humperton's death, we can still operate safely in the Shole. We mancers had a crisis meeting late yesterday, and the majority opinion was that the killer would be waiting to intercept and slay anyone who used a gate. I did not concur. I thought it likely that some aberration had simply stumbled upon the gate by chance. Nothing was waiting for us today – and so we have just proved the others wrong. I believe that attack is unlikely to be repeated. You may congratulate yourself! I think it is worth celebrating with ginger biscuits!' he exclaimed.

All at once he paused and frowned. 'Unfortunately, because of the crisis, we don't have time for that. Please return to the Waiting Room.'

Crafty was angry, but not because he'd missed out on a biscuit; he realized that, in order to prove his point, the mancer had just taken a massive gamble with Crafty's life. But he also understood that it wouldn't do any good to complain. As long as field trips continued, he'd have a job – and the chance to look for his father. Then he thought of something else.

'Could I ask you a couple of quick questions, sir?' he asked.

'Yes, but do make it *double*-quick, Benson,' the mancer said, sitting behind his desk.

'Sir, are you and Miss Crompton-Smythe now the only mancers who are able to operate the gates?'

Ginger Bob looked up. 'Of course not, Benson. We have several gate mancers at the castle, but most simply function in support capacities. I will summon one of them to replace Mr Humperton. As you know, Miss Crompton-Smythe now reports directly to the Duke but, given the circumstances, she has also agreed to cover some of our more routine work. It is in fact gate grubs that we are finding hard to replace at the moment. You are a valuable resource, Benson!'

The mancer dismissed him and Crafty left the office. *A valuable resource!* Is that what he was? Well, it certainly hadn't seemed like that until now.

He returned to the Waiting Room to find it empty. Until the replacement arrived, the only other mancer on duty was Lick: she must have taken Lucky.

Perhaps he's more 'valuable' than I am, Crafty thought crossly. Then he remembered that he'd already been selected by Ginger Bob, so she'd had no choice – which cheered him up a little.

He had plenty of time to mull over what had happened and what had been said. Although gate grubs had always been treated as the lowest of the low, the Chief Mancer's words had just contradicted that. The reckless waste of gate-grub lives, to which Viper had made a significant contribution, had resulted in a crisis. Gate grubs were in short supply – could that be used to better their circumstances? Crafty wondered. Surely people like the Chief Mancer must start to appreciate them more now?

But Crafty was a bit uneasy about the mancer's judgement. Crafty himself was now supposedly a valuable resource, but his life had just been put at serious risk. *Sometimes really bright people don't have much common sense*, he thought. *Their heads are too far up in the clouds to see what's staring right at them at ground level.*

Once it had killed and eaten most of Humperton, the aberration appeared to have gone back through the gate rather than continuing its grisly work in the rest of the castle. This suggested to Crafty that it had been able to exercise some control over the gate – and had been clever enough to remain safe. If that was the case, it could return and attack again.

Didn't the Chief Mancer see that danger? Surely they should put guards in every office, ready for such an eventuality? But Crafty knew he'd just be shouted down if he tried to warn his superior.

He just had to hope that he was wrong.

About an hour later Lucky came through the far door. He was smiling.

'You were right about Lick, Crafty! She's not the same girl she seemed earlier. And you're wrong about her thinking herself better than other people. She treats me well – she's really polite and doesn't talk down to me; she makes me feel like I'm a valued partner who's really contributing something.'

Crafty compared this to his recent experience with Ginger Bob, where he'd simply been used to test a theory.

'Where did you go?' he asked, trying not to feel a stab of jealousy.

'Oh, it was just more routine sampling along the canal bank. We got lots of stuff – some insects, a fish and a stray kitten. Lick was really pleased.'

Crafty opened his mouth to speak but no words came out. He had no doubt that it was the kitten he'd saved from Humperton. The trouble he'd got into had all been for nothing – though he couldn't blame Lick or Lucky. Getting samples was part of the job and they might be helpful in their fight against the Shole. But he still felt sad about the kitten.

Just after lunch the far door opened and Lick beckoned him over.

'We need to talk, Crafty.' There wasn't even a flicker of a smile on her face.

He wondered if he'd done something wrong, or whether she was still just annoyed with him.

Crafty followed her down to her office, took a seat and faced her across the desk. She wasted no time in coming to the point.

'I really do want us to work together, Crafty. We make a good team. But you must listen to what I tell you. I promise we will go looking for your father, but only when we've got a reasonable chance of success. We need to stay safe. I'm developing something that I hope might give us a fighting chance.'

Crafty understood what she was saying, but every day they delayed made it less and less likely he'd find his father alive. 'How long do you think it'll be before it's ready?'

Lick sighed. 'By the end of the month maybe, if things continue to go well. These things take time.'

'A month is too long!' Crafty could feel himself getting angry again, and soon realized that she was too.

'Look, we're going round in circles here!' she said, raising her voice slightly. 'I don't want to quarrel with you, but it seems we just can't see eye to eye at the moment. I suggest that, until we are ready to look for your father, you work with Mr Wainwright, and I work with Lucky.'

'That suits me,' Crafty replied through gritted teeth. 'But you might have a problem talking to Bertha if I'm not there.'

Lick frowned. 'Then we'll make an exception for visits to Bertha; for everything else I'll work with Lucky.'

So that was that, and Crafty returned to the Waiting Room feeling furious, as well as hurt. After all, he'd saved her life. Couldn't she help him now in return? His father had already been missing for a month. Couldn't she see that with every day they delayed, his life was at greater and greater risk?

Crafty had to try to save his father *now*.

And already a desperate plan was starting to form inside his head.

26

DOWN TO THE CELLAR

Two days passed before Crafty was able to put his plan into action.

He had considered getting Lucky involved, but finally decided to act alone. It would be very dangerous and it wasn't fair to put him at risk too. Crafty didn't even tell him what he intended to do, knowing that Lucky would insist on helping.

Those two days were spent collecting samples by the canal. He worked with Ginger Bob, and Lucky worked with Lick.

Crafty hadn't seen Lucky looking so cheerful since Donna's death, and he struggled to control his jealousy. His friend seemed totally at ease with Lick. Crafty hadn't spoken to girls very often – he'd had no sisters and had attended a boys' school. There was only Bertha, who was certainly no ordinary girl, and Donna, whom he hadn't known long.

Even their names seemed to belong together – Lick and Lucky! Crafty fought to control his feelings, but it was far from easy.

Then, on the third day, Lick entered the Waiting Room and called *his* name.

He buttoned up his coat, checked that the dagger was in his right-hand pocket and followed her down the stairs, his stomach full of butterflies. This was it. The chance he'd been waiting for.

Lick wasted no time in pleasantries. 'I've put together some questions to ask Bertha. Do you think you can find her now that we no longer have her finger?' she asked. 'And, by the way, giving that finger back to Bertha didn't go down well with staff in the Relic Room,' she told Crafty, shaking her head. 'I had to fill in half a dozen forms to explain it.'

He nodded; even though tapping into his emotional connection hadn't worked with his father, he'd found Sandy, and now he was confident that he could find Bertha.

He sat in the chair, stared at the silver gate and concentrated. Almost immediately the clouds cleared; the bog was directly ahead of them, steaming and bubbling.

There was no immediate sign of Bertha, but they knew that this wasn't unusual.

'I'll go first and see if she's around,' Crafty told Lick.

She nodded and he stepped through the gate.

It was noon, the safest time in the Shole. The visibility was good, it was relatively mild, and there was no sign of danger. Crafty imagined what a cold, terrible place this must be in winter, with just a few hours of light. At least in the cellar he'd never had to endure that.

In the distance Crafty could see the three houses, his old home in the middle. He wondered if he should call out to Bertha, but the very next moment there was a disturbance in the mud and her crowned head rose up. Seconds later she was standing facing him.

'Hello again, Bertha. The gate mancer you met before wants to ask you some more questions,' he said. 'Are you happy for her to do that?'

'She may ask and I will answer, if possible.'

'You mean you might not know the answers?'

'That in part. But there may be questions I do not *wish* to answer.'

Crafty wondered at that. Bertha had already admitted that she fed on anything that bled and was prepared to kill it with her own hands, which he assumed meant she ate it raw; and that she might be prepared to kill and eat a human being. What could be worse than that? What sort of information might she feel it necessary to withhold?

Putting this thought out of his mind, he waved towards the gate, and Lick came through and walked towards them. Giving her a reassuring smile, which she returned, Crafty went and took up his position halfway between Lick and the gate, ready to intervene and warn her if anything nasty tried to go through it.

After a nod towards Bertha, Lick asked her first question. Crafty was still within earshot and heard it clearly.

'Is there a beast or some kind of entity that rules the Shole?' Then, barely pausing for breath, she quickly asked two more questions. 'Has something created it, or is the Shole itself perhaps aware and sentient – is it some kind of bestial living being?'

They were three good questions, and Crafty would have been interested in hearing Bertha's replies – but he was already too far away to catch them: he was striding quickly round the edge of the bog, heading towards the three houses.

He saw Bertha glance at him, but Lick still didn't realize that he'd left his position in front of the gate. It was time to tell her.

'Hey, Lick!'

She turned towards him, the astonishment on her face quickly changing to an expression of alarm.

'The gate's unguarded! Get back inside!' Crafty shouted.

Then he started to run. He knew that there was only a slim chance that she would chase after him. After Humperton's death she wouldn't leave the gate unguarded in case something dangerous got into the castle.

Crafty sprinted as fast as he could. Lick might not follow him on foot, but she could follow him with the gate to intercept him . . . if the beasts from the Shole didn't beat her to it. It was not long after noon and most of them should be sleeping, he reckoned. But his target was the very place where some might now be doing just that – even though it had been one of the safest refuges in the Shole.

But it was no longer safe now. He was heading for the cellar.

Crafty was approaching the houses from the rear when he noticed that the hawthorn hedges along the back gardens had gone, swallowed up by the advancing bog; it now extended almost to the three back doors.

As he ran along the edge, kicking up mud, the blue circle of the gate suddenly flickered into life ten yards to his right. Crafty glanced at it and saw Lick's anxious face.

Sound didn't carry well into the Shole, but she was shouting at the top of her voice.

'No! No! Don't be a fool!' she yelled. 'Come back!'

He ignored her and kept running, and saw the gate flickering out; seconds later it reappeared to his left, much closer, almost within touching distance.

'Please, Crafty, don't do it. You'll get yourself killed!' Lick cried.

'Wait for me! I'll be back in a few minutes!' Crafty shouted back. At least, he hoped he would.

So far, his plan was working. Lucky had once told him that gates couldn't go into buildings because there was too much of a risk of colliding with something. Lick would have to wait for him outside.

He arrived panting at the back door of what had once been his home. He gripped the handle of the door, took a deep breath and eased it open. Stepping inside, he closed it carefully behind him, trying to make as little noise as possible. He kept perfectly still with his back against it, holding his breath while his eyes flicked across the gloomy kitchen, searching for danger. He listened too. The house was absolutely silent.

So far, so good. He started to breathe again, and then crept over to the sink and reached up to open a cupboard – the one high on the wall to the right of the draining board. It was full of useful items: balls of string, nails, a hammer and a pair of pliers. He felt around, and for a moment his heart sank. He couldn't find what he was looking for.

They'd always kept them here. Where could they be? There should have been a dozen at least. Had somebody taken them? he wondered. Maybe, before his father went missing, he'd been back to visit Crafty's brothers' graves and used them?

Crafty felt a moment of despair. What a fool he'd been. He should have brought one with him. Then his hand closed on what he was looking for: a candle.

He positioned it on the draining board and then reached into the left-hand pocket of his coat for the small box of lucifers he used to light the candle in his room at the castle. They'd kept boxes of matches in the cupboard, but by now they'd be damp and useless.

He struck a match and it flared with light. Crafty managed to light the candle at the second attempt, even though his hand was shaking with nerves. He returned the box to his pocket and then added a small hammer he'd found in the cupboard. It could be useful as an additional weapon.

Now he just had to go down into the cellar.

Crafty opened the door and began to descend the short flight of wooden stairs, aware that he would be heard below. There was no way to avoid it: however slowly and carefully he moved, there would be creaks. If there *was* anything down there, it would know that he was on his way.

Crafty was carrying the candle in his left hand, keeping his right free to grab the dagger if it proved necessary. He reached the second door, which led directly into the cellar, holding the candle out before him and peering down. The flame sent grotesque shadows flickering up and down the walls.

This had been his home for almost a year, though now it was clearly no longer his. Crafty could see nothing that might immediately threaten him, but he knew that something was here. Or had been here. The silver staircase told him that.

It had been built by his father as a defence against the Shole, constructed from silver alloy so that no aberration could use it. But now the staircase had been wrapped in something so that none of the metal was visible. He thought at first that it had been covered in a dense layer of branches and twigs.

No – it hadn't been covered. Something had grown over it. It was some kind of vine that had sprouted out of the earthen floor just at the foot of the staircase.

Had some kind of malign magic been used? Crafty wondered. This was clearly no ordinary vine. It had only been a few weeks since he was last here, but it had grown quickly and densely to shield every inch of the staircase, thus rendering the silver useless as a defence. Yet the steps were still clearly defined and it would be easy to walk down them. Something had wanted to use this staircase.

Crafty didn't move for a long time. He kept perfectly still and listened. Could he hear something breathing? No, it was probably just his imagination.

He slowly began to descend the steps – until at last he was standing on the cellar floor. Now he had to find what he'd come for and get out as quickly as possible.

A different kind of dread began to prickle at the back of his neck. Crafty had been relying on the fact that Lick would wait for him.

But what if she didn't?

27

WHAT COULD BE MORE TERRIBLE?

At first glance the rest of the cellar looked exactly as he'd left it.

The three tall metal candlesticks stood where they always had, the candles long since extinguished. There were the two beds, the leather couch, his father's black leather armchair with his stick still resting against it, the triangular table with one chair, the bookcase and, of course, the tall cupboard leaning against the wall. It would have almost seemed cosily familiar, if he hadn't been so terrified.

Suddenly Crafty's eyes were drawn to the cupboard again. Before he left the cellar, the doors had been open: he'd kept them like that to save himself checking whether any new food had been delivered. Now they were closed.

A sudden cold breeze came from nowhere, threatening him with darkness. The candle flickered and almost went out, making his heart lurch into a faster rhythm.

Then he heard a faint sound, a whispering. It was coming from his brothers' graves.

Crafty went over and knelt down between the two flat oblong gravestones. He pressed his ear to the ground.

'*Crafty! Crafty! Crafty!*' they whispered in unison – but the rest was too faint to hear.

'Hello, Brock and Ben. Try to speak more loudly. I can't hear. What are you trying to tell me?' he asked, keeping his voice low.

The whispering became louder, and a spike of fear went up his spine as he finally realized what they were saying.

'*There's something hiding in the cupboard . . .*'

Crafty came slowly to his feet and stared at it.

There were two possibilities. The first was that something was hiding in the cupboard because it was afraid of him. The second was that it was hiding in the cupboard because it wanted to leap out and kill him.

The second seemed much more likely. Crafty was trembling, and every bit of common sense was screaming at him to run for the steps.

But he'd come down to the cellar to find something, and he wasn't leaving without it.

Then his brothers started to whisper again. He knelt down once more and put his ear to the earth.

'*Don't open the cupboard door! Get out while you can!*' his brothers hissed, and then they began to cry.

Their muffled sobs brought a lump to Crafty's throat. It always wrenched at his heart when they cried. Were they crying because of the danger he was in or because they were afraid? Or maybe because being dead was so terrible and they were overwhelmed by their condition?

'Don't cry,' he whispered towards their graves. 'I won't open the cupboard. I'll be gone in a few moments.'

But first he had to get what he'd come for.

It was under his father's black leather chair. Crafty knelt down again and rummaged around beneath it, trying not to think what might be lurking there. He found what he was looking for, quickly slipping it into his left-hand coat pocket.

He turned, but had only taken two steps when a voice halted him in his tracks.

The voice came from the cupboard.

'Is that you, Crafty? Is that you?'

A whirl of emotions almost brought Crafty to his knees. He didn't know whether to laugh or cry, to be happy or afraid. The voice had changed since he'd last heard it – it was huskier and slightly deeper in tone. But there was no doubt: it was his mother's voice. Or could it be something just pretending to be his mother? he wondered.

But then Crafty had a thought; surely it was possible that she wasn't dead after all! Hope threw caution to the winds.

'Mother? Mother! Is that you? It *is* me. It's your son, Crafty!'

'Oh, I thought it was you, Crafty!' came the reply. *'It's so good to hear your voice again.'*

'But why are you hiding? Please come out and talk to me.'

Crafty reached towards the cupboard door, but at the last second remembered the warning from his brothers. He forced his hand down to his side.

The voice spoke again.

'I've changed, Crafty. I'm still your mother and you're my son and I love you, but I daren't risk coming out to talk to you face to face.' The voice paused, and then sounded even more hoarse. *'I'm . . . I'm not what I was. We can't get too close.'*

The blood froze in Crafty's veins; he began to shiver violently and tears came to his eyes. How had the Shole changed his poor mother? And why was he no longer safe talking to her? Bertha seemed able to talk to him without putting him in danger – what was so wrong with his mother that she couldn't?

But before he could ask, his mother had a question of her own.

'Why did you come back here, Crafty?'

'Father's missing. I came here to get his pipe. It's the only thing I've got left of him and it'll help me to find him.'

The voice became more urgent. *'If you find him, Crafty, don't bring him here. Whatever you do,* don't *ever bring him* here. *This is my refuge and I want to be left alone. He can't see me like this. Do you promise?'*

Tears began to run down his cheeks and he struggled to speak. 'I promise, Mother.'

'You too, Crafty. Don't you ever come back. I've changed so much that even your poor dead brothers don't know me. Even

they are afraid of me. Go now, while you still can. I'll always remember you.'

And with that, Crafty fled from the cellar. Still crying, he raced up the steps, through the door, then up to the kitchen door. There he blew out the candle and stuffed it into his pocket next to the lucifers, the hammer and his father's pipe. He might need it again soon, he thought.

Before leaving the kitchen, he wiped his eyes as best he could and tried to control himself. He had to be strong now. There was no turning back. He had to rescue his father.

Once outside the back door, Crafty was overjoyed to see the blue circle of the gate. Relief flooded through him. Lick hadn't let him down. He could see her staring anxiously through at him from only twenty paces away, on the very edge of the bog. Crafty sprinted towards it and quickly clambered through.

As he turned to face Lick, he saw that her eyes were blazing with anger. She came right up to him.

'You idiot!' she shouted, literally spitting the words in his face. 'If I tell the Chief Mancer what you've done, you'll be dismissed. I've a good mind to do it too. What on earth possessed you? Why did you go back to your house?'

'I had to go down to the cellar,' Crafty told her calmly.

'The cellar? That's probably the most dangerous place now! Something terrible could have taken up residence – it could have been waiting down there!'

What could be more terrible than a mother who had been changed? Crafty thought. *What could be more terrible than a mother who never wanted to see you again?*

But he didn't say that. He just pulled his father's pipe out of his pocket and showed it to Lick.

'I went to get this!' he told her. 'It's my father's pipe. We've finally got something that belonged to him – it'll take me to him, wherever he is. I'm sure of it.'

Then, before she could stop him, Crafty sat down in the chair and stared at the silver gate, concentrating as hard as he could.

This had been his father's favourite pipe, but after the loss of his wife, for some reason he'd never smoked it again. Crafty had happy memories of watching them sitting together in the garden. His father used to put his left arm around Crafty's mother, holding the pipe in his right hand. In summer they sometimes stayed out until after dark. You could hear them murmuring together, and see the glow of the pipe. Sometimes Crafty thought they kissed, but it was too dark to be sure. He knew that they had loved each other very much.

When he was smoking, his father had put the stem of the pipe into his mouth and tamped the tobacco down into the bowl with his thumb. Crafty could practically see him doing it now.

Now that he had the pipe, it *had* to work. It *had* to take the gate to him!

And it did.

The swirling clouds cleared, and Crafty found himself staring at a narrow cobbled street. At the end was a grim-looking stone building. In front of this was a metal gate with a sign:

MOUNT STREET ORPHANAGE

He knew that this was a very dangerous place; it was where the Chief Mancer had brought him to snatch the feral, changed child; it was where Crafty had pushed Viper out through the silver gate.

There's something tying me to this place, he thought.

Beyond the gate he could see the wooden door to the orphanage hanging off its hinges. It was very gloomy and nothing was moving.

Nothing that he could see.

But his father was somewhere inside that building.

GOOD NEWS AND
BAD NEWS

Lick tried to stop him.

Crafty couldn't blame her. As far as she was concerned, it was madness to go into that dark building.

But his father was in there. It had to be done.

Lick was strong. She grabbed hold of his clothes and his limbs – and finally even his hair – as he fought to free himself and scramble through the gate.

And as they grappled, she kept saying the same things over and over again:

'Please! Please! Don't do it or you'll die! Please, Crafty! Please! You'll die!'

But at last he gave her one hard shove, and then he was through and away. He staggered three paces, then turned back and stared at her through the gate, and saw that her eyes were wild.

He'd half hoped that she might wait there until he'd rescued his father. They were in Preston, deep inside the Shole. The walk back to Lancaster was fraught with danger, the chances of survival slim. How else would he get back to the castle?

But the blue circle winked out almost immediately. Crafty waited a few seconds to see if it would reappear elsewhere, as it had done by the bog, but there was no sign of it. Lick had left him to his fate.

He couldn't deny that this abandonment hurt. But he put it out of his mind; after all, he was here with a purpose – he was going to find his father. He turned and walked slowly towards that open door, listening for danger.

Hours still remained before sunset, but already the gloom was deepening. It would be very dark inside that building, with its thin narrow windows. No doubt there would be other creatures inside, similar to the one he'd snatched. Crafty remembered the hungry mouth and that triple row of sharp fangs. He prayed that such aberrations would still be sleeping.

At the entrance he took the candle out of his pocket and lit it. Then, with one hand on his dagger, he stepped inside, broken glass crunching underfoot.

The candle illuminated a large panelled hallway. There were corridors to left and right, a wide staircase leading upwards and, directly ahead, a pair of very big, dark-stained doors.

And there were cobwebs everywhere. Huge cobwebs.

They hung in drapes from the ceiling and covered the walls, undulating like grey waves on a turbulent sea. What was causing them to move like that? The air was chilly but very still. Crafty could see nothing that might cause it.

Then a terrible thought crossed his mind. *Spiders!*

He'd been alert to the threat from the feral children, but there might be other, even more dangerous aberrations here. Maybe huge spiders lay hidden within the webs!

Crafty hated spiders. He sometimes had nightmares about them. He'd find himself struggling to get free of a sticky web while a monstrous spider scuttled down, heading straight towards him.

The creatures that had spun those webs must have been a lot bigger than your average Daylight World spider. He glanced around nervously and tried not to imagine how the Shole might have made them bigger and more savage – with a need for blood and raw flesh.

He concentrated instead on locating his father. The pipe should have brought Crafty close to him but, as he knew from previous experience, gates were not always very precise. Sometimes they took you to within a few yards of your target; on other occasions they were much further away – his father could be in any of the rooms off these corridors. Or he could be up on the upper floors.

Should he go upstairs or try the corridors? Crafty wondered. Or was his father on the other side of those big wooden doors?

Some kind of intuition prickled at his neck, and he suddenly felt certain that this was where he was. He stepped forward and turned the left-hand door handle, trying to be as quiet as possible. But when he leaned his shoulder against the door and tried to push it open, it didn't yield an inch.

He tried again, this time setting his shoulder against it. The heavy door eventually yielded to the pressure, and he opened it just wide enough to squeeze through. Once inside Crafty lifted his candle high.

It was a scene from his worst nightmares.

A huge spiral web covered the whole of the wall directly in front of him and, hanging within it, head down, were three figures, each dressed in the greatcoat of a courier. He could see at a glance that one of them was dead. But which one?

Crafty crept slowly across the large room, prepared for the worst, hardly daring to hope that his father had survived. With his left hand he held the candle up to the web while gripping the dagger with his right.

The sight of the dead courier appalled him. All that remained was a dry husk: the blood and moisture had been drained from his body, making a mummified corpse of him.

Crafty knew what spiders did to insects. Once the insect was stuck to their sticky web, they injected them with venom to paralyse them. They became living food stored in the spider's larder, and whenever the creature was hungry it would feed on its prey, eventually sucking it dry. The same was happening here. But here the victims were human.

His gaze now turned to the other two figures tangled in the web. He saw immediately that his father was one of them! He and the other courier were still breathing – just – but their eyes were closed and they looked horribly thin. A lump came into Crafty's throat. Perhaps the spider had already sucked out some of their blood and fluids? Maybe the effects of the spider venom were irreversible and they were simply dying very slowly? Even if he could get them free, they might never wake up.

Another thought struck him: how was he going to get them out of the Shole now that Lick had gone? Such big men too. He'd have to drag them . . . two of them . . . He would have to deal with them one at a time, and might get only one out of the building before he was attacked. He felt a pang of guilt as he realized that he would free his father first.

Crafty pushed his worries to the back of his mind. *Concentrate! Take one step at a time*, he told himself.

He summoned up his courage and prepared to cut his father free of the web – maybe he *could* cut both men free and drag them outside, he thought suddenly in a flood of optimism. Maybe Lick would even have forgiven him and returned –

Then, out of the corner of his right eye, he glimpsed something moving. One of the changed children was watching him; the boy was standing close to a side door and, as Crafty watched, another came through the doorway, his movements jerky and unnatural. Then another.

This wasn't looking good. No doubt there were a pack of them; they would surely attack him and tear the flesh from his bones.

Crafty prepared to make the first cut into the web. He knew that this would bring fresh danger. If some big spider was lurking above in the darkness, the twitching of the web would warn it of his presence. It would be upon him in seconds – just as it had been in his nightmare.

He set the candle down on the floor and, keeping one eye on the changed children, began cutting the strands with sweating, trembling hands. He started with those closest to his father. They were sticky and kept attaching themselves to his hands and coat, but his blade sliced through them easily enough. Fear lent him speed. Within moments he'd cut his father's upper body free and dragged him to the floor.

He looked at him briefly, but was not reassured by what he saw. Apart from the slight rise and fall of his chest, his father was completely inert. And he was so thin, his face painfully gaunt.

Hardly able to bear the sight, Crafty worked away furiously, slashing at the strands still attached to his father's legs.

He decided to free both men before dragging them outside one at a time, and had just started on the other courier when the whole web began to vibrate. Crafty glanced up, expecting to see some huge, fierce spider.

The good news was that the spider wasn't as big as he'd feared.

The bad news was that there was more than one.

Each of the spiders' bodies was about the size of an adult human head, the span of the legs at least three times that. They were covered in thick, glossy black hair and their faces . . . Their faces were like something out of a nightmare so awful that the terror would stop your heart. The eyes were big, bulbous and disturbingly human, and the wide mouths were full of sharp fangs pointing in all directions.

The creatures didn't move. They just waited there, staring at Crafty.

He was frozen in position as if paralysed, like a rabbit transfixed by the stare of a stoat. But then he heard a sudden noise behind him – a heavy bang, and then the boom of the door closing. It had been shut to prevent his escape. Next he sensed something moving. Fear clutching at his stomach, Crafty turned his head.

The hungry-looking children had edged round between him and the double doors, and were now slowly advancing towards him. There were three ranks, gathered into a rough crescent, and he saw that they weren't all the same size. The ones in the front were as small as the child he'd snatched. The ones to the rear were much taller, some even larger than adults. Perhaps the larger ones were the staff who'd once been in charge of the orphanage.

But one certainly wasn't. Crafty recognized him because he was still wearing his blood-splattered white shirt.

It was Viper.

29

THE WARRIOR QUEEN

When Crafty pushed Viper through the gate, he'd been desperate. He hadn't been thinking about what might happen to the mancer – he was only concerned with saving his own life.

Afterwards, although Viper had always been in the back of his mind, he hadn't dwelled on his fate. He hadn't expected him to change and survive. Crafty had assumed he'd either been killed by the Shole or eaten by the aberrations. But now he was one of their number.

Viper looked like the others – vaguely human, with a torso, a head and four limbs. But it wasn't just the twitchy walk and bestial faces – particularly those wide, drooling mouths with the rows of sharp teeth – that marked them out as no longer human. It was their eyes, with those vertical, elongated pupils. They were hungry eyes, desperate for blood and raw meat.

But there were no other thoughts going on behind those eyes. The souls of these creatures had departed.

Crafty glanced at Viper again – and realized with a shock that he was different. His face was similarly distorted and bestial, but his eyes showed awareness. As Crafty stared at him, Viper's face twisted into a gloating smile. Somehow, he still knew who he was and remembered what Crafty had done to him. Now he sought revenge.

Crafty's attention was suddenly distracted by a more immediate threat. The front line of children was edging closer, and in the web above him he could sense the spiders creeping down. Nearer and nearer they came.

Crafty was surrounded, cut off from any hope of escape. Above him were the spiders. Now, as he turned, in front of him and blocking the double doors, the nightmare children were closing in, saliva dripping from their open mouths.

He glanced at his father on the floor; then back at the other courier, still trapped in the web. How could he get them to safety? It seemed hopeless. They were all going to die here.

Then, all at once, he heard something banging on the double doors as if demanding admittance. There was a thunderous fury to the blows.

Boom! Boom! Boom!

Crafty could see the huge doors bulging inwards with each rhythmical pounding. It had to be some truly terrible thing, an entity grown to monstrous proportions. Looking round, he realized that he wasn't the only one terrified by the sound. The spiders were no longer inching downwards.

The children had turned their backs on Crafty and were staring at those doors. Did they know what was on the other side? he wondered.

Another *boom!* – louder than ever – and suddenly the doors exploded into the room as if struck by a giant's fist. They slammed back against the walls, bringing down a shower of plaster and dust.

Then a bright light flared, hurting Crafty's eyes and illuminating the room, and something stepped forward, silhouetted in the light, striking fear into his heart. It looked huge, and cast a giant shadow against the walls. As it entered the room, though, he realized that it was smaller than he'd first thought, and human in shape. In its left hand it gripped a long spear, the haft resting on the ground, the sharp tear-shaped blade much taller than the creature that wielded it. In its right hand hung a chain that coiled at its feet, attached to something huge and round and covered in sharp spikes.

Then the source of the light, a small orb, moved forward and floated in front of the figure, illuminating it fully.

It was a moment before Crafty recognized her. It was the Bog Queen – though she looked very different to the kindly figure who'd visited the cellar to befriend Crafty and his brothers. She was so fierce, so terrible to behold.

Her scowling face was daubed with streaks of blue, and she had a ring in each ear and two through her lower lip. She still wore her crown, but there was now a green torc encircling her throat; below that was a vest and skirt of armour.

And what deadly armour! It was covered in sharp spikes, as were her knee-high boots – sharp spurs curved upwards from each toe. Her gloves were similarly adorned, each finger terminating in a cruel-looking metal talon.

The three ranks of aberrations had been facing her, but now they began to retreat, backing away towards Crafty.

All at once he heard a whirring, whooshing sound. Bertha was swinging the chain in rapid circles above her head. That deadly sphere of spikes began whirling faster and faster. Crafty realized that it was the weapon she'd had made but was never able to use in battle.

She gave a terrible cry – half scream, half howl, like a pack of wolves scenting their prey. It was a war cry; the challenge of the warrior queen of the Segantii.

She stepped forward so quickly, she was almost a blur, and the whirling, spiked sphere made contact with the first rank of enemies that faced her. As it did so, a sickening squelching sound was added to the whirring and whooshing.

Some of the aberrations remained standing for a few seconds after the weapon had made contact with them. They didn't know that they were dead. They didn't realize that they no longer had heads.

It seemed to Crafty that the Segantii had made a big mistake in sacrificing their warrior queen in order to defeat the Romans. They should have let her fight. She would have battered holes in those shield-walls, and the Romans would have run for their lives.

The chain and orb continued to circle Bertha's head, and the second rank of aberrations suffered the same fate as the first. They hadn't even had time to register what had happened to the previous row.

Crafty looked around for Viper. He'd been at the back, out of the reach of the spiked orb, but surely he couldn't last long. Though Crafty realized that Bertha was letting the spinning weapon slow and come to a halt before casting down the chain. She drew a sword, and now faced the remainder of her opponents with this and her long spear. Why had she relinquished the orb when it was so effective? Crafty wondered. There were still aberrations left – and he noticed the remaining ones beginning to regroup, snarling and hissing as they did so. Surely it would be harder to kill them with just a sword and a spear?

But then Crafty saw why Bertha had chosen to attack as she did. Wielding her weapons to deadly effect, she drove the aberrations back, away from the double doors. And now, running towards him through those doors, Crafty saw two people he knew well – Lick and Lucky! Bertha had had to stop swinging the chain in order to allow them through.

The glowing orb floating above her was beginning to fade, the shadows in the corners of the room growing ever bigger. Without even breaking stride, Lick threw up another one, which flared like sheet lightning before settling into a steady brilliance.

'Cut the other man free!' she shouted to Crafty as she picked his father up by the shoulders. Lucky gave him a nervous grin before seizing the legs, then together they quickly carried him towards the double doors and safety.

Crafty couldn't believe it. Lick hadn't abandoned him after all! She'd gone back for Lucky and had somehow managed to persuade Bertha to come through the gate with her. Even the Bog Queen surely couldn't have covered that distance so quickly by herself.

The only thing that dented his feeling of relief was the realization that Lick must have left the gate unguarded – but there was no time to dwell on that. He set to work with his knife and soon had the top half of the other courier free of the sticky strands. He'd just managed to free the man's legs when the first of the spiders attacked.

It didn't scuttle across the web towards him like the spiders in his nightmares. Instead, it dropped down like a stone, descending on a single silken strand extruded from its body. At first its hairy legs were curled up tight, but at the last moment it spread them wide, intending to grasp his head.

But Crafty's blade was waiting to slice it open, and it gave a cry, missed his head and ended up twitching and writhing on the flags, its black blood spraying around it on the floor. The next one he splattered with his hammer – though, looking up, he realized that there were more; lots more. Far too many to fight alone. But then he saw Bertha at his side; she was howling her war cry, slicing and jabbing at the spiders in a frenzy of slaughter.

Moments later he and Bertha were retreating towards the entrance, holding off further attacks from the last of the aberrations while Lick and Lucky joined them, now carrying the other courier to safety.

Just before they reached the doors, Crafty turned, suddenly sensing a malevolence that was like a sharp pain in his head. He glimpsed a figure standing staring at him from the far door of the chamber. It was Viper. He was no longer gloating, but his furious glare was filled with such hatred that Crafty could feel it like a force.

Then they were outside in the chill air, with the blue circle of the gate in front of them – and through it Crafty was amazed to see the Chief Mancer surrounded by what looked like half the Castle Guard, armed to the teeth. He watched Lick and Lucky ease the unconscious courier through the gate, and checked that his father had been safely taken through. Behind him, he saw that none of the surviving aberrations had followed them out of the orphanage.

Crafty turned to Bertha. 'I can't thank you enough, Bertha. You saved my life,' he said. 'Again!'

The Bog Queen spoke in her strange rasping voice. 'I enjoyed doing battle, Crafty. It was a good fight. One day soon we'll do it again.' Then she grinned at him – a strange, oddly chilling grin – and turned and walked away into the gloom, the spiked sphere dragging along behind her and making a deep furrow in the ground.

Crafty strode towards the silver gate, where Lick was waiting for him. She smiled and gestured that he should go through first, and he saw that the floor of her office was covered in stinking mud. That was the price you paid when you were an ally of the Bog Queen – but he had a feeling that Lick didn't mind.

Then Crafty came face to face with the Chief Mancer. He wasn't smiling.

'Go to your room, Benson. Stay there until you are summoned!' he commanded. 'You'll answer to the Duke at dawn.'

30

THE WOODEN DUKE

Back in his room Crafty had plenty of time to think. He didn't regret a thing – after all, he'd managed to bring his father back from the Shole! However, he knew that, in the eyes of Ginger Bob, he'd gone too far this time. He'd proved himself incapable of following orders; incapable of the behaviour expected of anyone who worked at the castle. At the very least he expected to be dismissed. At worst, he could end up in a prison cell. No – there was something even worse than that! He could be returned to the Shole, which would be a death sentence.

His fears seemed to be confirmed when his supper was brought up not by a kitchen server but a guard. The food was steaming hot and tasty, far superior to the prison fare he'd had before. But ominously, when he left, the guard took his key and locked the door of Crafty's room. It seemed he was as good as in prison already.

He sat there, hoping for a visit from Lucky or even Lick – although if he was locked in, he probably wouldn't be allowed visitors. If Lick did come, he intended to apologize for tricking and disobeying her. But nobody came near him.

He didn't sleep much. He lay there worrying about his father. Would he recover? Or was he dying? Might he even already be dead? He'd asked to see him after Ginger Bob ordered him to his room, but he was told he was still unconscious.

Then he thought of his poor mother: she wouldn't come out of that cupboard to talk to him because she didn't want him to see the change in her. Yet he understood what it must have cost her. The thought brought a lump to his throat and tears to his eyes.

At last, dawn light filled his room and the guard arrived to take him to the Duke.

Crafty was admitted to the Ducal Chambers. To his surprise, he found that there were no guards present.

He went forward to stand before the Duke, looking up at the grim, sombre face. He noted that the blond beard had grown even thicker and longer. The silk that covered his lower half, flowing over the container that held his roots, had been changed from purple to green.

When the Duke spoke, the warm voice Crafty remembered had gone. It reminded him of the tone in which the hanging judge had addressed him – though at least the Duke looked him in the eye.

'You have deliberately disobeyed the instructions of a gate mancer. It was an act of open defiance. You lived up to your nickname, using guile and deceit to carry out what you had already planned in meticulous detail, risking not just your own life, but that of the gate mancer and another gate grub, who had to come to your aid.'

The Duke paused, but when he spoke again, his voice sounded slightly milder.

'However, your actions have also resulted in locating and retrieving two of the three missing couriers – something that nobody else in the Castle Corpus was able to do. Not only that, you have formed an alliance with a truly formidable entity, the bog creature. We are in desperate need of such allies. You have demonstrated initiative too. You are young, and – for better or worse – not constrained by tradition or protocol.'

The Duke gave a wry smile, and Crafty couldn't help but wince at the reminders of his recklessness.

'I believe I need more young people like you to join our cause. Come here!' the Duke commanded, beckoning him up the steps.

Crafty climbed up until he was almost on the same level. 'Bend forward!'

When Crafty did so, he felt something being eased over his head. He looked down – and, to his surprise, saw that it was a silver key on a chain.

'This key represents the freedom of the castle,' the Duke said, smiling properly for the first time. 'Show it to anyone responsible for a department or a room, or guarding a door, and they cannot refuse you admittance. They may not like it, but I suspect that, because you are but a boy, they will not feel too threatened. This is to be our greatest advantage, Crafty.'

Crafty wondered what he meant, and looked questioningly up at the Duke.

'If you continue to be as crafty as you were in the Shole,' he continued, 'then you will soon gain access to all their secrets. For too long we have been a secretive operation – clogged by bureaucracy, constrained by jealous guilds, with departments refusing to cooperate and share knowledge with each other. They even withhold information from me. That is no doubt why Vipton was able to escape detection for so long. Whatever you discover you will bring directly to me. Do you understand? You will also be alert for any evidence of the presence of that vile cult, the Grey Hoods.'

'Yes, sir,' Crafty said. It seemed that he was to be a spy – he wondered what Lucky and Lick would have to say about that.

'Do you know what some people call me, Crafty?'

'No, sir,' he replied.

'They call me the Wooden Duke.'

Crafty remembered that those sensitive roots enabled the Duke to listen to anything that was said in the castle. No doubt it was useful, but in a way it was terrible to have to hear such tittle-tattle.

'Of course, that's only *half* true,' he went on with a sad smile, 'but I'd prefer another nickname. One day they'll call me the Iron Duke, because that's what I intend to be. I plan to fight the Shole with every means at my disposal. I cannot yield – for my people's sake, and indeed literally. I cannot move from this spot because my roots continue to grow. They have penetrated the floor of this chamber and run deep into the foundations of the castle, spreading ever wider.

'When the Shole engulfs this place, as it will surely do in the not-too-distant future, I will remain here, and I want others to stay and fight by my side. You have friends, Crafty. They came and begged audiences with me. Each one extolled your virtues and pleaded for clemency on your behalf. The first was young Miss Crompton-Smythe, closely followed by the gate grub you call Lucky. Finally even Mr Wainwright, the Chief Mancer, spoke up for you. They will also be part of the team fighting that final battle. For now, watch, listen, and learn what you can. Go back and continue your work as a gate grub. Maybe one day you will become much more than that. Maybe that is what you deserve.' He smiled as he said this.

But Crafty's heart skipped a beat on hearing this last phrase.

May you get what you deserve!

Before her hanging, this was the curse Old Nell had thrown at him, Lucky and Donna. It had happened before the Duke had been returned to the castle, so he couldn't have overheard her with his sensitive roots.

It was probably just coincidence. But Crafty thought about it all the same.

Did he deserve to get his father back, returned to full health? That's what he wanted.

Did he deserve a mother who never wanted him or his father to see her again? Crafty hoped not. Surely nobody deserved that. He'd experienced some terrible things in recent weeks, but that had been the worst.

Still, he wasn't alone in the cellar but living in the Daylight World, working with friends – Lick and Lucky. And the Chief Mancer, apparently.

And Crafty found that he was grateful.

As soon as he could, Crafty went to visit his father. He had been told that he was conscious, as was the other courier they'd rescued, though still very weak.

His father was in one of the sick rooms where patients stayed while they recovered from illness or injury. He was not in the bed, but sitting in a big chair with a rug over his knees, staring into the embers of the fire. He turned and, seeing Crafty, gave him a tired smile.

'Bring up a chair, Crafty, and sit beside me,' he invited.

Crafty would have liked to hug his father, but Brian Benson had never been one for hugs or any kind of fuss. In any case he didn't look like he had the strength to stand up.

Crafty brought a small chair from beside the bed and placed it next to him. 'You're looking better, Father,' he said as he sat down. 'You'll soon be on your feet and back to normal.'

His father gave him another weary smile. His appearance was much improved since he'd been freed from the spider's web, but it was clear that he had been changed forever. His hair was newly grey at the temples and his face was thinner, the lines on his forehead deeper. Crafty felt very sad. He knew that his father would never be quite the man he'd been before.

However, the doctor had said that, given time, both couriers would recover. That doctor belonged in the Optimists' Room. Crafty could only hope.

'Thanks for saving my life, son,' his father said. 'But for you I'd be dead now. You were brave, and I'm proud of you.'

Crafty didn't know what to say. He felt choked with emotion. So instead of acknowledging his father's thanks he asked a question.

'Please say if you don't feel like talking about it, Father, but I've been wondering – what happened when you were carrying the sedan chair, taking the safe route through Preston? Someone told me that there was probably some sort of malign magic used – a compulsion that lured you towards the heart of the Shole. What was it like?'

For a while Crafty's father neither spoke nor looked at him – it was probably too upsetting for him to think about, Crafty thought. But then he replied, speaking slowly and choosing his words carefully.

'It was as if my will had been snatched away,' he began. 'I remember releasing the chair, just letting it fall, and striding away up the hill. It was as if I was a puppet and someone was using strings to move my arms and legs. I knew it was my duty to turn back, but I was powerless. It was as if I was walking in a dream ... no – more like walking in a nightmare.'

'Did you know where you were going? I was told you headed directly towards the centre of the Shole – the most dangerous place of all. The location where it first began.'

His father nodded. 'Yes, I knew exactly where I was going, and I was terrified. Something was summoning me, moving me, and I was powerless to resist. When I got there, I knew there'd be something terrible to face. Something that wanted to eat both my body *and* my soul. Somehow I knew that – and I'd never been as scared in my life. The terror was overwhelming.'

'That orphanage was a terrible place all right,' Crafty agreed.

'Oh no! That's not where we were heading,' said his father, turning to face Crafty. 'We just passed by – and those fierce little creatures ran out and dragged us inside. For weeks we were locked in a stinking cellar with just water and stale bread to keep us alive. Then, just when I thought things couldn't get any worse, they gave us to the spiders ...

'I didn't expect to survive. When they tangled me in their sticky web and injected their poison into me, I cried like a baby. But, believe you me, being taken into that orphanage was a blessing in disguise. You see, we'd been heading towards something far worse – towards the very heart of the Shole, the lair of some terrible beast. It would have been impossible to rescue us from there, I know it . . .' His father's voice trailed off, and he stared blankly into the fire again.

Crafty had other important things to discuss with his father. He wanted to tell him that he'd been able to hear his dead brothers, and that his mother was still alive. But for now he didn't want to upset him any further. Maybe he'd wait until he was stronger, he thought. Maybe he should tell him all these things another day.

But the decision had been taken out of his hands. His father's chin was now resting on his chest, and he was snoring.

31

A NEW ABERRATION

The first thing Crafty did after getting out of bed on Saturday morning was look through his narrow window. That was his routine now. He always went to check that the Shole hadn't surged nearer during the night.

The sun was shining, though it no longer glinted off the surface of the canal, which was now hidden by the dark curtain of the Shole. As far as he could tell, it hadn't advanced any nearer.

It had been a week since the Duke had given Crafty the silver key. He'd had time to reflect on what had happened and plan for the future. Tomorrow was Sunday and he intended to use that key for the first time.

He was going into the Relic Room to see what secrets it held. Then he would pay a visit to the Grey Library, where he would begin reading up on the Shole and its aberrations.

Yes, I think I'll quite enjoy being a spy, he thought to himself.

After breakfast he went down to the Waiting Room. As usual, Lucky had arrived before him. To his surprise, Lick was also there. She gestured for Crafty to sit down, and he settled himself next to Lucky.

'Extra chess lessons?' he joked.

Lick had started joining them for lunch and, in addition to draughts, there was now a chess set on the table. While they ate, Lick had been teaching them how to play. She always won because she knew so many different methods of attack and defence. She could also remember every move in games that had been played years ago. But Crafty was slowly improving. He was very determined. One day he would beat her!

He liked learning how to play chess. It was interesting, and somehow seemed to mirror life. For example, there were pawns, the least powerful pieces on the board. Risks were taken with them – they could sometimes be sacrificed to gain an advantage later. So pawns were like gate grubs.

His favourite chess piece was the knight, because it moved across the board in a strange diagonal manner, and players who weren't concentrating could be taken by surprise. Crafty was going to be like a knight. He was going to surprise those people who wanted to hold on to their secrets.

The queen was the most powerful piece on the board – so that was obviously Bertha. But maybe they had *two* of them in their fight against the Shole. Lick was their secret queen.

And as for the chess piece called the king – that had to be the Duke. If your king was trapped, you lost the game. If the Shole engulfed the castle, the Duke would be hard to protect.

'Wake up, Crafty, and stop dreaming!' Lick commanded with a smile. 'We're going to change our routine. From now on we're going to start each morning with a fifteen-minute briefing. Bit by bit, I'm going to tell you what I know about the Shole.'

'So you're going to train us,' Lucky said, beaming at her.

'*Inform* rather than train. It's the Duke's idea. He thinks it will help you do your job better, and I agree. It won't be formal – just a short question-and-answer session, so go ahead and ask me something. It doesn't matter how stupid!' she said, grinning at Crafty. 'I'll do my very best to answer.'

Crafty smiled back, and without even thinking asked his first question.

'Is there any way to predict when the Shole will surge again, or is it always going to take us by surprise?'

'That's a good first question. It's something we're studying very carefully, Crafty. As yet we've no way of predicting a big surge, but we have just come up with a new theory. It seems that they take place each time a new aberration is created. Somehow the two events are linked. The surge that swallowed your house happened at the same time as the bog and the Bog Queen came into existence. If that's the case, then it's very worrying because aberrations and surges are definitely occurring more frequently.'

Crafty was stunned. That new information about his house hit him like a blow. He suddenly felt very sad. He owed a lot to Bertha, but she had come into existence because of something that had ruined his life forever – for that surge had changed his mother and led to the deaths of his brothers.

'What about the latest surge – the one that engulfed the canal?' Lucky asked next.

'I was coming to that. We're pretty sure that it was caused by a new, very strong aberration – the one that came through the gate into the castle. It's already killed two mancers . . .'

Earlier in the week, whatever killed poor Humperton had struck again. Doon said that it had seized the replacement gate mancer, chewed him up into tiny pieces and spat them out all over his desk.

'And those two deaths are probably only the start,' Lick continued. 'If it's anything like the previous aberration, the bog, it will grow in size and power. We have to investigate and deal with it somehow before it strikes again.'

'It could be Viper,' Crafty suggested. He had already told them about seeing Viper in the orphanage; about the difference he'd seen in him: unlike the other aberrations he'd seemed aware and motivated by something other than blood-lust. If it really *was* Viper, then Crafty was responsible for this new development. But he pushed away any sense of guilt. He had been fighting for survival – for Lick's life as well as his own.

'It's a possibility,' Lick admitted, 'though some boffins have speculated that it might be a witch brought back to life by the Shole. We know that it's something more dangerous than anything we've encountered, and we need to find out exactly what it is.'

Just then the far door opened and the Chief Mancer appeared.

'Sorry to cut your first briefing short, but this is urgent,' he announced, his face grim. 'One of our couriers has just crawled out of the Shole. He was in a very bad way, and before he died he was able to tell us a little of what happened. It could well be that he was attacked by the killer we're looking for. Proudfoot, you will come with me. You, Benson, will work with Miss Crompton-Smythe.'

They quickly got to their feet, and Crafty followed Lick down to her room. His mouth was dry and his heart was beating rapidly, so he took a few deep breaths to try and control his fear as he sat down in front of the silver gate.

This was what they did, he told himself. Their work would continue. Their priority was to hunt down and destroy that killer – the new aberration. They must find out what it was, and how it was getting through the silver gates. But above all, they had to be ready for when the Shole finally engulfed the castle.

That's when the fight would truly begin.

Glossary

Aberrations

The generic name given to creatures that dwell within the Shole. The majority evolved from creatures (including humans) who were engulfed and, instead of dying, changed their shape and adapted to life in that new environment.

Black gates

A type of gate that is believed to be under development by the boffins who work within Lancaster Castle. If successful, it would enable mancers and gate grubs to access the world of the damned dead as easily as they do the Shole.

Boffins

Highly skilled theorists, researchers and technicians who develop new methods to combat the effects of the Shole.

Bowland Fells
A range of hills south of Lancaster. Although enveloped by the Shole, most of the green summits rise above it into the Daylight World.

Canal
This runs from Preston to Kendal, passing through Lancaster. It is used by horse-drawn barges carrying all manner of wares. A large portion to the south has now been engulfed and only the northern section between north Lancaster and Kendal is still viable.

Castle Corpus
The collective name for the people who work from Lancaster Castle to learn how to counter the threat from the Shole.

Chair jobs
A task that is carried out from the chair facing the gate. The grub is often strapped in to minimize the danger of being dragged into the Shole by one of the aberrations.

Combined field operation
Where two or more gate grubs pass through their respective gates and work together in the Shole.

Courier craft
The skills used by couriers to protect themselves when travelling through the Shole. Some are magical, others

technological. For example, a triangle of three candles can be used to ward off aberrations, while the use of silver alloy is applied science.

Couriers

These are recruited from the Fey and thus largely immune to the effects of the Shole. They carry messages and sometimes medicines to the Daylight Islands encircled by the Shole. They also make regular patrols, noting areas of change and danger, and are skilled in map-making. They are also skilled in the use of courier craft.

Daylight Islands

Pockets of the Daylight World cut off and surrounded by the Shole after a sudden surge. Why they are untouched by the Shole remains a mystery.

Daylight World

The ordinary world, as yet untouched by the Shole.

Duke of Lancaster

The ruler of the Palatine of Lancashire, answerable only to the King. He has the power of life and death over the county's inhabitants.

Fey

The Fey are humans with potential magical ability which may or may not manifest itself as they grow up. Some have a single ability while others have several. Couriers and gate grubs are traditionally recruited from the Fey. Mancers (from the managerial staff of the Castle Corpus) are not recruited from the Fey, who are sometimes thought to be reckless and unreliable. They are considered to be a necessary evil – except for the few with extremely high academic ability, who become boffins.

Field operations
These are jobs involving a gate grub passing through a silver gate to carry out some task in the Shole.

Fixed locations
Only gate grubs can find new locations within the Shole, but subsequently they can be revisited by mancers using the ratchet-dial on the side of the gate. They are then termed 'fixed locations'.

Forensics Room
Those who work here apply magical theory and practical technology to the study of deaths and changes in the Shole. Any samples are routinely handed over to the Relic Room within seven days unless the Chief Mancer authorizes an extension.

Gate grubs
Fey humans who are able to venture into the Shole without fear of either dying or changing. Using a silver gate, they

also have the ability, using sympathetic magic, to find aberrations, locations and objects within it. Most gate grubs do not survive much longer than a few months.

Geographical aberrations

These types of aberration consist of local changes in the landscape of the Shole rather than to a human or an aberration.

Grey Hoods

This is a cult that worships the Shole. Its members believe that one day it will engulf the whole world and they will then live forever. They actively work to undermine the efforts of the Castle Corpus.

Grey Library

This contains the cumulative knowledge gathered about the Shole over a period of almost seventy years. The name refers firstly to the Shole, which is grey and murky; and secondly to the books in the library, all of which have grey jackets. Thirdly, metaphorically speaking, it refers to the understanding that the facts about the Shole are neither black nor white. All is uncertain and in a state of change – the known facts are grey.

Guillotine

A sharp blade suspended above the area between the chair of a gate grub and the silver gate itself. It slides down between two vertical poles. A gate mancer controls it, by means of a foot pedal, to kill any aberration attempting to enter the Daylight World through the gate. Unfortunately, gate grubs are sometimes killed or maimed by the blade. For them, it is the second most likely cause of death. (The first is failure to return from the Shole after a field operation, when the precise cause of death is usually unknown.)

Lancaster

The chief city of Lancashire, lying on the river Lune. At its centre is Lancaster Castle, which is the focus of attempts to contain the threat from the Shole.

Lancaster Castle

This castle is very old and was once the centre of the county's judiciary and military. Now it is the centre for research into the Shole and home to the mancers and other experts who hope one day to reverse or destroy it. It also has its own guard, a quasi-military force which is responsible for the security of the castle and for policing the city. They also patrol the boundaries of the Shole to prevent its aberrations entering the Daylight World.

Lure

This is an illusion with which a mancer entices an aberration towards a gate so that a gate grub may snatch it.

Mancers

Specialized mages who have magical and technological power within just one field of expertise. Their magical abilities are developed over time using discipline and meditation, whereas Fey magic is innate and chaotic, and potentially much more powerful. *Gate mancer*s are one of many such categories; *necromancers* are another. The Chief Mancer manages and has authority over all types of mancer.

Menagerie

This is where live specimens from the Shole are kept for study and experimentation.

Ouroborus

This is a great serpent sometimes called the Earth Dragon. It is a symbol of rebirth as its head is joined to its tail. It was important to ancient tribes like the Segantii and was often represented on their weapons and amulets.

Porter magic

This is used to transmit objects over a distance. It is the means by which many of the Daylight Islands are fed. But the Shole waxes and wanes in strength, and sometimes porter magic does not work.

Preston

A market town on the river Ribble about thirty miles south of Lancaster where the phenomenon known as the Shole first began. At first it merely covered a terraced house in a small street called Water Lane, which is next to a busy thoroughfare called Fylde Road.

Relic Room

This is where artefacts taken from the Shole are stored by its curators. They jealously guard its contents, sometimes undertaking further study of the items without sharing their findings with the Forensics Room.

Samples

Items from the flora or fauna of the Shole, removed to be studied in the castle. Samples may be large and active, or small, or even dead. All or a piece of them is taken for further study.

Segantii

An ancient warlike tribe inhabiting Lancashire before the invasion of the Romans. Some believe that they had a port on the west bank of the river Wyre.

Shade

This is an alternative term for the Shole which is in popular use. Another variant is the *Shadow*. Mancers always use the term *Shole*.

Sheol

This is one of the ancient names for Hell. Some believe that the word Shole was derived from it.

Shole

This first manifested near the centre of Preston, in a house in Water Lane, close to a busy thoroughfare called Fylde Road. It gradually expanded to cover most of the town centre. After seventy years of sporadic growth it has extended thirty miles north and now threatens the heart of Lancaster. The Shole changes or kills most creatures within it, including humans (except the Fey). The changed are termed *aberrations* and they are at their most dangerous after dark.

Silver gates

These are mediums resembling circular framed windows through which a gate grub may access the Shole.

Snatches

When performing a snatch, a gate grub (secured in his or her seat by restraining straps) seeks to drag an aberration out of the Shole into the Daylight World for the purposes of research.

JOSEPH DELANEY used to be an English teacher, before becoming the best-selling author of the Spook's series, which has been published in twenty-four countries and sold millions of copies. The first book, *The Spook's Apprentice*, was made into a major motion picture starring Jeff Bridges and Julianne Moore.

IF YOU'D LIKE TO LEARN MORE ABOUT JOSEPH
AND HIS BOOKS, VISIT:

www.spooksworld.co.uk

www.arena13.co

www.penguin.co.uk

THE SPOOK'S SERIES

WARNING:
NOT TO BE READ AFTER DARK

DO YOU DARE ENTER THE WORLD OF ...

WHEN LEIF'S FAMILY IS DESTROYED BY AN EVILCREATURE, BATTLE IS THE ONLY WAY TO GET REVENGE . . .